SCRIPT TO SCREAM

SCRIPT TO SCREAM

A Novel

JAMES & LYDIA HICKS

mango PUBLISHING

MIAMI

Published by Mango Publishing, a division of Mango Publishing Group, Inc.

Cover Illustration & Design: Andrew Swainson (@andrew_swainson)
Layout & Design: Megan Werner
Map Illustration: Helen Poulteney (@helenpoulteney)
Author Photo: Nisha Jayne

For permission requests, please contact the publisher at:
Mango Publishing Group
5966 South Dixie Highway, Suite 300
Miami, FL 33143
info@mango.bz

For special orders, quantity sales, course adoptions and corporate sales, please email the publisher at sales@mango.bz. For trade and wholesale sales, please contact Ingram Publisher Services at customer.service@ingramcontent.com or +1.800.509.4887.

Script to Scream: A Novel

Library of Congress Cataloging-in-Publication number: requested
ISBN: (pb) 978-1-68481-896-9 (e) 978-1-68481-897-6
BISAC category code: FIC015000 FICTION / Horror / General

Printed in the United States of America

To our daughter, Freya.

CONTENTS

Tinseltown. NV.

Where it's Christmas all day, every day!

"The holly-est, jolly-est place in the West!"

Ronald "Ron" Burnett-Turner,
founder of Tinseltown

PROLOGUE

Evil Elf (1985–1992): The Complete DVD Box Set

Reviewed by Peter Morton for HackandSlashMovies.com

At the bottom of the DVD bargain bin in any given supermarket across America, you're bound to find at least one *Evil Elf* movie. But if you don't want to sift through piles of plastic to complete your collection, you can now own the entire franchise in one definitive box set (yes, even the contentious sixth installment).

The *Evil Elf* movies are the kind of cheesy horror that you resort to after exhausting your reruns of *A Nightmare on Elm Street*, *Friday the 13th*, and *Halloween*–and when your copies of *Hellraiser* and *Leprechaun* are out of reach.

While this franchise hasn't been my go-to for a horror movie marathon, the *Evil Elf* series has been a satisfying-enough guilty pleasure. A delightfully campy franchise filled with mullets, mallets, blood, guts, and–of course–Jennifer Hawkins. I think I can speak for all horror fans when I say her performance as the doe-eyed "final girl" Rebecca Sommers in parts I to V remains to be one of our main motivations for pressing that "play" button.

Unfortunately for the franchise's villain, Plucky the Elf (primarily portrayed by Douglas King) didn't achieve the legendary status of Jason, Freddy, or Michael in the '80s

Slasher Hall of Fame. But he still gave us a handful of quotable catchphrases that look great on a T-shirt, along with some inventive kills. Nutcracker, anyone?

Campy and low-budget, the first installment of *Evil Elf* hit screens in 1985, introducing us–and Plucky's unsuspecting victims–to a deranged Christmas elf determined to cross misbehaving teens off Santa's naughty list. It's schlocky fun that doesn't take itself too seriously. And despite meeting the sharp end of a candy cane shiv, Plucky returned for a sequel just one year later.

Checking It Twice ditched its iconic Christmas theme park setting for the bright lights of Las Vegas. From there, the series only got more ridiculous, changing locations with each film. Plucky slashed his way through Santa Cruz in the third installment, New Orleans in the fourth, New York City in the fifth, before finally, boldly going where all slashers have gone before...*space.*

(Because, as we all know, in space, no one can hear you suck!)

Some fans theorize the last movie's dire performance at the box office could be in part due to Hawkins's and King's absence from the sci-fi installment–which is a shame, but I can't say I blame them. In retrospect, signing on would've been complete career suicide.

It's been thirty-three years since that last underwhelming entry, so it looks like Plucky, and the franchise as a whole, won't be coming down our chimneys again anytime soon.

So, grab the complete box set if you want to *slay* ten hours–now with an exclusive candy cane scented vinyl sticker.

Three out of five stars ★★★

CHAPTER 1

Zara Westbrook's line stretched around the convention hall, snaking through booths of overpriced merchandise, tables overflowing with collectible figurines, and into the farthest reaches of the room–where Jennifer Hawkins sat, unnoticed, like a relic collecting dust.

Across the hall, a fan watched as Zara's pen glided over a glossy 8x10 photo, her signature looping across her blood-soaked yet beautiful face. "Thanks for coming," she said, flashing a flawless, practiced smile.

Before the fan could even stammer their thanks, they were hurried away by security, giving the young actress barely enough time to cap her pen before another stepped forward, a crisp hundred-dollar bill held out in their shaking hand.

Jennifer's pen, however, lay unused atop a stack of untouched photos. But she wasn't picky. You didn't *have* to buy one of her photos. As long as you paid her forty-dollar fee, she would sign anything you put in front of her. She once signed a 1989 October issue of *Penthouse* when she was their "Pet of the Month." Sure, the centerfold was suspiciously sticky, but she signed it all the same.

As Jennifer sat, picking at her long, manicured nails, she took in convention-goers of all ages, shapes, and sizes dressed as their favorite fictional characters. She counted three Freddys, nine Harley Quinns, fifteen Jasons, and one screaming toddler dressed as Chucky.

Some glanced her way, while others stared, trying to recognize her semi-familiar face before moving on.

This was getting embarrassing. Telling herself that they must have missed the large banner hanging behind her, Jennifer turned to straighten it in a bid to remind them. The ink had faded, and her finger traced the beginnings of another rip. She brought this banner to every meet-and-greet, and after years of being folded and unfolded, it was now 90 percent tape.

Jennifer Hawkins a.k.a. Rebecca Sommers—
EVIL ELF I-V

She couldn't resist stealing another look at Zara's booth and her towering banner that stretched the entire height of the convention hall. Her face was twenty times her actual size and the freshness of the ink only enhanced the shininess of her dark locks, the brightness of her blue eyes, and the plumpness of her red, wet lips.

ZARA WESTBROOK—
STAR OF* TERRORDOME *(2025)
FINAL GIRL OF THE YEAR!

Jennifer's gaze lingered long enough to witness yet another one of Zara's fan interactions, complete with the perfect hair flick and giggle.

Yeah, enjoy your prime real estate while you can, Jennifer thought. *Give it forty years and your table will be hidden away in the shadows–just like mine.*

Jennifer leaned on her table, which wobbled under her weight. She sighed, grabbing a copy of her memoir, *Behind the Blade: Confessions of a Final Girl*, and wedged it under the table leg. She could spare it; a towering stack sat in front of her, and an extra box permanently resided in the trunk of her car.

Jennifer tucked her hands under the table, only to brush against a furry ball of gum on its underside. She gagged.

Around her, other booths were manned by faded and forgotten faces of Hollywood's past. They all looked as bored as she felt. The only one who was enjoying himself was Douglas King, her old *Evil Elf* costar. But, to her horror, he was committing one of the cardinal sins of conventions–interacting with fans *in front* of his table.

Maintaining a barrier between herself and her fans was integral–unless, of course, they paid for a photo. This would grant them the privilege of leaning across her table for a quick snap.

But there was Douglas, back in the rubber Plucky the Elf mask, waving a plastic knife at a fan who crouched to match his four-foot height. Nearby, the fan's friend took photos on his phone, tapping away incessantly.

Douglas peeled off the mask, revealing a flushed red face and a grin that stretched from ear to ear. Though his copper curls had faded to gray, he was still the same guy she had met on set four decades ago–cheerful, playful, and far too generous with his time.

Across the room, he caught Jennifer's eye and waved. She returned the gesture with a raised palm and a smile that didn't quite reach her eyes.

Her gaze drifted to her cracked phone screen. Ten in the morning. It was going to be a long day. She reached into her pocket and pulled out a pack of cigarettes, but as she tipped one into her hand she heard a weak cough beside her. It was the young girl the convention organizers had assigned to her. Jennifer had forgotten she was there–a small, quiet thing who had introduced herself that morning as Sarah...or was it Susan?

Jennifer couldn't recall which one it was, and frankly did it matter?

"I'm sorry, Ms. Hawkins, but you can't smoke in here," she murmured.

Jennifer sighed, tucking the pack back into her tight jeans. She missed the good old days when you could light up wherever you wanted, back when she was a Zara. Red carpet rolled out, a hefty appearance fee, security, the lot. Now, Jennifer had to pay out of her own pocket to appear at these crappy conventions and have a crummy booth. Sure, a couple of fan interactions would cover the cost, but she also knew the demand for her was dwindling. Would today be the day that she couldn't break even?

As Jennifer ruminated on her career's demise, hope arrived in the form of two men sporting matching Pennywise shirts.

The men shifted their gazes from her banner to her face, then back at the banner again. Jennifer had gone to great pains–and great expense–to combat aging: a consistent skincare routine, chemical peels, lasers that zapped away lines and veins, and regular salon visits to salvage a fragment of her "blonde-bombshell" persona. But as they scrutinized her with such intensity, all those efforts felt wasted.

They shuffled over to her table as Jennifer pretended to blink herself out of a daze, a convincing smile spreading across her face. She was still a great actress.

"Hi there," she said.

"Uh, are you Rebecca Sommers from the *Evil Elf* movies?" one of them asked, as if the answer wasn't already emblazoned on the banner behind her.

"Uh huh," she replied through a smile.

"Told you," the other blurted out.

"Ah man, I loved those movies," the first guy exclaimed before turning to his friend. "Do you remember watching them in college? Man, we'd get so wasted." His voice was loud enough for a few heads to turn. He continued, recounting every rule of his drinking game on his fingers. "Drink every time she falls, when someone has sex, when someone can't open a door, when the weapon's left behind for Plucky...and wait, oh no, they're having sex again, better take another shot–"

"It's always great meeting a fan," she interjected. "So, who should I make it out to?"

She clasped her pen and paused, waiting expectantly.

"Huh?"

She pointed to the pricing sheet on her table.

"Oh, right." He dug into his back pocket and thrust out four warm, crumpled ten-dollar bills.

"She handles the money," Jennifer said, jolting her pen toward the young volunteer beside her. Susan/Sarah took the money and counted the bills before nodding.

"My name's Brian."

Jennifer began writing his name in gold ink on a glossy photo when her wrist twinged. This stiff, dull ache again. It had been creeping in more and more. If she could no longer manage the simple task of scribbling her name, then what would she do? She persevered.

Dear Brian, Stay Spooky. Jennifer Hawkins. X

Jennifer slid the signed photo across the table, pulling her hand back before it could touch his. But the motion sent a sharp jolt right through her wrist again. She winced.

"Thanks." He lingered for a few moments. "I've seen all the *Evil Elf* movies. And, sure, they were crap fests, but they were enjoyable crap fests, you know? I hope that doesn't offend you." Brian looked at her for reassurance.

She didn't offer any.

"To me, they're comforting. Like those movies where you can smoke a joint, switch off your brain, and laugh with your buddies. Know what I mean?" Brian chuckled.

Forced to reply, Jennifer sighed. "Sure."

"Although the last one *was* absolute trash," Brian said. "The one in space. Like, not even ironically bad–just awful. No offense. But then again, you weren't in that one, were you?"

Jennifer shook her head.

"You must have smelled a stinker when you read the script and dipped. Don't blame you. I remember watching it with this girl I was trying to date and I would say..."

As Brian rambled on, Jennifer nodded, making sure to maintain a polite smile. She had learned early on that horror fans could be very blunt when they disliked a movie, which was often the case with her work. Fortunately, she had no illusions about the quality of her filmography–choosing instead to protect herself with a quiet pride in her acting ability. A talent often praised, and one that she could adapt for a variety of roles. Like pretending to be interested in Brian's pedantic critiques.

"Can I get a photo?" Brian asked, already pulling out his phone.

She pointed to the price list again.

He pulled out another couple of crumpled bills; they unfurled in his sweaty palm. Sarah/Susan took the money.

Jennifer didn't bother to stand up, so Brian passed his friend the phone and squeezed his way around the table. With the last barrier between herself and Brian broken, all she could do was stare at the lens. Realizing she wasn't going to stand, he contorted himself into a crouch beside her, his knees popping as he bent.

"Say *Evil Elf*," his friend directed.

"*Evil Elf*," Brian huffed.

Jennifer forced a smile.

"Okay, one more."

After what seemed like the hundredth snap, Brian stood up and made his way back around the table.

"Thanks," they said in unison.

Before they had even turned their heads, Jennifer reached for the nearby bottle of antibacterial gel and squeezed a generous amount into her hands before lathering it up her arms like sun lotion. The aroma of alcohol filled her nose, and she could almost taste a tall glass of something that awaited her back at home.

"Ms. Hawkins, I know you've been hearing this all day, but I really am such a big fan of your work," Sarah/Susan said. She said this with such conviction that Jennifer was convinced that the assistant had been building this conversation up in her mind.

"Aw, thanks," Jennifer replied, looking down at her phone again. *How has it only been five minutes?*

"Do you think they'll do another sequel?" she asked.

"Six not enough for you?" Jennifer said, flexing her aching wrist. Had her veins always bulged like that?

"I've always wanted to be an actress," Susan/Sarah pushed on.

Jennifer turned to study the girl. Her skin was soft and smooth without a single line or blemish, except for freckles that kissed the apples of her cheeks and the tip of her nose.

"Got any advice?" the girl asked, her bright green eyes sparkling with hope.

"Yeah, get a good agent so you don't wind up doing this in thirty years."

Sarah/Susan tugged on her sleeves before excusing herself to use the restroom.

Alone at last, Jennifer took a sip of her coffee, spotting the remnants of red lipstick on the plastic lid. She ducked under the table to rummage through her handbag for a touch-up.

"Ms. Hawkins?"

She jumped, banging her head hard against the underside of the table.

"Son of a–" Jennifer yelped, clutching her scalp.

The sudden movement dislodged the book balancing the table, sending her photos and the rest of her books into a sprawling mess on the ground before her eyes.

A young man's head popped into view.

"I'm so sorry," he said. "Here, let me help."

Jennifer pushed herself to her feet as the boy stacked the now coffee-stained photos into a loose, uneven pile. He couldn't have been older than twenty-five.

Just when she was about to let him have it, his T-shirt caught her eye. It was the most worn, threadbare *Evil Elf* shirt she'd ever seen. The fabric was faded to near transparency, but Plucky still grinned over the washed-out Vegas skyline. Then she noticed his arms, both inked with *Evil Elf* tattoos. She could even spot the bottom half of her face, peeking out from under his sleeve, her expression in a silent scream–Jennifer's iconic pose from the first film's poster.

Die-hard fans like this, who literally wore their fandoms on their sleeves, were common at movie conventions. But they weren't common for *her* movies. But when they did show up, they spent big.

The boy was turning into a dollar sign before her eyes. Jennifer's growing headache, along with her worries about old gum stuck in her hair, slipped from her mind.

"Oh, it's fine," she said, still rubbing the sore spot on her head as she flashed her well-practiced smile. "I'm used to doing my own stunts."

The fan relaxed into a laugh. "You sure do. Like when you wrestled with Plucky on top of the Empire State Building in *Evil Elf IV*. No stunt double, just you. Now that's what a 'final girl' looks like."

In reality, Jennifer almost never did her own stunts. She fabricated this detail for her book, after hearing that Sigourney Weaver had done hers in *Alien*.

"Well, it wasn't *really* the Empire State Building," she said, before picking up a copy of her book. "It was a set built out of cardboard, which we filmed inside a warehouse. But it was still dangerous...which I discuss more in my book."

"Yes, I know. I already have it."

"Oh," she said. "Then how about a signed photo?"

"No, thank you, I have lots of those too."

Jennifer blinked, unsure of her next move.

"Did you bring something you wanted me to sign, then? Just to let you know, custom items cost extra."

"That's kind of you, but you've already signed all of my *Evil Elf* merch."

"We've already met?" She figured she should feel embarrassed for not remembering him, but all she could think about was the money she wasn't going to make.

"Three times, in fact," he replied. "My name's Vincent Shepard, and I'm here to give *you* something." He pulled out a plastic binder from a satchel slung over his shoulder and set it on the table.

Jennifer flipped it open. "A script?"

The fan grinned. "I called your agent a few times, but seeing as I didn't hear back, I thought I'd come here to see you in person."

She glanced at the script. "Okay...what's the role?"

"You're already well acquainted with her. It's Rebecca Sommers."

Jennifer considered Vincent. "Wait, you're from the studio?" she asked. "I didn't know they were interested in bringing the franchise back."

The latest update she'd heard was that the children of the original–now deceased–writer were squabbling with the studio over the franchise rights.

Vincent shrugged. "I'm not affiliated with the current rights holders."

Jennifer raised an eyebrow.

"It's an independent, unlicensed project. A fan film, to be more precise," he rushed his words out, as though ripping off a Band-Aid. "And I want you to reprise your iconic role."

"You're saying you want me to star in your student film?"

He shook his head. "*Fan* film."

"What's the difference?" Her eyes flicked toward the restroom, silently urging Susan/Sarah to come back and rescue her from this conversation.

Vincent wasn't deterred by Jennifer's obvious impatience. "There's a few. For starters, we know what we are doing. And, most importantly, we have a budget. A rather big one. We've raised over $80,000 from dedicated, hardcore fans of *Evil Elf*."

He paused, allowing for the most important parts of his pitch to sink in. "Fans are sick and tired of waiting for the franchise to return. They want this. They *need* this. *Plus*, we've even got some of your old costars on board too."

Jennifer scoffed. Most of the *Evil Elf* cast were even worse off than she was. She had made up her mind. "Well, that's great. But I'm afraid I don't work in student films–"

Vincent opened his mouth, but Jennifer cut in. "–or *fan* films, and I certainly don't work for free."

"I'm not asking you to work for free. We've got a proper budget, and I'm offering you $60,000 for the role."

"$60,000?"

Jennifer's hand shot for the script. She began skimming the words, then she froze, meeting his gaze. "You're serious?"

"Deadly."

Her eyes flicked to the script, then back to him. "When does filming start?"

"Tomorrow."

"Tomorrow?"

$60,000 was more money than she made all of last year doing conventions. Then again, a lifetime in Hollywood had taught her to be jaded, and, from experience, if something seemed too good to be true, it usually was. She set the script down on the uneven table, her fingers lingering. When she looked up, Vincent had disappeared into Zara Westbrook's ever-growing line.

And within a few moments, Jennifer's booth was swallowed in its shadow.

CHAPTER 2

The second half of the day dragged even longer than the first. After demanding that Sarah/Susan shoo away Zara Westbrook's relentless line of fans blocking her booth, Jennifer snagged a few more people to pay for autographs. But that had been over an hour ago, and the convention was fizzling out.

Jennifer, resigned to the fact that she wasn't going to make any more money, got up to use the restroom. When she returned, her battered red collection tin was left on her chair with a note that read:

Hope to see you next year.
–Sarah

As she picked up the tin, her eyes lingered on Vincent's script on the table. She hesitated before picking it up. It was heavier than the tin.

Jennifer sighed and turned to take down her banner. As she tugged at the corner, her nail ripped straight through the fragile paper.

She should replace it, but deep down knew that she'd tape it together in time for her next convention...which, she realized mid-fold, was only five days away. A knot tightened in the pit of her stomach.

Screw it.

She pulled out a cigarette and lit up.

Some event workers glared at her, but Jennifer didn't flinch. She met their eyes, took a slow, deliberate drag, then exhaled a curl of smoke into the stale air of the convention-turned-bingo hall.

Most of the other "celebrity" guests had left long ago. Zara had been hurried off a full two hours before closing. The few who remained looked as haggard as she felt, all except for Douglas, who was still smiling as he shook hands with his booth assistant across the hall.

As soon as he spotted Jennifer, Douglas's smile spread even wider. He rushed over and gave her a hug.

"Alright, Jenny?" he said in his Yorkshire accent. "How's my favorite 'final girl'?"

"Couldn't be better," she lied. "How's my favorite evil maniac?"

"Great. It's been a fantastic turnout, which is great for me because I've basically given up the acting gig, well, except for a few smaller projects. You know, my back's never been the same since that stunt in part five." He pressed his hand against the small of his back. "But Linda's happy. I'm not away as much, and you can't beat meeting the fans at these things. Look at what they've given me." He gestured to his table, where a collection of items were piled together. There were crochet Plucky dolls, friendship bracelets, decapitated-head Christmas decorations, and cupcakes covered in fake blood and impaled with little candy cane shivs.

"There was also this one fan who told me about a cool project he wants me to be involved in," Douglas continued. "It's all very mysterious, though. I don't know if he came up to you, too?"

Jennifer was distracted by the table full of junk. *Where the hell did he store all this stuff?*

"Well, yeah, anyway, what about you, Jenny? You must be beating the offers off with a stick?"

"There's one audition coming up that's promising," she lied.

"I'm sure you'll get it," Douglas smiled. "Say, are you up to anything now? I'd love to have you round for dinner. Linda always makes too much, and the kids would be thrilled to see you again."

"Not tonight, I'm exhausted. Rain check?"

"Absolutely. Well, I best get going, otherwise the wife will think I've been kidnapped by a crazy fan."

She gave Douglas another hug before making her own way toward the exit.

* * *

Jennifer pulled into her apartment parking lot, leaving everything in the car apart from the script, her phone, the money tin, and a canvas bag that clinked as she traipsed to her door. She fumbled with the key in the lock, that familiar dread prickling at her–the fear that the landlord had changed the locks again.

But when it clicked open, she exhaled in relief.

She pushed open the door, stepping into the eternal pile of mail on the floor. Pushing aside the bills with her foot, she caught sight of the SAG-AFTRA logo on one of the envelopes. Her heart leaped–it was a residual check. She snatched it up, tore it open, and went straight to the number in the bottom corner.

Our Broken Hour: $0.20.

After walking away from the franchise after the fifth film, her career seemed promising. She landed the role of sharp-tongued attorney Olivia Montgomery in a primetime courtroom drama–only for it to be canceled after only ten episodes. She then transitioned into daytime soaps, securing a role on *Our Broken Hour*. This lasted seventeen episodes before her character met a dramatic demise–a car explosion orchestrated by her vengeful adopted sister.

This abrupt and brutal act was written in after rumors spread that she was "difficult to work with on set." All she had wanted was to make the character–and the show–better. But word traveled fast in Hollywood, and soon, the phone stopped ringing.

She balled up the residual check and tossed it into the trash.

Peeling her shirt over her head, she caught the stale scent of recycled bingo hall air on the fabric. She dumped the rest of her clothes into an overflowing laundry basket, already relishing the prospect of washing away the day's grime–that is, if she had remembered to take out the last load.

Too exhausted for a shower, she slipped on a robe, raked her hair into a loose bun, and trudged to the kitchen clutching the canvas bag. Her bare feet slapped against the sticky vinyl floor.

From the bag, she pulled out a fistful of miniature gin bottles, swiped from the convention green room. One by one, she twisted off the caps and emptied them into a giant Big Gulp cup, finishing the mix with a splash of cranberry juice.

Jennifer sank into the sagging sofa, propped her feet up on the cluttered coffee table, and took a long swig of her lukewarm cocktail. She let out a small sigh as the tension of the day melted away.

Her next order of business: the remote. Flicking through channels, she bypassed countless infomercials until her younger self appeared on screen. Covered in blood and clutching a tangled web of Christmas lights, Rebecca was in a face-off against Plucky the Elf, who had descended down the chimney with a burst of smoke. "Have you been naughty or nice?" the elf taunted.

And there it was–the ear-splitting screech that crowned her as a certified scream queen.

Jennifer mocked her character with a yawn whilst Rebecca Sommers screamed for her life. She took another gulp of her drink as her younger self tussled around with Douglas. Though it was cheesy, she couldn't help but appreciate the effort. The blasting synthesizer score, the shaky camera work, and the gallons of fake blood–she had to admit, it was impressive for its time. But all Jennifer could remember was her and Douglas giggling through the scene, ruining take after take.

Jennifer turned the TV volume down and shifted her focus to the collection tin. Spilling its contents onto the coffee table, she formed a messy pile of crumpled bills and scattered coins. She didn't bother counting it; she knew the takings were less than last time, and even less than the signing before that.

Taking another swallow of her drink, she pushed the small mound of money aside and glanced up at the TV. There she was, gaining the upper hand on Plucky. She coiled Christmas lights around his neck, lightbulbs popping and sparking as she tightened her grip. Plucky kicked and wriggled while she wielded a sharpened candy cane in her free hand. The camera zoomed in on the weapon, glazed in a green and red glow, as she plunged the pointed end down and pierced the bastard through the eye. His eye exploded, blood bursting from the socket. Jennifer winced away from the TV. Though she knew it was all staged, the sight of blood–even if only red food dye and corn syrup–made her stomach churn. She'd been on the edge of vomiting for many of her days on set.

The script, abandoned on the kitchen countertop, caught her eye next. Stumbling over to it, she read the title. *Evil Elf: The Revenge of Plucky–A Fan Film by Vincent Shepard.*

Not the most original title, she thought between swigs.

Needing more downtime before tackling the thick stack of pages, Jennifer tossed it on the sofa and picked up her phone. She had no messages–not even a spam email. Opening her phone app, she selected the only contact listed.

There were two rings before a peppy voice answered. "Hello, Magnum Agency. This is Clarissa speaking. How can I assist you today?"

Her chipper tone grated on Jennifer. "Is Andrew there?"

"May I ask who's calling?"

"It's Jennifer."

"Jennifer..." Clarissa's voice trailed off as she scanned through a contact list.

"Hawkins," Jennifer sighed.

There was a brief murmur in the background. "I'm sorry, but Mr. Lewis has stepped out. Can I take a message?"

"Yes, do you have a pen on hand?"

"I do indeed."

"Great, are you ready?"

"Yes, ma'am."

"Tell that lazy son of a bitch if he doesn't answer my call, I'm going to come over there and shove his head so far up his ass he'll be picking sweetcorn out of his teeth for weeks."

There was a long pause.

"Jen, baby, how are you?" Andrew's voice came through. "I heard you've been terrorizing my poor new receptionist."

"What future sexual harassment lawsuit did you hire this time?" Jennifer muted the TV.

"Whoa, who put a stick up your ass?"

"You try being grabbed and groped by sweaty basement dwellers for hours on end, and see if you're still as peppy as Little Miss Sunshine over there."

"You're getting paid to sit on your ass, sign your name, and take photos."

"Did you follow up about that audition or not?"

"...Yes, I asked."

"And?"

"It was a no."

Silence.

"They said you weren't right for the part, Jen."

"But I'm perfect for it."

"*I* know that," he said. "But they decided to age the character down."

Her eyes drifted back to the TV. Dressed in that awful Christmas sweater and drenched in blood, *she* didn't recognize the girl staring back. She switched off the TV.

"Jen, you still there?"

"I can't do this anymore," Jennifer said, staring at the stained ceiling. She reached for her cigarettes, slipped one between her lips, lit it, and took a long drag before exhaling.

"These conventions, it's humiliating. I'm an actor, I need to act."

"Jen, please relax," Andrew said. "You'll be happy to know I've got a few auditions lined up."

"Yeah?" Jennifer refocused.

"There's an exciting role playing a landlady in *Tower Block Six*. It's a direct-to-streaming sequel, but it sounds promising."

Silence again.

Andrew cleared his throat. "There's also a guest role as Great Aunt Sally in *The Family Flip*. It's a new sitcom on CBS."

"Andrew," Jennifer began, "I've told you a hundred times. I want to do real movies. I want real roles. That means no shitty sequels, and I definitely don't want to be anyone's Great Aunt Fucking Sally."

She heard a deep sigh. "Look honey, you need to be realistic. You're hot, I find you crazy sexy, you know I do–everyone at the office does, I've got your headshot right here in my office–but, come on, you're a..." He paused to muster the least offensive phrasing. "*Mature* woman, known for starring in..." Pausing again. "A certain kind of genre."

"Just say it, Andrew, schlocky horror shit." She threw back the rest of her drink. "I don't even know what you do for me anymore. I've been with you for, what, forty fucking years? Talk about me sitting on *my* ass–what about you in that big office, sitting on your ass, watching your receptionist's ass while *being* an ass..." She found her voice trailing off as she sank further into the couch.

"In this business, as it's always been...there aren't many options for someone of your age, and many actres–"

She hung up before he could finish, drawing in one last drag of her cigarette.

CHAPTER 3

Jennifer's eyelids, fused together with sleep crust and cheap eyeliner, peeled open. There was a loud buzzing.

Hazy memories of overweight stormtroopers carrying tinfoil weapons spun in her mind. Then, a horrific thought came to her. Did she take one of them home? It wouldn't be the first time she had woken up next to a Ferengi or a Jawa. She turned her heavy head and was relieved to find that the left-side of the bed was empty.

Once the world had settled, Jennifer staggered and swayed over to the bathroom, where she buried her face in the toilet bowl and unloaded the contents of last night's liquid dinner.

"Never again," she promised herself for the hundredth time.

In the mirror, stained with greasy fingerprints and toothpaste splatters, she studied the smudged mascara under her eyes. She filled the sink with hot water, tossed in a washcloth, and let it swirl amongst the rising steam. She doused her hands with cleansing oil and massaged it into her face, before pressing the cloth on top. She met her reflection's eyes once more. Unfortunately, some things couldn't be washed away, like the deep laugh lines around her mouth. Were those jowls? A visit to Dr. Cardwell was long overdue. Each month, she set aside a generous portion of her earnings for touch-ups and tightening. But the only thing that was tightening in the meantime was her budget.

Jennifer grabbed a near-empty pot of anti-aging cream and pried off the lid. Scraping her long, chipped fingernail into the bottom, she scooped up a tiny morsel of cream and applied it to the deep grooves under and around her tired eyes. At $100 a pot, she was already conservative with the amount she used, but she found herself needing a new one every two weeks.

Buzzzz...

She clamped a hand on her throbbing head.

Buzzzzzz...

She stormed over to the door intercom.

"If you little shits don't stop pressing that button, then so help me, I'm gonna come down there and shove my foot so far up your–"

"Uh," a voice cracked through the intercom. "Your ride is here."

"My ride? You've got the wrong apartment, hun. I didn't order a ride."

"This is Ms. Hawkins, right? Jennifer Hawkins? I'm here to take you to the shoot."

"Shoot? What shoot?"

"The *Evil Elf* shoot. Vincent sent me."

"Vincent? I don't know a–" Then, from the murky recesses of her mind, it came to her. A hazy memory from the night before took shape. She now remembered messaging the number on the front of the script, a decision motivated by five miniature bottles of gin. Jennifer dropped her head against the intercom. "Shit."

"I'll be waiting for you down here, ma'am," the voice said.

"No, wait," she cried. "There's been a mistake."

No response.

Jennifer paced the cramped apartment, weighing her options. She could leave him waiting.

She hadn't signed anything legally binding yet. Besides, she was under the influence when she agreed. Surely that doesn't count...right? Or did it? She rubbed her temples. Was there such a thing as deciding-under-the-influence?

She continued to pace, but one thought shouted the loudest. She needed the money. $60,000 would be more than she could ever make as an occasional TV guest star. It could cover her rent for the year, and leave a little for Dr. Cardwell, too.

She could either star in this fan film, something that nobody would probably ever see, and make some easy money, or she could keep doing the convention circuit, repeating the events of yesterday over and over. At least with the first option, she could afford a break from the second. Her stomach churned, remembering she had another con scheduled for next week.

Jennifer took three deep breaths, knowing full well what she was going to do.

She threw whatever clean clothes she had into a suitcase, skipping showering and makeup. There would be hair and makeup artists on set. Besides, she wouldn't be expected to start acting right away.

* * *

Jennifer stepped outside with her heavy suitcase to find a twenty-something-year-old in gray sweatpants and a baggy black shirt, fully absorbed in his phone. When he noticed Jennifer struggling with her bags, he rushed over.

"Hi, I'm Michael, your driver."

"So, where's the car?" she asked, scanning the parking lot.

"Right here." He gestured to a small sedan caked in sand and dirt.

"What is *that*?" she scoffed.

"A 1993 Geo Metro ma'am." He stored her suitcase in the trunk before opening the passenger-side door for her.

Her eyes shifted from his sweatpants to the car, then back to her apartment. It was no Rolls-Royce, but she had to remind herself that this wasn't a studio movie–it was a fan film. Considering that most of the budget was probably going to her, she supposed she could forgive the unimpressive transportation–as long as no one saw her, of course.

Instead of settling into the passenger seat, she pulled the lever to lean it forward and then clambered into the back seat.

"Uh, okay..." Michael muttered, before settling into the driver's seat.

The car huffed and spluttered to life as it set off.

Jennifer leaned back in the worn seat and stared out of the smudged window, catching a glimpse of the Hollywood sign in the distance as the car merged onto the highway. Despite the uncomfortable seat, the monotony of the passing nodding donkeys lulled her into a drowsy state and she drifted to sleep.

* * *

The car jolted as it hit a pothole, and Jennifer's head smacked hard against the window.

"Son of a bitch," she cried out, rubbing her temple while shooting a glare at her driver through the rearview mirror.

"Sorry," he winced. "The roads out here are terrible."

Jennifer peered out the window to see where *here* was and was greeted by a vast expanse of barren desert stretching as far as the eye could see.

"How long have I been out?" she asked, rubbing her itchy eyes.

"About four hours."

"Four hours!"

He nodded, keeping his eyes focused on the pockmarked road ahead.

"Where exactly is the shoot?" she asked–probably a question better asked *before* climbing into a stranger's car. Only now did it hit her: she had no idea where they were going or how long they'd be gone. A new thought crept in–was this all some elaborate setup to abduct her?

"You don't know?" he asked.

She shook her head. Her fingers inched toward the front seat's lever. She imagined herself flinging the car door open before tucking and rolling. She'd seen one of her stunt doubles pull it off once–it hadn't seemed all that hard. But even if she somehow survived rolling on hard dirt and rocks at sixty miles per hour, where could she run off to? She'd be stranded in the middle of nowhere. There were no other cars, no houses, and no nodding donkeys in sight.

"We're going to where it all began."

She caught his grin in the rearview mirror.

As if on cue, they drove past a rusted, bullet-riddled sign: *Now Entering Tinseltown, NV. Where It's Christmas All Day, Every Day.*

"You've got to be joking," Jennifer stared out the bug-smeared windshield.

"Welcome ho-ho-home, Ms. Hawkins."

Without warning, he jerked the wheel hard and veered off the road, tires spitting dust as they hit the packed desert floor.

Jennifer grabbed the front seat headrest. "Are you trying to kill me?"

"Relax," Michael replied. "I need some fuel. We're running low."

"Where the hell are you going to find gas out–"

Up ahead was a derelict gas station slumped off the side of the road, a rotting relic under the penetrating sun. A faded sign reading "Santa's #1 for Reindeer Refuel" hung crookedly over the sagging canopy that shaded the old store door.

"You sure this place is even open?" Jennifer asked.

But sure enough, the door swung open and out stepped a man in dusty blue overalls. Gray, stringy hair spilled out from under a tattered blue baseball cap. The man perched himself on a splintered rocking chair by the entrance. His pale eyes locked onto Jennifer's as he hacked a ball of black phlegm into the dirt.

"Are you sure you need gas this bad?"

"Unless you want to hike to Tinseltown." Michael pulled up next to one of the pumps and got out.

He wrestled with the gas pump while the attendant made no move to assist, simply rocking back and forth, his jaw grinding tobacco.

Jennifer debated waiting in the car, but the lure of a fridge stocked with cold drinks called to her. The station might have looked like it was from the 1920s, but surely it could offer at least a chilled bottle of water–maybe even something stronger to take back to her trailer. That last thought alone forced her to step out into the blistering heat.

They were deep in the middle of nowhere. The wind whistled across the barren desert, rattling the loose boards of the canopy.

She walked up to the store. The gas station attendant remained in his chair. She glanced at his overalls, where a peeling name tag identified him as Bob.

"Hi Bob," Jennifer said. "I take it you have some drinks here?"

He huffed, then struggled to his feet. Without a word, he yanked open the door and stepped inside.

"Well, you coming or what?" A thick Southern drawl drifted from inside the dark store.

Jennifer turned back toward Michael, who was still struggling with the pump. She hesitated for a moment before stepping inside.

It was stiflingly hot, the air thick and still, lit by a few dim, flickering fluorescent bulbs. Old newspapers plastered the windows, blocking out most of the sunlight. Shelves held only a handful of dusty items. Dirty floor tiles were caked with layers of dirt and sand–no one had cleaned this place in years.

By the door stood a bargain bin filled with DVDs. As Jennifer leaned in, she realized they were all copies of *Evil Elf*. It was strange seeing her old franchise being sold way out here in the desert, but she figured Bob here was cashing in on being near the original filming setting. Then she noticed something else–they were all *Part VI*, the only installment she and Douglas hadn't been in. Figuring that she should be grateful that none of hers were here, covered in thick dust, she picked one up. Turning the case over in her hand, she could see why they were here. It looked awful. Set in space, Plucky had become some kind of cyborg–painted silver, eyes glowing red, with parts of his costume replaced with wires and cheap robotic panels. She took in the cover, noticing how the iconic candy cane shiv was now a candy-cane-shaped laser staff. She stared into the off-brand Plucky's eyes, with the words "They wanted holiday cheer. They got interstellar fear." emblazoned above him. Saying no to the film had been a good move.

Bob leaned over the counter, his pale eyes tracking Jennifer as she moved farther into the store.

"Nice place you got here," Jennifer said.

Bob only grunted, his eyes never leaving hers.

At the back of the store stood a lone, unlit refrigerator. Jennifer reached inside for a bottle; it was warm to the touch. She made a face.

Bob shrugged. "Damn thing on the fritz again."

Jennifer could only guess the water had been in there for God knows how long, but she couldn't afford to be picky out here. Given her hangover, the heat, and the long journey, she placed the bottle on the counter.

"Where you headed?" Bob asked, his pale eyes dropping to take every part of her in.

"Tinseltown," she said. "It's been a good few years since I've been back. In fact, I had no idea it was still open."

Bob burst into laughter. It was startling. When he threw back his head, she caught sight of the black tar stuck between his teeth and gums.

"You're a little late, darlin'. Tinseltown ain't open. That place closed down over a year ago."

She wondered how they were going to film their movie in an abandoned amusement park. Would it even still have power?

"Yup. When Tinseltown closed up, so did everything else around here. Except for me, of course. Ya can't get rid of ol' Bob. That's what the ladies used to say, anyway."

This sent him into another fit of laughter, harsh and rasping, before he started gagging. He spat out a wad of black tar behind the counter before grabbing a tin and popping two fresh lumps into his mouth.

As his jaw worked the tobacco, his face shifted. He leaned over the counter, his eyes clamped onto Jennifer's.

"Don't go there."

"What?"

Bob's eyes flicked to the window, where Michael was waiting by the car, then back to Jennifer–their faces inches apart. She fought the instinct to pull away.

"It's dangerous," Bob croaked.

"Dangerous, how?"

"Some say there's a force there, some kinda creature. Folks who've gone there don't never come back."

"A creature, you say?" Jennifer stifled the urge to laugh. She didn't want to upset the old guy; besides, she didn't know how he'd react if she did.

He nodded. "Think me crazy if you must. But don't say I didn't warn ya. There's a monster waiting for ya there. And there's a reason why no one comes this way no more."

"I'll take that advice on board, Bob," Jennifer said, eager to end the conversation and get back on the road. "Can I pay for this, please?"

Bob drew back, crossing his arms. "Five dollars."

Jennifer put her card on the counter.

"We don't take cards here, lady. Cash only."

"You're not serious."

"Ma'am, does it look like this place has the internet?"

"I don't carry cash," she snapped. "No one does."

Bob spat another wad of tobacco into a bucket. It landed with a loud *twang* against the metal.

"Fine, I'll leave it," Jennifer muttered, unwilling to argue with the old man any longer.

As she turned to leave, his voice called after her, low and gravelly. "Remember what I told ya, ya hear?"

CHAPTER 4

As soon as the rusted doorbell tinkled shut, a voice crackled into the gas station.

"Cut."

"Thank God," Bob muttered, his thick Southern drawl falling away.

He grabbed the beat-up metal bucket by his feet, leaned over, and retched, hawking up a glob of black spit.

"Jesus Christ," he gagged, his West Coast accent coming through as he wiped his mouth with the back of his hand. "Tastes like death."

From under the counter, he grabbed a bottle of mouthwash and took a large swig. He swished the blue liquid, washing away the tar that coated his tongue and teeth, before spitting into the bucket again.

"It's too hot for this shit." He slid his fingers under his sweaty baseball cap, careful not to knock the hairpieces that were already sliding over his clammy scalp.

Grabbing the radio underneath the cash register, he squeezed a button on the side.

"So, what did you think, boss?" he asked, turning to the shelving behind him where a GoPro camera sat hidden between two dusty boxes of cereal. “Was I hamming it up too much at the end there? I feel like I was. Can we do another take?”

An engine roared to life outside. He crossed to the window to squint through the cracks between the newspaper.

“Wait...she’s leaving?” he cried, as the car disappeared in a cloud of dust.

The radio crackled to life. “No, that’s great, Dan. Honestly, you were awesome. We’ve got everything we need for that scene and we’re ready to move on to the next, so get yourself back into Bob mode and let’s reset the scene.”

“Don’t you think this character is a little too cliché?” Dan said into the radio. “I mean, isn’t the freaky gas station attendant trope a little overdone?”

A deep sigh hissed through the radio.

It was not the first time Dan had raised concerns, and every time, he was shot down. Besides, he was used to being treated like shit by directors. He shut his mouth and pressed his sideburns firmly against his skin in the grubby mirror.

“Can I at least do the scene without the tobacco?”

The radio crackled again. “No. It’s integral to the character.”

It was Bob’s turn to sigh. He grabbed the tin of chew and popped a black lump into his mouth. The bitter tar clung to his gums and he grimaced, fighting the urge to gag. He reached for the script hidden under the counter and flipped to the next scene. Again it was vague, offering little to no dialogue and minimal stage direction.

When he first spotted this job posting on Craigslist, Dan was instantly drawn to it–not only for the generous day rate, but for the heavy emphasis on ad-libbing. He had been taking improv classes for years, sandwiched in between his long driving shifts for Uber. By this point, he knew pretty much every teacher in Hollywood–all with their own styles. But one thing they all emphasized was how things went wrong on set all the time, and it was a necessary skill to be quick on your feet and come up with lines on the fly. Even when miserable old actresses give you absolutely nothing to work with. But still, Dan was quietly confident he had pulled it off. He could not believe that she was happy with that single take and left. So unprofessional. She wouldn't make it in the business.

The radio squawked. "Action."

Ever the professional, Dan pushed his doubts aside and slid back into being Bob. When he landed a role, he fully committed to the part, no matter how small or ridiculous it was. So, he made sure his jaw worked the tobacco, chewing on it like it was the most delicious damn thing in the world, all while wiping down the filthy countertop with a greasy rag. He was desperate to break out of extra work, and this could be his chance.

Five minutes crawled by as he scrubbed and scrubbed. Just as he was about to break character and demand some actual direction, a sharp bang jolted him upright.

Something had fallen off a shelf at the back of the store.

Was this part of the scene? Or just an accident? If it was planned, he had no idea how they had rigged it. As far as he knew, he was the only one in the building.

Dan glanced at one of the three unblinking GoPros mounted high in the corner before forcing himself to relax and stay in the moment. His character would not panic. His character would lumber over to check it out.

Dan muttered a low curse under his breath, dragging his left foot behind him as he moved. He had decided his character was an ex-college football player who had wrecked his knee and ended up stuck here; that's why he was such a miserable ass.

A can of beer rolled across the floor, foam hissing from its split top as the amber liquid bled across the filthy tiles. He ran his tongue across dry lips. His throat burned. Sweat clung to his shirt, and the heavy, stagnant air pressed in from all sides–this place was a goddamn oven.

As he bent down to pick up the can, he heard a jingle–like the tinkering of a bell.

His head whipped toward the door, half-expecting the woman to have returned to redo their scene. But the door was firmly closed. His brow furrowed.

Another thud echoed through the store, this time from somewhere back near the counter.

"Hello?" Dan called out, using his character's Southern accent.

Peeking past the shelf, he caught a flash of green. Whatever it was, it was fast.

"Anyone there?"

Grunting, he straightened up and shuffled toward the cash register. But he found nothing. The store was empty.

Dan sighed, his sweat-soaked shirt clinging to his back. His character's frustration matched his own. This was getting tedious.

The bell chimed again.

He spun around, maybe too sharply for his character, and caught a glimpse of something ducking behind the far aisle. His heart lurched. It vanished as quickly as it appeared. The store was dim, but even in the poor light he had made out a pale, mangled face.

His eyes flicked to the GoPro, then to the radio on the counter. If the director was still watching the live feed, which Dan had to assume he was, then he hadn't called cut. Which meant the scene was still on.

"Hey," he called out. "You there. What are you doing in my store?" Spitting out a glob of tobacco for good measure.

The only reply was the faint jangle of bells.

Dan stormed through the aisle, ready to catch whoever it was. But once again, he found it empty.

The heat of the room was smothering. The only sound was the buzz of the fluorescent lights and a few lazy flies that danced beneath the dim glow, until the bulbs cut out completely, leaving only a single stream of light struggling through the newspaper-plastered windows. And the red camera lights that indicated that they were still rolling.

Dan wiped his brow, careful not to remove the makeup he applied that morning. He needed this scene to end. He wanted to go home.

Another bell rang. Closer this time. And he knew for sure it wasn't the one hung above the store's door.

Dan spun around and spotted the head again, now behind the second aisle. But it didn't lurch back like before. It was frozen, its angle unnatural.

Through the shadows, Dan could make out a lopsided grin stretched on its face. Around the smile, the skin was bone-white, cracked and flaking.

Dan dropped the faux Southern accent. "You scared the shit out of me, man."

The figure didn't respond. It only twisted its head farther into a disjointed tilt.

Dan's eyes darted to the GoPro again. *What if this wasn't part of the scene?*

He stepped back. His eyes locked on the exit.

He slipped on something. He went down hard, his head slamming against the floor tiles with a crack. The spilled beer soaked into his sweat-drenched shirt.

The lump of tobacco caught in his throat, choking him. He gagged, spitting black phlegm into the brown puddle.

"Fuck this," Dan croaked. "The scene's over. We're done."

The radio crackled on the counter. "Actors don't call cut. You know that. Stay in character, please."

Dan gagged again, twisting onto his stomach as he hacked up the last of the tobacco.

When he looked up, he froze.

The thing was closer now, standing behind the nearest aisle. It was only feet away, with the same unnatural head tilt.

Dan scrambled to his feet, but a sharp jolt knifed through the back of his knee, buckling him mid-step.

He screamed and hit the floor again, face down.

Something heavy slammed down on his back, crushing the air out of his lungs. His ribs pressed against the floor.

Dan's fingers scrambled across the filthy tiles, searching for something to hold onto but finding nothing.

His head twisted just enough to catch the unblinking red light of the GoPro mounted overhead, silently recording.

"Please," he gasped.

Over his exposed cheek, he could feel the pant of hot, sour breath. The creature pressed closer. Dan could smell old rubber.

"Have you been naughty...or nice?"

Before Dan could answer, a hand clasped around the back of his skull.

His head was yanked back and then slammed down with force, again and again.

The world tilted, warped, and blurred with each blow. Dan's last memory was the sight of his blood swirling with the beer-soaked floor.

Still, the camera's red eye stared, unblinking.

CHAPTER 5

Jennifer pressed her forehead against the warm glass, watching Tinseltown's entrance approach. An imposing, disembodied Santa Claus head loomed over the road as they drove closer. Parts of his once-jolly face were rusted away to reveal tangled honeycomb chicken wire beneath, and his pupils, now bleached white from the unforgiving sun, still seemed to follow them as they drove through Santa's gaping mouth.

Gravel crunched under the tires as they pulled into a wide-open parking lot. It was empty, except for a minivan, a bus, and three large gazebos.

She swallowed, the dryness scraping her throat like sandpaper. "God, I need water. Where's catering?"

"I don't know about any catering, but you can grab some water from over there." He pointed to the black gazebo.

As soon as he parked, she got out of the car and rushed over to it.

"I guess I'll get your bags then?" Michael called after her.

Inside, she found a table of bottled water. Rushing over, she grabbed one and drank. It was warm, but she didn't care as she finished the whole bottle. At least it was marginally cooler here than it was outside, thanks to the shade and an industrial fan that was working overtime, powered by a loud diesel generator.

As she reached for another bottle, Jennifer noticed a woman, perhaps in her late fifties, early sixties, her hair streaked with white and silvery tones. Sitting in a fold-up chair, the woman wore brown suede cowboy boots dusted from the desert. Bangles jingled softly on her wrists as she flipped through a magazine, completely absorbed and oblivious to Jennifer's arrival.

While most production runners onsets were young, overly enthusiastic film students trying to break into the industry, it wasn't unusual to find much older adults in these roles as well–often retirees looking for extra income or wanting to get out of the house.

"Hey," Jennifer said.

The woman glanced up from her magazine, her eyes lighting up as they met Jennifer's. "Oh my goodness," she said in a warm Southern drawl.

"Can you grab me some food?"

"Excuse me?"

"A Danish if you have any, and a coffee. Black with sweetener. Oh, and some aspirin."

The woman's smile faltered. "You don't know who I am, do you?"

Jennifer rubbed her temples. "It's been a long drive, my head's pounding. Can you just do your job, please?"

The woman threw down her magazine and stormed out of the gazebo.

"Wow, that was rude," came a voice from behind her.

Jennifer turned to see another woman sitting by the entrance, a script draped over her crossed legs. She had a short black pixie cut and deep plum lipstick that contrasted harshly against her pale skin. Her arms were also crossed, obscuring a purple sequined dress and a tangle of Mardi Gras beads. There was something familiar about her. Vincent had mentioned she'd be working with actors across the franchise, so it was possible they'd crossed paths before. But after filming five *Evil Elf* movies over seven years, Jennifer had seen countless actors come and go. It was understandable that she couldn't recall every single one.

"Right?" Jennifer said. "I guess good help is hard to come by these days."

"I'm talking about you."

"What did *I* do?" Jennifer said, taken aback.

"You really don't recognize her, do you?"

"No?"

"I'll give you a hint: you were in a movie together," the woman said, rocking back in her chair, part playful, part smug.

Jennifer blinked.

The woman stopped rocking, letting all four chair legs thud against the ground. "*Evil Elf III.*"

"Oh," Jennifer paused, "Well, I've worked with a lot of people over the years. I can't remember everyone."

"Apparently not," the woman said coolly as she strode out of the gazebo.

Still trying to process the exchange, Jennifer was soon distracted by Michael popping his head in.

"Ms. Hawkins? If you'll follow me, I'll show you to the trailer."

Jennifer followed Michael across the gravel parking lot while he wrestled with her suitcases, the wheels catching on every bump. He led her to a large, rusted blue vehicle–less of a trailer, more like a battered old school bus.

Michael shoved the vehicle's stiff sliding door open before trudging with her luggage up the steps. Jennifer climbed aboard and froze. The bus was cramped and chaotic. There were six narrow bunks lining either side, leaving only a slim aisle down the center to shimmy down. Four of the bunks were already claimed, cluttered with personal items and overstuffed luggage.

Michael grunted, heaved, and dropped Jennifer's suitcases onto one of the last available bunks at the end.

"Here you are," he said, between deep breaths.

"Here I am, what?"

"Your accommodation, your bed, your boudoir."

"No, no, no," Jennifer shook her head and marched back down the bus. Scrambling out, she scanned the parking lot and spotted the guy she recognized from yesterday's convention: Vincent.

He was hunched over a little contraption that had propellers attached. He wore a faded baseball hat emblazoned with *Evil Elf VI* and was wearing yet another *Evil Elf* shirt. This time Plucky wore Mardi Gras beads and brandished a rusty alligator hook with a beignet pierced at its end. The words "Silent night? Not in the Quarter, sugar" were printed below. Jennifer suspected Vincent's entire wardrobe consisted exclusively of Plucky the Elf merchandise.

He raised his head and smiled. "Jennifer, it's so wonderful to see you. I can't tell you how excited I was when I received your text message last night."

"Where's my trailer?"

"It's right over there."

"That's a bus, not a trailer. I hope you're not expecting me to sleep in it."

"They're not strangers. You've worked with them all before. They're your costars."

"It's not professional," she said, crossing her arms. "I need my own private accommodation. A trailer or a hotel room. Anything but *that*." Jennifer couldn't even bear to look at the heap of rusted metal twenty feet away.

Vincent scratched beneath his hat, his sandy-colored hair clinging to his scalp with sweat. "I'm afraid that's a no-go. Look around you, Ms. Hawkins, we're in the middle of nowhere. There isn't a hotel or motel for miles."

Jennifer glared at him. "This is unacceptable. Every film I've ever worked on, no matter how small, always gave me my own private room."

Vincent sighed. "Ms. Hawkins, please remember, this is a fan film. We're not on a studio lot. We don't have the luxury of giving every actor their own trailer. Every single cent was spent on production, most of which, I might add, went toward your pay. Besides, you won't have to put up with these conditions for much longer."

"And why's that?" Jennifer crossed her arms.

"Because we're filming your death scene tomorrow."

CHAPTER 6

"I die?"

"Believe me, the scene will be tastefully done," Vincent boasted, his eyes drifting off past her shoulder and into the distance.

Jennifer snatched his copy of the script off the ground and flicked through the pages.

"Page seventeen."

Jennifer found the page and read it, then read it again. She glared at him.

"A fucking heart attack? That's how you decide to kill off Rebecca Sommers? One of the most beloved 'final girls' in horror movie history?" Her blood boiled.

"Exactly, the audience will never see it coming."

Jennifer rolled up the script and stepped toward Vincent. "She's gone toe to toe with this little shit for five movies. She pushed him off the Empire State Building, for fuck's sake. Now you've written her to go out like some frail old bitch? Really?"

Her grip on the script tightened as she considered swiping Vincent's head with it. Sensing the imminent attack, Vincent stepped back, raising his tattooed hands. The faded words "Naughty" and "Nice" were inked on each palm.

"Ms. Hawkins, please," Vincent winced. "You have to keep in mind that this isn't an official sequel. Think of this Rebecca

Sommers as separate from the one you know. Like a different reality. As I'm sure you know, there are five different timelines in the *Halloween* franchise alone. Jamie Lee Curtis's character of Laurie Strode in *Halloween H20* is separate from the one she played in the 2008 *Halloween*. Same character, but different versions. Do you understand what I'm saying?"

Jennifer narrowed her eyes. She wasn't going to make it easy for the kid. But Vincent continued calmly. "Basically, even though you die in this film, your character is still very much alive in the main continuity."

Jennifer crossed her arms, tucking the script under her arm. With her weapon now out of the danger zone, Vincent's shoulders relaxed. "How many times have we seen you defeat Plucky? Five? Six if you include his two deaths in *Mischief in Vegas*. Everyone knew before they even walked into the movie that you'd end up on top. It's repetitive. Predictable. So, why not subvert the audience's expectations?"

She considered it only for a moment, before shoving the rolled-up script into Vincent's chest. "No. Rebecca Sommers doesn't die. She's *the* 'final girl.' Change it."

"Let me put it this way: the sooner we kill off your character, the sooner you can go home. Sound good?"

He patted Jennifer on the arm and edged past her before she could respond.

"Please familiarize yourself with the script. We start filming in a few hours, Ms. Hawkins," Vincent called over his shoulder as he strolled away.

* * *

Back in the bus, Jennifer stormed up and down the narrow aisle.

"Fucking arrogant asshole," she muttered to herself. Her hands shook as she rummaged through her purse for the cigarettes buried deep inside. She considered grabbing her bags and demanding that Michael take her back to her apartment. She hadn't signed a contract; she could leave whenever she wanted. Not finding the pack, she threw her purse hard onto the floor. Thankfully, Jennifer found a limp cigarette in her pocket, jammed it into her mouth, and slumped onto her bed. But then, of course, she wouldn't get paid. Without pay, she'd have to do double the amount of convention appearances to cover her rent.

Jennifer stared up at the bus's ceiling. Pinpricks of sunlight filtered through rusted holes, the faint beams catching the dust drifting in the air.

Besides, what did she care if they killed off Rebecca Sommers? She hadn't played the role in three decades and wasn't expecting to again. This could be her final chance to say goodbye to the character that held her back. Plus, like Vincent said, it was just a fan film. If anything, that took the pressure off–she doubted anyone would ever see it.

As she considered all of this, the bus rocked and shook. Was it about to drive off with her inside? She wouldn't be surprised. Jennifer popped her head into the aisle to investigate, but her view was blocked by a large man clambering onto the bus holding a duffel bag. Huffing and wheezing, sweat pebbled and dripped from his forehead. He paused by the entrance to catch his breath, lifting his chin up to inhale the hot air. Jennifer found his face oddly familiar but couldn't quite place it. Vincent had mentioned she'd worked with everyone on the bus–so who was this guy?

The man caught Jennifer staring.

"Holy shit. Long time no see," he said.

The man squeezed himself closer. Jennifer sat up.

Scared of repeating the same awkward mistake in the gazebo earlier, she went along with the interaction and kept things vague. "Hey, yes, it's been so long!"

"What's it been? Like, forty years? *Forty-five* years?"

She shrugged and forced a smile. "Your guess is as good as mine."

He studied her face. "You don't recognize me, do you?"

"Of course I do," she insisted.

"No, you don't. I could always see right through you. It's me, Johnny. Johnny Holt? I guess my hair is a little thinner and I'm a bit more...well, fuller around the middle. But come on, I haven't changed that much," He laughed, patting his stomach.

She couldn't believe it was the same person.

Johnny played her love interest in the second *Evil Elf* installment. Unlike many of her forgotten costars, whom she rarely spent any time with between shoots, she found herself sharing pretty much all of her downtime with him from day one. She remembered that during auditions, the director's daughter hailed him the next big heartthrob. The guy that would be plastered over girls' lockers all across America. And so, he was hired.

Johnny was tall, broad-shouldered, and had effortlessly tousled dark hair. He would have been the boy in school who rode in on a motorcycle while the other guys grouped around their sweet sixteen LeSabres, the kind of guy that would joke with you by the lockers while your friends looked over in envy.

All the girls on set fawned over Johnny. The makeup artists would fight to apply his face powder, adjust his collar, read lines with him, or run their fingers through his already perfect hair. She was often told how lucky she was to have his arms wrapped around her, even if it was in front of the cameras. But that was the thrill for her.

As production continued, they started "rehearsing" in her trailer, and, before long, fiction blurred into reality as Jennifer and Johnny became an official item. The director said their chemistry bettered their performances, and the studio suits weren't blind to the fact that their relationship would generate buzz for the film. Having Hollywood's new and young "it" couple star in their movie was a hot commodity–even if they were being chased by a crazed elf.

Jennifer's manager, Andrew, pushed them to capitalize on the exposure, dragging them to Hollywood's most exclusive parties so they could mingle with the right people. But once the movie premiered and the press tour wrapped, Johnny vanished from her life. He stopped answering her calls and ignored every letter she sent. She'd heard he still attended some parties in the Hills, but as for their relationship, it was over.

They could have been in all the magazines. The paparazzi would have loved them. It was a wasted opportunity on what could have been a strong start to their careers. She was livid, and so was Andrew.

Her manager started bad-mouthing Johnny all around town, claiming Johnny was only hired for his looks and not for any real acting talent. She would have felt bad for him, if what Andrew was saying wasn't true. She could still remember when she glimpsed their performance playing in her local Blockbuster.

"That dude is shit, man. I've seen better acting in pornos," the teen at the counter said as Johnny was mutilated on screen. Jennifer smiled, finding the irony in the statement–after all, that's exactly how Johnny's career had started. Perhaps that was why his performances were only truly convincing during their sex scenes.

Fast-forward four decades, the shirt that would have once hung loosely over his six-pack now stretched tightly against a bulging stomach. His hair had thinned to a few wispy gray strands, damp with sweat and clinging to the sides of his head.

"Johnny? Yes, of course. It's so nice to see you again." She forced a smile.

"Yes it is..." His gaze drifted up, taking in every inch of her. His once piercing blue eyes were now swallowed by flesh–small, beady, and hungry. Jennifer was suddenly aware how alone they were on this bus, and that a man she barely recognized was now ogling her chest.

"Oh, hey," he said, gesturing to the bed across the aisle from hers. "Looks like we're bunk buddies. Just like old times, aye?" He winked and threw his duffel bag on the floor and sat himself on the edge of his newly claimed bunk. His knees touched hers as he leaned in.

"Say, remember when we used to sneak off between takes and uh..." He shifted his eyes left and right, even though they were alone on the bus. "Hang out in your trailer?"

His face was so close that she could smell his stale, hot breath.

"Nope, can't say I do."

"Oh, I think you do," he reached over and stroked her exposed knee with a finger. The shiver crawling up her spine twisted into something sour. The air thickened. The bus pressed in from all sides, and her breaths became shallow, each one tighter than the last. Johnny's finger was soon joined by his hot sweaty palm which wandered up her leg, his fingers soon wrapping around her thigh. But before Johnny's hand could roam any farther, a firm hand clamped onto his shoulder.

Johnny jumped up and turned to find Douglas King staring up at him.

"Holy shit. It's Dougie," Johnny said, having regained his composure. "Last time I saw you, you were only this big." He bent down and leveled his hand to the height of Douglas's neck.

Douglas batted his hand away.

"Alright, don't get *short* with me," Johnny said, turning to Jennifer proudly.

She crossed her arms.

Not getting the reaction he was obviously after, Johnny shuffled awkwardly before bending down to tousle Douglas's hair. He winked back at Jennifer as if she was in on the humiliation.

After failing to garner any further entertainment from either Jennifer or Douglas, positive or negative, Johnny threw his hands up. "Oh, lighten up, I'm only having some fun."

"You haven't changed a bit, Johnny," Douglas said.

"Thanks, dude," Johnny said, not catching the tone.

After a moment of icy silence, Johnny started rocking back and forth on his heels. "Well, I've got some lines to memorize. It's been a few years since I had to read a script, or read anything for that matter." His loud laugh rattled through the bus. "It was good to see you, Jennifer. I guess I'll catch you on set."

Douglas stepped aside and let him pass.

"Wow," Jennifer said, as soon as Johnny had exited the bus. "I can't believe how much he's changed."

"Are you serious? He's always been an assclown. I don't know what you ever saw in him."

"A chiseled jaw and a rock-hard six-pack?"

"Ah yes, I remember now."

Jennifer stood up and hugged Douglas. "Honestly, I'm so happy to see you."

"Me too. I didn't expect to see you here."

"To be honest, neither did I. So how did you get roped into this?"

"Vincent, the director, spoke to me at the con. And it was quite simple, he asked if I wanted to be involved and I jumped at the chance. I said, 'buy me a beer and you're on,' " Douglas laughed.

"Wait, you're doing this for free?" Her eyebrows shot up.

"Sure. The fans have done so much for me over the years, I wanted to give a little something back. Just don't tell my agent," he whispered conspiratorially.

A part of Jennifer pitied Douglas. Why does he do this to himself? You don't have to say yes to every fan who wanders over, especially when they're not even paying for your time.

Still, guilt twisted in her gut. They were paying her–generously. No one could know that.

"So, excited to get back under the mask?" she asked, shifting the conversation.

"Oh, I'm not playing Plucky."

"What?"

He shook his head. "I'm playing a different role. After having my face covered for my entire career, I guess it was about time I debuted this handsome mug on screen. Ryan Gosling watch your back."

"Then who's playing Plucky?" Jennifer asked.

He shrugged. "Beats me. But whoever it is, I don't envy him in this heat. It's already hot as hell under that damn rubber mask, let alone out here. I tried to find him to offer some pointers, but I haven't seen him. I even asked Vincent, but he said the actor's choosing to stay out of sight until they film his scenes."

"Hey, maybe it's Daniel Day Lewis?"

"I think he's a little tall for the role," Douglas smiled.

Michael popped his head into the bus. "Ms. Hawkins, are you ready for your hair and makeup?"

CHAPTER 7

The dressing room was less of a room and more of another large gazebo. Inside was a cheap, rickety clothes rail and a couple of small folding tables. Jennifer sat at one facing a mirror smudged with fingerprints and splattered with white specks.

"Because you woke me up so early, I didn't have any time to put my face on, so I hope you're one hell of a hair and makeup artist," Jennifer called out.

"Only the very best, darling," a deep voice came behind her, smooth as butter.

A tall man strode into the gazebo. He had dark skin, a bald head, and salt-and-pepper stubble. Finally, someone she could immediately recognize–her costar from the fifth *Evil Elf* movie.

"Thomas?"

He smirked. "So, you do remember me then? From what the other ladies have said, I was starting to think you might have dementia."

"Oh God, you heard about that?"

"This is a small parking lot, honey. Everyone's heard about that."

Jennifer whispered playfully, "Now that I'm in a safe space, can you tell me who the hell they were?"

"Don't worry, you'll meet them again during the table read. I'm sure that's when Vincent will formally reintroduce us all." Thomas checked his watch. "Shit, twenty minutes. We need to get you ready."

"Wait, hold up. So, you're acting in the movie *and* doing the hair and makeup?"

"What can I say? I'm a jack of all trades."

Jennifer glanced at his bald head. "No offense, Thomas, but you don't have hair and you're not wearing makeup. How can I trust you to do mine?"

"My husband does drag part-time. His face has been my canvas for years."

"Great, so not only am I going to be killed off, but I'm gonna look like RuPaul while dying?"

"You wish you'd look half as good," he laughed. But when Jennifer didn't, he bent down beside her. "I also ran my own salon. Is that good enough for you, Ms. Gloria Swanson?"

Jennifer rolled her eyes. "Fine. But if I look like I should be in *To Wong Fu*, you're fired."

"Deal." Thomas unrolled a black bag on the dresser, revealing a line of makeup brushes. He then opened a case with tiers of compartments filled with lipsticks, glosses, palettes, tubs, and tubes, all covered with a thin layer of powder.

"So, for my hair I was thinking–"

"Sorry, but Vincent gave me strict instructions."

"And what are they?"

He pulled out a picture from his back pocket, unfolded it, and stuck it to the mirror. It was a promo picture of Jennifer from the first *Evil Elf* movie. She was leaning against the Santa head she passed under earlier. Only here Santa was fully intact and freshly painted. The young Jennifer beamed, her hair extravagantly teased. If there was a hairstyle that defined the '80s, this was it. Her hair was a towering monument–teased high, sprayed stiff, and cascading in a wild blonde mane that looked like it had been struck by lightning. The top was a voluminous explosion of crimped bangs and lifted roots, while the bottom spilled down in frizzy waves.

"You can't be serious."

Thomas shrugged and set out a bowl of water with a towel. Jennifer dipped the cloth and pressed it to her face. The warmth spread across her skin, loosening the tightness.

"So, how did you get roped into this?" Jennifer asked as he applied toner to a cotton pad and swiped it over her skin. It stung, but Thomas continued, whipping out a fan to cool her face.

"Do you mean the acting or the makeup?" he asked, applying a thin layer of moisturizing primer.

"Both."

"I haven't acted in years. A couple of small gigs after *Evil Elf*, but that was it. So, I packed up my bags, moved my sorry ass out of LA, and went back home to Chicago. I haven't done many conventions, but at every one, Vincent showed up and paid for my autograph." Thomas tipped some foundation over the back of his hand, dabbed a brush over it, and gently applied it over Jennifer's face.

"It wasn't until a con in Illinois last week that he told me about *The Revenge of Plucky*. And after not acting for over thirty years, you could say I was a little hesitant. But when he sweetened the pot by offering me a little extra to double as the head of the hair and makeup department, I said 'Sure, why not?' Although, when I got here, I found out that this 'department' consisted of only me."

"You didn't do it for the love of the franchise like Douglas?" Jennifer asked.

He laughed, blending the foundation into her skin. "I needed the money after my salon went under. And honestly, I've never even seen one of the *Evil Elf* films. Even the one I was in. They're corny as hell." He paused, catching himself. "Sorry."

"Don't be. I've heard far worse," Jennifer said.

He smirked, twisting open some concealer with a pop. "To be honest, it's not just *Evil Elf*; I can't stand horror movies in general. I find them terrifying. I just needed the money and I wanted to be famous."

"And why are you making a horror movie now?"

"Duh, 'cause I still need the money. Maybe you do have dementia."

Thomas stepped in front of Jennifer to pencil in her eyebrows, blocking the mirror. She shifted her focus to the script in her lap, deciding now was as good a time as any to finally read her lines.

Thankfully, Jennifer's short stint as a soap opera star had taught her to memorize lines fast. You hit your mark, said your line, and moved on–no second takes unless you completely blew it.

She wished she had more time to go through all of it, but chose to focus on today's scenes for now. She could finish the rest of it tonight on the bus.

Jennifer turned to the first page. The movie opened with her character, Rebecca Sommers, returning to where it all started, Tinseltown, to hunt down Plucky. But this time, she's accompanied by five other legacy characters from the franchise. Jennifer's character is the only one from these movies to have survived Plucky, so it wasn't exactly clear why they were alive again. She guessed it had something to do with the timeline nonsense Vincent was talking about.

It didn't matter anyway. She had to keep reminding herself that this movie wasn't official. It was a low-rent fan film. Who gave a crap about continuity? Especially seeing as they were going to kill her off.

The script outlined how she and her costars explore the abandoned theme park. She read on, past the pedantic descriptions and exposition, skipping straight to the dialogue. It was pretty decent, at least by slasher movie standards. Jennifer spent the next fifteen minutes rehearsing her lines to herself as Thomas silently applied her makeup and styled her hair. Finally, he stepped back and admired his work.

"So, what do you think?"

Jennifer lowered her script and braced herself. She fully expected to see a sad, old clown stare back at her. But she was pleasantly surprised. Sure, her hair was ridiculous, the blush was too pink, and the eyeshadow far heavier than usual–but she had to admit she pulled it off. Her skin was smooth, her lips were drawn to plump perfection, and she admired the small glimmers of highlight that helped lift her face and give her a healthy glow.

"You know, this isn't half bad," Jennifer said, leaning closer to inspect her reflection.

"Coming from you, I'm sure that's high praise," Thomas teased. "Oh, and there's one more thing: your costume."

"Don't tell me you're in charge of wardrobe as well?"

"No," he laughed, "I'm afraid I can't be blamed for, well, I'll show you..."

Thomas turned to the clothes rail. "Vincent chose the wardrobe all by himself. I have to get that detail out of the way first."

He handed Jennifer some garments before holding up his hands as though he had deposited a ticking time bomb. She studied the faded blue jeans, acceptable. Some scuffed tennis shoes, also acceptable. And a Christmas sweater, totally unacceptable. She unfolded the woven monstrosity as though it carried a deadly disease. It was bright red, heavy, and had white fur around the wrists. Right in the center was an embroidered Rudolf the Red-Nosed Reindeer. And if that wasn't dreadful enough, stitched along its antlers were little jingle bells. She shook it. They tinkled.

Thomas just stood there, obviously trying to suppress the urge to laugh. "Oh yeah, and there's one more thing..." He pressed a button on the inside sleeve. A cluster of blinking red LED lights pulsed on Rudolf's nose.

Jennifer's stomach dropped.

"Vincent told me it's an exact replica of the sweater you wore in the first movie. He wants everyone wearing the same clothes their characters wore in the films... I guess you don't remember it?"

Oh, Jennifer remembered it. How could she not? She still has the scars from scratching herself crazy at the end of every shoot.

"Does he seriously expect me to wear that thing in ninety-eight-degree weather?"

"I know it sucks now, but trust me, when the sun sets, you'll be grateful. It gets pretty cold at night."

"I don't care if I'm freezing my fucking tits off, there is no way I'm wearing this shit," she said, throwing it down on the floor. "Surely there's something else I can wear?"

He shook his head. "Vincent was insistent. He didn't bring alternatives. He said he wants you looking exactly like you did in the original movie–with the original wardrobe."

"He's forty years too late for that."

"With my makeup skills, I'd say twenty at the most," he said, picking up the sweater and folding it loosely.

She cracked a smile, eyeing it before extending a hand to take it. Thomas helped to maintain her hair as she slipped it on. The wool had barely touched her skin before the itch began.

Vincent poked his head through the curtain and gasped. "Oh my God. Jennifer, you're the spitting image of yourself in the first *Evil Elf*."

Jennifer couldn't help but blush. "Oh, I don't know about that."

"Well, I do. Great work, Thomas."

Thomas bowed theatrically.

Vincent beamed at the both of them. "Okay, so if you'd both like to follow me, we're gonna do a table read before we head out on set."

CHAPTER 8

Vincent was practically skipping ahead of Jennifer and Thomas as they ventured into the largest gazebo on the lot. Michael was standing in a corner, filming everything with a DSLR camera on top of a DIY shoulder rig. A folding table was set up in the center and seated around it were four people: Douglas, Johnny, and the two women from earlier. Johnny gave Jennifer a wink and waved her over to the empty chair next to him, but she slipped into the seat next to Douglas.

Douglas leaned over and gave her a low whistle. "Loving the threads."

"Don't start. I've seen your holiday cards; you and your family wear sweaters just like this. Unironically, might I add."

He laughed.

"Hello, everyone." Vincent stood. "Before we begin principal photography, I wanted to gather us all for a quick table read. My name is Vincent Shepard, and I'm the producer, director, and writer of this little picture. I've been an *Evil Elf* fan since I was five. I've seen every single film more times than I can count, and, in my humble opinion, it is the greatest horror franchise in history. My body is a testament to that."

He held out his arms to show off his many, many *Evil Elf* tattoos.

"Like every other *Evil Elf* fan, I have been impatiently waiting for the next entry in the series. But over two decades have come and gone, and there's still no word of any follow-ups. While the studios and producers duke it out over the rights, it's the fans that suffer. I was sick of waiting. So, one day, I thought, 'If they aren't going to make another movie, I will.' With help from fellow fans, I've crowdfunded enough money to make it. *Evil Elf: The Revenge of Plucky* is a film made by fans, for fans. I well and truly intend to make this the best movie in the franchise–the most authentic. Which, to be fair, is a big task. As you all know, the movies are almost flawless."

Thomas met Jennifer's eyes from across the table, his lip trembling. She couldn't hold it together and a snort of laughter burst out.

"Yes, Jennifer?" Vincent said.

"Come on, kid. You're fucking with us, right?"

Vincent's brow furrowed. "No, I'm being very serious. I believe that *Evil Elf* is significantly better than *Friday the 13th*, *Nightmare on Elm Street*, and *Halloween* combined. So, I've brought you all together, the best *Evil Elf* alumni–from every single installment–to celebrate and extend its legacy. I want to bring back slashers, revive the horror genre, and wake Plucky up from his slumber."

"Hell yeah," Johnny cheered, pumping his fist.

Vincent smiled as he eased into his seat. "I'm sure you all know each other already, either from working together on set or crossing paths at conventions. But let's go around anyway. Say the character you played in your respective film, and how you were killed off."

Johnny launched himself to his feet. "Hi, I'm Johnny. And I played teen heartthrob Calvin in *Evil Elf II*, and that little shit over there sliced me open with a reindeer antler." He pointed over at Douglas, who gazed back at him with a blissful smile–Jennifer was sure he was replaying that very scene in his mind right now.

The woman with the black pixie cut stood up. "Hi, I'm Christy, I played the role of Britney in *Evil Elf IV*, Rebecca Sommers's roommate in college and *supposed* best friend." Christy glared at Jennifer.

"Yes, who could forget?" Vincent clapped his hands.

Me, apparently, Jennifer thought.

"And unfortunately, I was killed with a pickaxe to the neck." Christy feigned sadness.

Douglas jokingly pulled on his collar to release some imaginary steam. "Yeah, sorry about that. No hard feelings?"

Everyone laughed, except Johnny, who rolled his eyes.

Thomas stood up next. "Hey guys, so I was in the fifth film, *Evil Elf: Plucky Takes Manhattan*. And as the only Black guy in the entire franchise, I, of course, was the first to be killed off–I think I lasted all of fifteen minutes."

"Hang on a second," Douglas said. "You didn't say how Plucky killed you."

"Uh, I don't remember," Thomas said, crossing his arms.

"Uh, I think you do," Douglas teased, leaning back on his chair.

Thomas sighed. "You killed me with a nutcracker to the balls. Happy now?"

Douglas broke into a toothy grin. "Yes, very."

Jennifer had always admired how Douglas could warm up a crowd, whether it was on set with the crew or hosting events at conventions. Within minutes, he could have anyone in the palm of his hand. Entertaining came naturally to him; his ability to lift up an entire group of people was a perfected art.

As the laughter died down, all eyes shifted to the woman Jennifer had mistaken for a runner.

"Hey everyone," she said in a Texan drawl. "Well, my name is Luna–"

To be fair, even taking into account that forty years had passed, she was still unrecognizable. Back when they worked together, Luna had long red hair that tumbled down to her waist, a belly button ring that was always on display (thanks to her rotating collection of cropped band tees) and baggy jeans that hung off of her hips. On set, she was never seen without a cigarette hanging loosely from her lip, continually frustrating the director.

The last time Jennifer saw Luna was on a July night in 1988– one that had replayed in her mind ever since.

Now standing before her was a far more timid Luna. Her hair, still long, had been touched by age and was streaked with white and silver. It was bundled up with a tortoiseshell claw clip which revealed her freckled face. Thick-rimmed glasses magnified her large green eyes. Her fingers, adorned with many rings on each hand, gripped the script, while the bangles clinked on her wrists.

"–I played Sophie in the third *Evil Elf* movie," Luna continued. "*Slay in the Sand*...I think?"

"*Slay in the Sun*," Vincent corrected her.

"Right, that's the one," Luna said, retreating to her seat before adding, "Oh, and Plucky hung me with Christmas lights."

The next person in line was Douglas, who stood up and rubbed the back of his head. "Well, this is a little awkward. I'm Douglas and, first of all, I'd like to formally apologize for killing all of you. I was going through some things at the time. But rest assured, I'm in a much less stabby place now...a lot less *nutty*." He winked at Thomas who laid a hand over his own crotch and winced. Everyone laughed; even Johnny couldn't help but crack a smile.

"But seriously, it's great to see you guys all here. Playing the role of Plucky was an amazing experience, and your deaths are some of my fondest memories." He wiped away a fake tear, and the group laughed again.

"My only regret is not being able to kill you all again, for I am handing over the title of the Killer on Candy Cane Lane to someone else. Yep, this old-timer has been given a brand-new role: Douglas. Who is basically a fictionalized version of myself." Douglas nodded toward Vincent, who confirmed with a smile.

After Douglas sat back down, all eyes shifted to Jennifer. Michael swung the camera around to aim, and she could feel the lens zoom in on her. And when Jennifer didn't stand up, Vincent announced her himself.

"And last, but not least, we have the legend herself, the ultimate scream queen, the 'final girl' of all 'final girls'–Jennifer Hawkins," Vincent said, leading a round of applause. Nearly everyone joined in, except Christy, who crossed her arms and leaned back in her chair.

Jennifer stood up. "Thank you, Vincent, and it's great to see you all again. And yes, like Douglas, I'm so excited to work with you all...again."

Her eyes swept the room before settling on Vincent, who stared at her, clearly expecting more. When he realized she had finished, he stood and clapped his hands together. "Great, thank you, Ms. Hawkins."

"So, with introductions out of the way, I want to stress that this will be a much smaller film crew than you're used to. Me and my brother here, Michael, will be doing all of the filming." He wandered over to Michael and laid a hand on his shoulder. "And you will be seeing DSLRs attached to steady cams, like the one here, that we made ourselves. But in addition to those, we will also be using these." Vincent held up a small GoPro camera.

"Dozens of these are planted around the park to capture that found-footage vibe. Think *Blair Witch Project* or *Paranormal Activity*. It's going to look stylistically different than any *Evil Elf* movie before. But that's not all–we'll also be filming with this drone." Vincent held up the small machine from earlier.

Up close, Jennifer could make out the tiny camera fixed to its underside.

"The plan is to shoot all the daytime scenes today and tomorrow," Vincent continued, "and after that, we'll be filming exclusively at night."

Vincent checked his *Evil Elf* novelty watch. Jennifer could just make out Plucky the Elf in the middle with his green-and-white-striped arms pointing to eleven and four. "We will be doing a quick read through of the first few pages now, but I'm afraid that's it. We're working on a tight deadline here, so that doesn't leave us a lot of time to thoroughly rehearse every single line together. But you guys are professionals, so please have your lines memorized when it comes to filming your scenes. If you'd like to open your scripts in front of you, we can begin."

The group moved through the script, with Vincent reading aloud the scene headings and actions while the actors delivered their lines. He struggled to contain his excitement as each actor brought his writing to life, his hands gripping the edge of his seat and his eyes wide like a child on Christmas morning.

Jennifer and Douglas were the only ones at the table who still acted semi-regularly, so they got through their lines without any issues. The others, who hadn't even read a script in at least a few decades, stumbled over a few of their words and had a lot of work to do on their intonations and cadence. But none more so than Johnny, who chose to over- and underemphasize certain words, seemingly at random. Jennifer would have assumed that he was doing some sort of avant-garde performance if she didn't know him. It was then that she recalled that Johnny had won a Razzie award for his acting as Calvin in the second installment, which if memory served, was the only award the *Evil Elf* movies had ever won.

After going through the first thirty pages, Vincent checked his watch and sprang to his feet.

"Bravo! Bravo, everyone," Vincent cheered, eyes glistening. "Incredible performances from all of you. Sorry to cut this session short, but we're running out of daylight. Luna, Johnny–please go with Thomas to get your hair and makeup done. We'll start filming in forty-five minutes."

"Forty-five minutes?" Jennifer heard Thomas gasp under his breath.

"In the meantime, everyone else please feel free to enjoy the selection of food and drinks while myself and Michael get set up."

CHAPTER 9

Vincent's "craft services" was a platter of mostly broken chocolate cookies, a half-empty bowl of potato chips, stale crackers, and cheese slices that were about as plastic as their packaging. Generic brand soda cans sat nearby in a bowl of warm water. Jennifer opted for a cup of coffee, only to be horrified to find that there wasn't a machine. Instead, a small pile of off-brand sachets were scattered next to a stack of Styrofoam cups and a rusty hot water dispenser. Pouring several of the sachets into a cup, she added some water. After giving the mix a quick stir, she took a sip and instantly grimaced at the bitter sludge. Still, she forced it down; it was her only hit of caffeine for the day, and she wasn't about to give that up.

Douglas and Christy were laughing together, giving Jennifer the perfect moment to sneak outside for a smoke. She stepped outside into the blinding light and dry heat, heading away from the gazebo and toward the bus. She reached into her purse but still couldn't find the pack of cigarettes. She searched every one of its pockets–until it hit her. It was still at home.

Jennifer wondered if she could ask Michael to drive back to that creepy gas station, but she doubted that weirdo Bob even sold cigarettes; his store was practically empty. There had to be a town nearby. She pulled out her phone to check Google

Maps, but there was no signal. Not even 3G. Holding it up, she wandered around, hoping for a single bar to appear. And after five minutes of searching, it was no use. She was officially in the middle of nowhere.

Jennifer steadied her cravings with the thought that she was going to leave tomorrow.

I can live without cigarettes for a single day. Right?

To distract herself, she turned to her phone. Even without internet, she could still record a short video for her TikTok and upload it later. Her agent, Andrew, had pushed her to use various social media platforms as a self-promotion tool. But honestly, aside from the occasional creepy message sliding into her inbox, it was like shouting into a void. She flipped to the front-facing camera anyway and held it up high. Thomas had done a fantastic job; she looked great. After admiring herself for a few moments, and a fair few selfies, she slapped on a smile and tapped the record button.

"Hi guys, I'm out on location filming a secret project, and I think you're all going to be very excited." She gave a playful shush to the camera, making sure to pout her lips, before turning it around to capture the Tinseltown theme park sign. "That's right, I'm back where it all began, and–"

"You know you're not supposed to be recording this, right?"

Jennifer spun around. Christy was leaning against the bus.

"What?"

"I said, you're not supposed to be recording this," Christy repeated. "Vincent made us all sign NDAs. He was super strict about us not spoiling anything. We didn't even know we were filming here until he drove us out."

"I didn't sign any NDA," Jennifer said.

"Of course you didn't." Christy rolled her eyes.

Jennifer bit her tongue, remembering that she had to work with this woman, even if it was just for a day. "I can't get any signal out here anyway. It's kind of a blessing, really. Don't you hate having to do all this social media crap?"

"I love it," Christy said. "In fact, it's my job."

She wasn't making this easy.

"You really don't remember me at all, do you?" Christy asked, a hint of amusement in her voice.

"Of course I do. We worked on the fifth movie together."

"Fourth, actually," Christy sighed. "But seeing as we only had a few scenes together, I guess I can't be too hard on you. But maybe you remember my podcast, *The Horror Haven*?"

Jennifer was getting tired of being quizzed. "Should I?"

"Douglas knows it. He's been on it twice."

Good for Douglas, Jennifer thought, glancing past Christy toward the gazebos, silently hoping Vincent–or anyone, even Johnny–would appear to rescue her from this conversation. With no end in sight, she attempted some damage control. "Well, why don't we schedule a day for me to be on your podcast soon?"

"I've already asked you. Douglas gave me your number a couple years back, and I thought it would be great to have you on the show to reminisce about our time on set." Christy pulled out her phone and scrolled through her messages. After a few seconds, she found what she was looking for. "Here it is. You replied with, 'How much?' to my invite. Then, when I explained that podcasts generally don't pay guests, you ghosted me."

Jennifer's eyes darted around, but all that surrounded them was the endless, empty desert. There was nowhere to run.

But then a thought struck her. She didn't have to stand here, being lectured by someone she hadn't seen in decades. Who did Christy think she was? Jennifer had clawed her way up, earning every scrap. Why should Christy expect freebies for her dumb podcast? Between the hangover, the heat, the itchy sweater, the cramped bunks, and the terrible coffee, Jennifer had reached her breaking point.

"Look, I'm sorry you didn't get the response you wanted, but to be honest, I don't owe you anything," Jennifer said. "So why don't you–"

She paused, her attention drawn to a faint whirring sound above. Jennifer and Christy glanced up to find the drone, its lens locked on them. Without warning, the drone darted behind the bus; Christy and Jennifer exchanged puzzled glances before following it to find Vincent tapping away on his cell phone.

"Hey," Jennifer called, marching over. "Are you spying on us?"

"Spying?" Vincent said, not looking up from his phone. "No, I'm only grabbing some B-roll for the BTS features."

He tapped the screen, sending the drone soaring high before diving sharply toward the ground. Then he stopped it just above his head, making it hover in place.

"Isn't this great?" Vincent said. "I can control this little guy with my phone." He pointed underneath the drone. "It's got a 4K resolution camera, perfect for those hard-to-reach shots. It can fly so sneakily, you won't even notice... Well, except for now, I guess." He met Jennifer and Christy's eyes with an unapologetic grin, then carried on.

"I've studied all the behind-the-scenes features on all the DVDs. For the first movie, the director, Hank Tarwell, talked about blowing a huge chunk of their budget on aerial shots using a helicopter. But fast-forward forty years, and you can buy a drone that fits in the palm of your hand with a terabyte of storage for only a couple hundred bucks."

Vincent held out his palm and the drone settled on it. "This is going to be the most cinematic *Evil Elf* movie ever made."

"Boys and their toys." Christy shook her head.

As Vincent continued on about the movie's cinematography, Douglas joined the group wearing a green sweatshirt that read "Tinseltown: the holly-est, jolly-est place in the West." Jennifer smirked at him, and he gestured toward both of their festive costumes. "At least I'm not the only one celebrating Christmas in July." Jennifer would have laughed if she wasn't distracted by Luna emerging from hair and makeup.

Luna looked as though she had stepped out of a time machine. Her hair, now a long cascade of molten copper, flowed down her shoulders–each curl capturing flecks of sunlight as they lapped against her black leather jacket. Her black cowboy boots scuffed the ground, kicking up little clouds of orange dust as she moved. And now, without her glasses, Luna's green eyes sparkled like persistent embers beneath the dark haze of her smoked-out eyeshadow. Jennifer's mind snapped back decades, drawn into a past she thought long buried.

"So, what do you guys think?" Luna addressed the group as she performed an awkward twirl.

"Incredible," Vincent exclaimed. "Exactly what I wanted. Fans are going to freak out when they see you all in your original costumes." His eyes glazed over as if imagining the applause.

Luna grinned, and then peeked over at Jennifer.

Heat rose in her cheeks. "Honestly, you look..." she faltered, searching for the right words. "You look great."

"You guys haven't commented on *my* look yet!"

The group turned to find Johnny stroking the side of his wig, a long, curly, chestnut-colored mullet. It was safe to say that his transformation wasn't quite the same as Jennifer's, Luna's, or anyone else's on set. Yes, he was dressed exactly like his character from the second movie–open Hawaiian shirt, white wife-beater underneath, and green visor–but it didn't have the same effect. He didn't carry the vibe of a man living it up in Las Vegas, but seemed more like a greasy regular at a strip club or a degenerate gambler glued to a slot machine for days on end. Johnny's days of being the buff poster boy, plastered on the back of every teenage girl's bedroom door, were long gone.

"Very sharp, Johnny," Vincent said, though with less enthusiasm than when he'd complimented Luna. "We just need Thomas before we start rolling."

"Don't worry, I'm here," Thomas said. Unlike the others, he wasn't wearing a wig, but instead sported a red snapback cap, a white basketball jersey, and an oversized lime green bomber jacket. He had gold chains hanging from his neck and zebra-striped baggy track pants.

"Oh my God," Jennifer exclaimed.

"Not a single word," Thomas warned her.

"What the hell are you wearing?"

"What? Don't you remember my iconic costume from *Plucky Takes Manhattan*?" Thomas said, rolling his eyes. "You know, the film that was exclusively written and directed by white guys, whose only knowledge of Black culture came from MC Hammer and Sinbad? Cut me some slack."

"I'll try," Jennifer said, suppressing the urge to laugh.

Vincent scratched his shin, unconvinced. "Thomas, you're almost perfect, but there's something not quite right. I just can't put my–ah, I know."

He adjusted Thomas's hat, tilting it to the side, then stepped back. "Perfect. Very fly."

Jennifer let out a giggle. Thomas shot her a look. "One more word out of you, and I'll sew more bells onto that hideous sweater of yours."

Jennifer theatrically mimed zipping her mouth and throwing away the key.

Vincent stepped back to survey his cast. He held up both hands, bringing his index fingers and thumbs together to form a makeshift frame. "Perfect," he exclaimed, peering through it. Michael handed out lav mics to the cast to capture their audio. Jennifer clipped hers onto the waistband of her jeans, concealed the device under her sweater, and ran the wire through before securing it in place.

Jennifer's eyes swept over her costars–actors well past fifty–all dressed like teenagers again. They were like some weird, midlife-crisis ragtag ensemble. Thomas resembled a budget version Will Smith from *The Fresh Prince of Bel-Air*, while Johnny's mullet looked like a startled woodland creature. Christy, draped in a glitzy sequined dress and weighed down by Mardi Gras beads, could've passed for an overexcited aunt crashing a bachelorette party. Luna, on the other hand, pulled off a wild rock-chick vibe. Then there were Jennifer and Douglas: she in a blinking red reindeer sweater, he in a Tinseltown sweatshirt, shifting awkwardly as if unsure what he'd signed up for. All together, they were a ridiculous sight.

Vincent clearly didn't feel the same. He beamed, rubbing his hands together. "Let's make a movie."

CHAPTER 10

Vincent led his cast across the parking lot away from the massive Santa head toward Tinseltown's ticket-gated entrance, flanked by sun-bleached candy canes. The sun was unrelenting, and Jennifer could already feel her makeup starting to melt. She turned to Thomas, who had his makeup kit tucked under one arm, and offered a silent thanks. She made a mental note to keep her teasing in check. She needed to stay on his good side, if only for vanity's sake.

As they got closer, it struck Jennifer that this was her first time back at the amusement park since they'd wrapped the original film in August of 1985. The same nerves she felt as a young actress didn't feel so distant now. She could almost hear Hank, their director, giving his pep talk as they hurried production in order for *Evil Elf* to meet its December release. The filmmakers wanted to capitalize on the Christmas season and make it *the* definitive Christmas horror film. But that didn't exactly pan out.

Jennifer approached the tall fence surrounding the park. The steel tips curled in a half-hearted imitation of candy canes. Once bright with festive red and white, the paint had been bleached by the sun and chipped away, exposing streaks of dull, reddish-brown rust beneath.

The gates were wide open. From the corner of her eye, she spotted a severed metal chain coiled on the ground. She wasn't the only one who'd noticed.

"No key?" Douglas asked.

Vincent shrugged. "Lost it."

"We do have permission to film here, right?" Jennifer asked.

"Uh huh." He walked through the gates toward a small red wooden hut, its frame warped and leaning off-center. A carved wooden sign clung onto it from a rusted iron hook, swaying in the breeze: Ticket Office Booth.

The hut's only window was shattered, revealing a cashier's desk covered with old, sun-bleached park pamphlets. Vincent reached through the fractured window, searching through the pamphlets until he found one where at least some words and illustrations were still visible. The paper crackled under Vincent's touch, brittle with age. He unfolded it, revealing the map inside. Stepping back to the group, he held it open for everyone to see. The map was brightly colored, its hand-drawn illustrations vivid and kitschy. Jennifer couldn't help but think of the *Frosty the Snowman* cartoon she'd watched as a child. At the center of the map, a bright green Ferris wheel stood tall, crowned with a glowing star. Four themed areas surrounded the wheel, each illustrated with reindeer and elves and promising a host of rides and a festive wonderland.

"This is where we are now," Vincent said, pointing to the entrance indicated on the map. His finger then traced along a green gumdrop road to an area titled Reindeer Park. "We'll be filming here next. Over the following days, we'll move on to the other areas of the park, like Elf Village, right here." He pointed to the north of the map, before running his finger down to the western area entitled Toy Town. "And then over here. But some of you needn't worry about that." Vincent glanced at Jennifer.

He then folded up the map, put it in his back pocket and held his arms up high. "Our first scene takes place right here by the entrance. To set the scene, you've all arrived at Tinseltown. Jennifer, this is the first time you've been here since the 1985 massacre. And for the rest of you, this is your first time ever seeing this park. Okay, let's start rolling, and *action!*"

In the first scene, all of the characters arrived at the park and greeted each other like old friends. It was strange in that there was no discussion, explanation, or acknowledgment that all of them, except Rebecca Sommers and "Douglas," were now somehow alive and well after being killed by an evil Christmas elf. Jennifer assumed this would be a little confusing to the audience, but then again, horror movies weren't exactly known for their logic: especially in the *Evil Elf* franchise, where Plucky was forever inexplicably returning from the dead. Jennifer considered asking Vincent about this, maybe even suggesting adding a line or two to explain their sudden resurrections. But she assumed he'd give her a throwaway answer like, "It's a fan film" or "Continuity doesn't matter" or some bullshit like that. Besides, she would be gone after the first quarter of the movie at the most, so did she need to exhaust any extra energy? She chose to ignore logic and instead focus on her lines.

Setting aside her doubts about the project, Jennifer had to admit that slipping into the role of Rebecca Sommers was second nature. Yes, it had been around thirty years, but she'd played the character five times–six, if you count her 1996 appearance on *Mad TV* in an *Evil Elf* spoof. This role had been her big break, and much of Rebecca's personality had been shaped by Jennifer herself when she was starting out in the industry. Back then, Jennifer had been wide-eyed, naïve, and vulnerable–traits that fit perfectly with the "scream queen" persona. But as the films progressed, her career matured, and so did Rebecca. She'd battled Hollywood just as much as she'd battled Plucky, and those experiences had turned her into the "final girl" of her own life. Bruised, scarred, but undeniably strong.

Jennifer was confident in her performance, and for the most part, her costars held their own. Even Luna, who hadn't acted since *Evil Elf III* in '88, did fairly well. She was a little wooden at times, but nothing too terrible. The only truly awful performance was Johnny's. Given just three lines, he flubbed every single one.

"Are you *sure* my character would say this?" Johnny asked Vincent, not for the first time.

Vincent sighed. "You mean the line: 'I don't think we should go in, guys'?"

"Yeah, I don't think Calvin would ever say such a pussy line like that. He'd be up at the front, leading the group into the park. Who am I? Shaggy from Scooby-Doo? The fans have been waiting since 1986 for Calvin to return to the franchise. We can't let them down."

"The fans?" Douglas said. Jennifer could tell he was biting his cheek trying not to laugh.

"Yes, the fans," Johnny said, turning on Douglas. "Calvin is a fan favorite. I can't tell you how many times I've been asked when he's returning to the franchise. In fact, many people have told me that they think Calvin survived."

"Didn't I slice open your stomach–sorry, I mean, *Calvin's* stomach–and watch your intestines spill out?" Douglas teased.

Johnny rubbed a hand over his stomach. "People have survived much worse."

"Yeah, like this conversation," Thomas said, rolling his eyes.

Johnny shot him a glare, but Thomas simply crossed his muscular arms and stared him down. Johnny's gaze dropped to the floor.

By this point, Vincent was squeezing the bridge of his nose and taking some controlled breaths. But he wasn't deterred, continuing to yell "cut" and "action" over and over until Johnny nailed his lines.

Aside from Johnny slowing down production, Jennifer thought Vincent was a pretty efficient director. Getting the shots and scenes he needed before moving on to the next. He and his brother used two cameras at once, meaning they could get different angles of the actors talking instead of filming them one at a time, which was standard on single camera productions. Fortunately for Vincent, he was shooting digitally, which meant he could record as many takes as his SD card could hold.

Back when Jennifer filmed the first *Evil Elf* movie, they shot entirely on film. She remembered the crew loading and unloading the massive reels–everything felt more tangible, more authentic. That's what classic Hollywood cinema was, and that's what Jennifer was mesmerized by when she toured the studios as a child. So, when it came to her career, she couldn't help but feel disheartened when she was filmed digitally for the first time. Film seemed reserved now for Hollywood auteurs like Quentin Tarantino, Martin Scorsese, and Christopher Nolan. It didn't matter if Johnny fucked up his lines a thousand times–Vincent could keep rolling.

"Cut," Vincent yelled, dropping his shoulder Steadicam. "Everyone, that was fantastic."

Johnny puffed up his chest proudly. Douglas rolled his eyes.

"For the next scene, you'll be entering the park. Please stay in character as I'll be filming with this." He held out the drone, then tapped his phone to send it soaring into the sky. Jennifer moved closer, peering over his shoulder. On the screen, a breathtaking aerial view of the park unfolded, the Christmas tree Ferris wheel perfectly centered ahead.

"Wow, this is incredible," Jennifer admitted.

"Isn't it?" Vincent said. "I used to watch your first movie every single day as a kid. And as much as I loved all the characters, yours most of all, my favorite was the park itself."

"You're telling me out of all the actors in *Evil Elf*, all the running around we did, and all the corn syrup that was thrown at me, your favorite character was an inanimate theme park?" Jennifer was as amused as she was confused.

"Oh, absolutely. Locations are more than just backdrops; they can become characters in their own right. What's *The Shining* without the Overlook Hotel? *The Texas Chainsaw Massacre* without the farmhouse? Or *A Nightmare on Elm Street* without, well, Elm Street? The setting of a movie can feel as real and as memorable as a character or any living person. What's your favorite movie?" Vincent asked.

Jennifer thought for a moment before replying, "*When Harry Met Sally*."

Vincent's eyes narrowed. "Wait, your favorite movie isn't one of the *Evil Elf* movies or *any* kind of horror movie?"

Jennifer raised an eyebrow. "Let's just say that when you work in a sausage factory the last thing you want to eat is a hot dog, kid."

"Well, anyway, like I was saying, New York is basically a character in *When Harry Met Sally...* When you think about it, generally, it's a story about love, not specifically about Harry or Sally. And New York is the epicenter for all these love stories buzzing around. That's why you have those talking heads throughout–all New Yorkers. And take the scene of Billy Crystal and Meg Ryan walking through Central Park in the fall: the changing season coincides with their lives, and relationship, at that time. Reiner used several wide shots to emphasize that Harry and Sally are just two neurotic individuals in a city filled with other neurotic people."

Jennifer didn't expect an essay, but decided to concede that it was a great point. And even though his taste in horror films was questionable and he *was* pretentious, Vincent knew what he was talking about.

He continued. "The Tinseltown theme park and *Evil Elf* are so entwined. Forty years ago, if you filmed your movie at any other location, I doubt it would have had the same success."

"Why's that?"

Vincent's jaw dropped. "Isn't it obvious? Look where you are."

Jennifer's eyes swept across the crumbling ruins of the holiday theme park and raised an eyebrow.

Vincent pressed on. "Back when you filmed in this park, it was the ultimate Christmas setting, right? The kinda place families came to year after year. But shooting after-hours in an empty park turns that focus on family and togetherness into something darker and more relatable. Horrors always capitalize on real-life fears. That's why it's so impactful as a genre. And *Evil Elf* specifically focused on those who didn't have that happy family. Those that felt lonely or alienated by the holiday. *Evil Elf* captures this contrast perfectly, using the festive sparkle of Tinseltown to mask something sinister."

"But what about the sequels?" Jennifer said. "They weren't filmed here and you still love them."

"True," Vincent nodded. "But each of them was deeply tied to its respective location–Vegas in part two, Santa Cruz in part three, New Orleans in part four, and New York in part five. And, of course, space for part six. Even still though, if you were to ask any fan what they think of when you say 'Evil Elf,' they undoubtedly will say Tinseltown. That said, I truly believe *Evil Elf VI: Christmas in Space* is a massively underrated gem. If I had a Tom Cruise budget, we'd be filming it up there next." He pointed at the sky.

"You know, you may be the only fan I've met who liked the sixth movie," Jennifer said.

"I know that's the general consensus," Vincent said. "But I think all those people are completely sleeping on it, and they're unable to comprehend its quiet brilliance. Wouldn't you agree?"

"I wouldn't know. Haven't seen it."

As Vincent went to respond, most likely as animatedly as before, Michael tapped his shoulder and pointed to his watch. "Oh yes, of course. I could talk about the franchise all day, but we have a lot to shoot and the daylight is running out." Vincent turned to the rest of the group and held his script up in the air. "We'll be continuing on from page ten. Ready...and action."

CHAPTER 11

The group walked toward the next location, Reindeer Park, with the drone overhead. Thankfully there were no lines, meaning Johnny couldn't possibly fuck it up.

The actors walked past the ticket office and stepped onto what the map called Gumdrop Road. Back when Jennifer filmed the first *Evil Elf* movie, they filmed it after hours when the park was closed to the public and all the rides and music had been turned off. But in the mornings, when they weren't filming and the park was open, Jennifer used to sneak in and just walk around by herself. She hadn't thought about it in years, but now that she was inside the gates, it all came rushing back.

Back then, as soon as you entered the park, you stepped onto a biscuity pathway dotted with multicolored gumdrops and sprinkles. Christmas music played softly from hidden speakers, and the sweet aromas of peppermint and bubblegum cotton candy forever lingered in the air. On either side of the path, faux snow made from soft white blankets shimmered with a pearlescent sheen.

Flash forward to now, and the magic was gone. There were no jolly jingles playing, not a trace of cotton candy, and no vibrant Gumdrop Road. Instead, lifeless pastel shapes marked the path, cracked and uneven, with jagged gaps where pieces were missing entirely. The ground was now gritty, strewn with desert sand and brittle leaves that crunched underfoot.

Gone, too, was the artificial snow that once lined either side of the path, exposing the dry dirt beneath. Derelict huts stood along the path, their windows and doors boarded up. Jennifer remembered when these had been lively giftshops and bustling eateries. Back then, the place was like a miniature version of Main Street, USA, at Disneyland.

Vincent directed the actors to channel concern and mild fear while they walked through the deserted park, a task that didn't require much acting on their parts. The sight of the once-thriving family theme park, now empty and abandoned, was unsettling even in broad daylight. Johnny, whom Jennifer had expected to overact and ham it up for the cameras, appeared genuinely disturbed by the desolate surroundings.

As they walked a little farther, the Gumdrop Road forked into three directions. At the crossroads stood a tall signpost designed to resemble a swirly lollipop. The striped pole, once crimson and white, had now bleached to a dusty pink and leaned to the left, pushed by the harsh winds or trespassing teens. Three arrows extended from the signpost: to the left was Toy Town, to the right Reindeer Park, and straight ahead was the Christmas tree Ferris wheel.

The centerpiece of Tinseltown once stood tall and proud. It was designed to be visible from every corner of the park and for miles around. Jennifer, who had been terrified of heights since childhood, had avoided riding it when she was last here in 1985, even when the entire crew ran riot through the park on their final day of filming. Still, the memory lingered: the way it spun, carrying families and lovers in carriages shaped like giant glass ornaments. No two were the same, each one painted with its own intricate design. As the nights drew in, its crown of glowing starlight sparkled in the sky, and the wheel stood like a beacon over the park.

It was sad to see it succumb to rust and ruin. The green paint had cracked and eroded, exposing its rusty skeleton, and a few ornament carriages hung askew, creaking on their hinges as though they could fall at any moment.

Johnny gasped, staring up at the Ferris wheel. "That's awesome."

"Vincent said to stay in character," Thomas whispered to him. "No talking. You'll spoil the shot. Again."

Johnny spun to face him. "Well, I think my character would be wowed by a hundred-foot Ferris wheel that looks like a freakin' Christmas tree. Ain't that right, Vincent?" He waved at the hovering drone filming them.

Thomas smacked Johnny's hand down. "What did Vincent say about *not* acknowledging the camera? This isn't one of your shitty old pornos. On a movie set, you don't stare straight down the barrel of a lens."

"Oh, you've seen my movies then, Tommy boy?" Johnny said with a wink. "That figures. Tell me, what's your favorite?"

Thomas rolled his eyes. "Wow, so many to pick from, it's so hard to choose. Speaking of which, I wanted to ask you, how is your current performance somehow worse than your acting in *Pleasure Patrol 10*?"

"I'll have you know I won a Thrusty XXXcellence Award for my role in that," Johnny snapped.

"That's great. Did you put it next to your Razzie?"

Douglas burst out laughing, causing Johnny to go beet red. He went to open his mouth but closed it again, obviously lost for words.

"Guys, I am sweating balls under this sweater, can we get back to the scene and get this over with? That would be awesome." Jennifer said, scratching under her itchy collar.

"So, where do we think we need to go next?" Luna asked.

"Vincent said to walk to Reindeer Park, so I guess we should head this way." Douglas pointed right.

Johnny shoved past Thomas and stormed off down the path. Thomas shook his head, muttering under his breath, before following. One by one, the others trailed after them.

They passed another sign; The North Pole Express, its letters faded and peeling. The train had been a big deal once. The bright red steam train chugged around the park, allowing visitors to hop on and off at the three main stops. Though the train was long gone, the tracks remained.

Douglas sidled up next to Jennifer, his voice low. "Do you remember when this train was still running?"

"How could I forget?" Jennifer smiled. "I seem to recall the park owners gave us explicit instructions not to touch it or go on it while we were shooting here."

"I remember," Douglas said, smiling to himself.

"But do you also remember that, after one particular shooting day when the owners and staff had left, you started the steam train and took us all around the park? A security guard caught us and our entire production nearly shut down because of you."

Douglas put his hands up. "In my defense, I was method acting."

"Method acting? How do you reckon that?"

"I was being Plucky. Plucky is mischievous, Plucky would've hijacked a train if it meant torturing you sorry group of misfits."

Jennifer laughed. "I wonder if this new Plucky is the method kind too."

Douglas shrugged. "Whoever's playing him hasn't shown himself yet. Which is strange because there aren't many places to hide back at base camp."

They walked a little more until they came across a large curved wooden sign that hung above an open gate welcoming them to Reindeer Park. Jennifer spied another cut lock and chains coiled beside the metal gates, just like at the main entrance.

Reindeer Park used to be where guests could find and feed Santa's reindeer. The animals were housed in a large, New-England-style red barn. Jennifer remembered twisting a quarter into a small vending machine that dispensed food pellets. A warmth pulsed in her palm and she smiled, recalling how the reindeer tickled her hands as they licked up the treats.

Even though the reindeer were long gone, the barn remained–just barely. The red painted siding was either missing, faded, or covered in graffiti. The windows were clouded with dirt and cobwebs.

Not far from the barn stood a carousel, frozen in time. The circling herd of reindeer were caught mid-stride, their mouths agape in silent screams, almost as if each one was reacting to the spiraling brass pole that pierced their abdomens. Jennifer stepped up onto the carousel, running a hand over each of the fiberglass reindeer. On their reins, each one bore a gold engraved name tag–Dasher, Dancer, Prancer, Vixen, Comet, Cupid, Donner, and Rudolph. Surprisingly, apart from a few broken ears, and a missing Blitzen, the reindeer were in decent condition all things considered. Jennifer wondered if the carousel still worked.

"What's that?"

Jennifer turned to find Johnny staring up at a long metal rail that wound its way through Reindeer Park. It hung twenty feet above the ground, and perched on top sat a single cart shaped like a sleigh.

"If I remember right, it was some kind of monorail ride," Douglas said. "Guests rode in sleighs and pedaled their way along the track. That sound about right, Jen?"

"I believe so," Jennifer said. "Though I never rode it myself." If she refused to ride the Ferris wheel, there was no way that she was going to cycle a rickety peddle sleigh that high above the ground.

"Yeah," Douglas said, "There's the entrance." He pointed to a nearby sign that read "Santa's Skyway."

"That's terrifying," Luna said, craning her neck up at the cart. "There's no railing either. That's a death trap, especially with kids."

"That's exactly what I used to think." Jennifer shivered.

"This was made way back before safety regulations were a thing," Douglas said, waving a hand.

"Yeah, before people weren't pussies and didn't care about this woke nonsense," Johnny said. "Back when we were younger, we weren't coddled. If we fell off something and hurt ourselves, we'd rub some dirt on it and carry on. Kids these days are too soft."

"Health and safety is woke now?" Christy said, rolling her eyes.

"Everything is woke to these people," Thomas said, nodding at Johnny. "He doesn't even know what that word means."

"What do you mean by *these people*?" Johnny said. "You mean people who remember the simpler, better times? Back when things were great? Everywhere we go, we're persecuted by lefties like you."

Thomas laughed. "Persecuted you say?"

"That's right. Canceling people you don't agree with because they don't share your opinion."

Before Jennifer could process how a conversation about an old ride had turned into a debate on identity politics, Vincent and Michael appeared.

"Hi guys," Vincent said, his voice cutting Johnny off mid-rant. "We got some fantastic aerial shots of you walking through the park. But we're running out of daylight, so we need to move quickly and wrap these next scenes."

CHAPTER 12

Filming resumed, and almost everyone stumbled over their lines–the heat didn't help, nor did the tension simmering on set. Even Douglas, who was composed in most situations, fumbled a few times. He wasn't used to this kind of performance. Most of his career had been spent behind rubber masks, his face hidden as he delivered exaggerated, campy lines. But now his mask was off, and for the first time, he was tasked with acting as himself–a human, not a caricature.

Frustration was building in him with each flubbed line. Jennifer felt for him, especially knowing that he was putting himself through this whole ordeal without even getting paid. It also didn't help that Vincent's direction was vague and Johnny's constant, unsolicited acting tips only made things worse.

"Doug, you're killing me here," Johnny exclaimed. "I'm not buying what you're giving me, man. I need to believe what you're saying, otherwise I can't give you anything back."

Ever the professional, Douglas bit his tongue and delivered his lines. Jennifer urged him on, eager to spite Johnny, who was holding up production more than anyone.

After Johnny's tenth retake of a single line, Vincent called "cut" and announced a short recess. Everyone was free to take a ten-minute break, except Johnny, who Vincent kept behind to go over his lines again.

While Christy, Thomas, Luna, and Douglas went over their lines together, Jennifer used the opportunity to slip away. She dreaded those awkward moments after the director yelled "cut," or when the cast and crew broke for lunch. In larger groups, she never knew what to do with herself. After hours of hiding behind a character, slipping back into her real self was draining. To shield herself from that discomfort, she'd retreat to her trailer and wait to be called back. She knew the crew whispered about her–*diva, standoffish, cold*.

But with no trailer to retreat to, this would have been the perfect opportunity for a smoke break. Jennifer reached for her pocket–then remembered she had none. Her mouth felt dry and tight, aching for a cigarette. To distract her herself from her cravings, she took out her phone and opened her inbox–nothing. No signal, not even one bar. She raised the phone and wandered, arm stretched overhead.

Jennifer's foot snagged on something solid, sending her stumbling forward. She managed to catch herself–and her phone–before hitting the ground. At her feet lay a fallen wooden sign. The gold paint, chipped and dulled with age, spelled out "Santa's Post Office."

Ahead stood a log cabin. Above its doorless frame hung a rusted hook that once held the sign. A large red mailbox was nailed beside the entrance, the words Letters to Santa Claus painted in gold lacquer across the front. Behind her, Johnny was still tangled in an argument over his lines. With some time to spare, Jennifer stepped through the threshold to investigate.

Dust motes danced in beams of sunlight that filtered through cracked windows. The air hung thick with the scent of mildew. Dust coated every surface. An ornate golden cash register sat on a long desk at the back of the room. Behind it, boxed shelves stretched across the wall. Most compartments stood empty, but a few were stuffed with letters or glass jars filled with red-and-white boiled candy. The old floorboards sagged underfoot as Jennifer stepped farther inside. Letters and papers with hand-drawn pictures of toys were scattered across the floor. She knelt down to pick up an envelope; its red seal was cracked and faded but unbroken. The address to Santa was written clumsily in gold glitter gel pen. Jennifer guessed that this was where kids would write their Christmas letters before handing them to an elf who'd then deliver them directly to Santa himself.

Jennifer placed the letter on a side table next to a large glass cabinet that displayed various pieces of the park's merchandise and memorabilia. There were ticket stubs, T-shirts, badges, pennant flags, pins, gift cards, and magnets, all displayed in a circle around a plaque. She wiped the dust from the glass and read its inscription.

Back in the '40s, Tinseltown could have easily been called Sandy City, what with all the dust and desert lying around. But there was one man, Ronald "Ron" Burnett-Turner, who saw something special in those dusty acres. Inspired by Hollywood's knack for turning dreams into reality, Ron set out to do the same, just a hop, skip, and a jump from Route 66. So, in 1950, we welcomed our very first guests to follow our Gumdrop Road and hop on the North Pole Express to find their own meaning of Christmas–and we've been doing so ever since.

Jennifer then peered into a framed black-and-white photograph of a mustached man standing proudly in front of the Christmas tree Ferris wheel. She assumed this was the original park's founder, or "Ron." He was surrounded by a large cast of jolly characters wearing whimsical uniforms and costumes.

Jennifer wondered what this man would think if he could see his beloved theme park today and how he'd react to someone filming a cheap horror movie in the ruins of his dreams. She remembered the constant arguments between the *Evil Elf* producers and the park's managers during filming. It was clear that the only reason they'd agreed to host the production was the park's dwindling ticket sales.

Johnny's voice rose from outside, arguing with Vincent on the complexities of his character. Knowing that she still had some time, Jennifer pulled out her phone and balanced it on a nearby shelf. She wedged it between a sad-looking teddy bear and nutcracker, careful not to let it fall. A long crack ran down the center of the screen, a reminder that replacing it wasn't an option yet. Maybe after this shoot, she'd splurge on an iPhone that wasn't seven years old.

She opened her camera app and switched it to the front-facing mode. Her image filled the entire frame. As the day had worn on, her makeup had started separating, and no amount of Thomas's touch-ups could mask the cracks of heavy drinking and light sleeping. But in the dim light of the cabin, and with the help of a few blur filters, it might not be too obvious. She tapped the record button and stepped back until her whole body fit in the frame. After a quick glance to make sure no one was watching, she closed her eyes, counted back from three, and danced. It was a routine she's rehearsed after seeing a few influencers pull it off. It took a few attempts to get the rhythm right without the music. She would've played the song on Spotify, but without any internet, she had to play it in her head. Just as she was about to nail the routine, something caught her eye–a small white face peeking through the cracked window in the corner of the screen. She held her breath and spun around. Nothing there.

Then, a floorboard creaked on her left. Jennifer froze.

"*What* are you doing?"

Luna was standing in the empty doorway, wearing a bemused look. Heart pounding, Jennifer rushed to the shelf, snatched her phone, and shoved it into her back pocket.

"Oh my God, don't creep up on people like that."

"Sorry, I didn't mean to disturb you," Luna said, looking a little startled by Jennifer's reaction.

"It's fine," Jennifer said, her heart settling down.

"Are you filming a TikTok?" Luna asked as she stepped inside.

Jennifer avoided eye contact. "My manager said I should start making them. Insisted actually. Apparently, to get noticed these days, you have to put yourself through public humiliation."

Luna nodded like she understood, but Jennifer knew she didn't. Not really. Almost forty years ago, she threw away a promising film career, abandoning Hollywood for Buttfuck Nowhere, Texas. She had no idea what it took to stay relevant in today's climate. Back when they acted alongside each other, social media wasn't even a thing. There was no Facebook, Instagram, X, or TikTok. Hell, not even a MySpace.

These days, acting wasn't enough. You needed followers. And to get them, you had to chase the latest trend–learn a dance, lip-synch to some K-pop song, or throw a bucket full of ice and water over yourself, all for forty likes, and that's if the algorithm felt generous.

"Well, don't let me stop you." Luna turned to leave.

"Fuck it, I won't be able to get any signal to upload it anyway."

"Same here. I've been trying to get through to my daughter all day."

"It's funny to think that the last time we saw each other, cell phones weren't even a thing."

"Exactly. My grandkids have no idea how easy they have it now. I remember having to use a pay phone to call my mother back on set."

Grandkids? How could she possibly be a grandmother? Luna had been one of the few people on set Jennifer could truly be herself around. A free spirit.

Looking at her now, Jennifer could still picture all those long evenings on the beach in Santa Cruz–cheap beer in hand, Aerosmith's "Angel" playing on the boombox, and the sweet taste of deep-fried funnel cakes as the sun slipped below the horizon. They talked about everything–their careers, their fears, their passions, and their futures. A husband wasn't ever included in either of their plans. And it was Luna's independence that heavily inspired Jennifer as she navigated her own.

"Times change."

Luna nodded. "Yes, it does. Except time hasn't changed you. You look amazing."

"I'm not so sure about that," Jennifer replied, her fingers instinctively moving to her face, conscious to cover her ever-dropping jowls.

"Oh shut up," Luna said, smiling. "You haven't aged a day. What's your secret?"

About a fortune in cosmetic surgery, Jennifer thought. "Just clean living and exercise."

"Right." Luna smiled politely, clearly not buying it. "Well, it's definitely working,"

The women shared an awkward silence, the only sound was the soft whistle of air slipping through the wooden slats. It was almost a relief when raised voices erupted from outside. It was Johnny and Vincent locked in yet another argument.

"If that carries on any longer, I don't think we're going to finish all our scenes today," Luna sighed. "Wasn't he this bad when you worked with him in part two?"

Jennifer nodded. "Back then I found it kind of hot the way he fought against the director," she laughed, almost in disbelief of her past self.

"I can't believe you dated that guy. I hope you have better taste now." Luna laughed, dimples appearing on her cheeks.

Jennifer remembered the same dimples from almost forty years ago. She couldn't help but smile.

"Well, you did always like your bad boys," Luna jibed. "I seem to recall you had a thing for the camera guy with the mullet just because he had a Harley and a leather jacket."

Jennifer groaned as the memory came flooding back. "I'm going to be honest, I wasn't actually into him."

"You weren't?" Luna asked.

"I think I was just trying to make someone jealous..." Jennifer's words fell away as her eyes met Luna's.

Before Luna could speak, Vincent's voice rang out. "Okay, everyone, back to set."

CHAPTER 13

Production continued for another hour until the sun set and they lost light. One of the biggest issues with filming on location was the constant battle against time. This was why pretty much everything was shot on sound stages. You can film for as long as you want without worrying about the weather or the daylight. Directors could be filmmakers, God, and mother nature all at the same time.

Vincent finally yelled, "Cut," and a collective sigh of relief rippled through the cast. They all trudged back to base camp in silence, utterly drained from a day of filming beneath the punishing sun.

By this point, Jennifer was running on a few hours of sleep, a cup of sludgy coffee, and a protein bar. Her stomach growled, and every inch of her body ached. She stretched her arms and leaned back, wincing as she heard a pop. The sour stench of last night's alcohol oozed from under her thick sweater. All she needed was a hot meal and an even hotter shower.

As they followed the crumbling Gumdrop Road through the park, Jennifer caught up with Vincent. "Where are the bathrooms? I'm dying for a shower."

Vincent turned to her with the same expression he'd had when he told her they were killing off her character. That alone sent a familiar sinking feeling through her gut.

"Please tell me you have showers here."

"Yes, there are showers here."

She let out a relieved breath.

"They're just not exactly...warm," Vincent said.

Jennifer's frustration with the production was at her limit. "Vincent. I can get past the sleeping arrangement. Kind of. But I draw the line at not having a hot shower."

"There is a shower room here. It was used by the staff members. It's right near the entrance to the park. Thankfully, it's still connected to the water mains. But it might only be warm if the sun heated up the tank–I'm not sure how it works. I'm not making any promises. Just please be mindful of everyone else and try not to use it all up."

Jennifer sighed. "Fine. I assume you brought towels?"

He nodded. "My brother will go fetch you one. He'll meet you by the gates when you're ready."

* * *

As soon as they got back to the parking lot, Jennifer made sure she was the first on the bus. She grabbed her bag, tossed in some sweats, and hurried to the park's entrance. She wanted to make sure no one else used up the limited hot water. Micheal was waiting with a towel hooked over his arm. The fabric was hard and scratchy, and she couldn't help but think of the last person who'd wiped themselves with it as she followed him toward the showers.

"The bathrooms aren't far," Michael said, veering off Gumdrop Road to the right of the ticket office.

Jennifer stayed close to Michael, aware that even though the park had been abandoned, it hadn't been abandoned by its wildlife. Scorpions, rattlesnakes, or spiders could crawl out at any moment. She shivered, already afraid of journeying back to the bus alone. Michael came to a quick stop before pointing to a small white building ahead.

"It's in there," he said. "Don't worry, I gave it a quick clean." Without another word, he turned and marched back to camp.

Jennifer pushed open the door. "Clean" was generous, but at least it resembled a functioning bathroom. She dropped some flip-flops down on the ground, switched out of her shoes, and made her way past the row of toilet stalls lining the right wall. At the far end were the showers. Careful not to let her Louis Vuitton cosmetic bag touch any questionable surface, she pulled out one of her facewipes, placed it on the sink, and put the bag on top.

At last, she did what she'd been yearning to do all day: yank off the itchy, hideous sweater. Her skin was blotchy and raw, and the thought of a hot shower was more than enough for her to forget about the black mold on the tiles and the limescale-caked showerheads.

Jennifer got undressed and threw her clothes next to her cosmetic bag. Then she stepped into the shower, armed with a curated lineup of bottles from her bag. The setup reminded her of the gym showers in high school, complete with a push-button that triggered an automatic timer. She pressed it and heard a rattling sound as the rusty pipes tinkered and groaned before sputtering out a stream of water. To her relief, it was warm. She lifted her face toward it, smothering her skin with cleanser. She could almost feel the day being washed away.

She was knuckle-deep into scrubbing her hair with shampoo when the water turned ice cold. Jennifer screamed and lurched backward. Shivering, arms wrapped tight around herself, she cursed under her breath as the last bit of warmth spiraled down the drain.

A low whistle cut through the air. She spun around. Johnny leaned against the doorframe, arms crossed, wearing a smug grin.

Jennifer rushed to the sink, almost slipping on the tiles, and snatched her towel to cover herself.

"There's no need for that. I've seen it all before, remember?" Johnny chuckled.

"Don't remind me," she said, tightening the towel.

Johnny placed a hand over his heart. "Oh, you wound me, Jennifer. At one time you couldn't keep your hands off me."

"That was a *very* long time ago." She grabbed her bag and slipped into the nearest stall, bolting the door shut behind her. Even though she wasn't dry, she pulled out her sweats and got dressed.

Only after hearing Johnny huff out of his clothes, turn on the shower, and start singing the Rolling Stones's "Start Me Up," did she dare open the stall door.

Between lines, he bellowed, "You can come and join me if you want, Jen."

Without glancing back, Jennifer headed straight for the exit.

"Your loss, sweet-cheeks," he called after her, resuming his off-key singing.

As soon as the door closed behind her, she heard a high-pitched scream as Johnny's warm water ran out. Smiling to herself, she walked back to base camp, feeling a small sense of victory.

* * *

The sky bled shades of pink and orange as the sun dipped below the horizon, casting an eerie, yet beautiful glow over the parking lot. Jennifer shivered, reminded of how quickly the desert's daytime heat could plunge into a bone-chilling cold at night. Despite the chill though, there was no way she was putting that itchy Christmas sweater back on.

She crossed the parking lot, her eyes drawn to a fire pit where a few people sat in a circle of lawn chairs. Thomas, Christy, and Luna were engrossed in their own conversation, the sounds of laughter mingling with the crackling of the fire. They had changed out of their costumes and into more casual clothes. Jennifer's gaze lingered on Luna, who had removed her red wig and had bundled her silver hair into a high messy bun.

Now slightly more relaxed, Jennifer dropped into an empty chair next to Douglas, who sat slouched, his eyes lost in the flickering fire. The old plastic webbing sagged beneath her, but after a long day on her feet, it was a welcome rest.

Jennifer shifted in her seat, watching Douglas. "Hey, Dougie, you okay?"

"Huh?" He blinked, as if surfacing from somewhere far away. "Oh, sorry, Jenny. What's up?"

"You seem distant."

"I'm fine." He flashed a smile, but it didn't reach his eyes.

She leaned in slightly, catching his eyes.

Douglas sighed, his smile fading. "I'm thinking of Linda and the kids. It's been a long time since I've spent the night apart from them."

"Have you tried calling them?" she asked, already knowing the answer.

"No signal. Worse still, they don't even know where I am."

"You didn't tell them you were filming?"

"I told them that much. But Vincent never told me we'd be here. He kept the filming location very secretive. Even made me sign a nondisclosure agreement. I think he was terrified of any information leaking out and spoilers getting online before filming had even begun. He said he didn't want to spoil anything and wanted our reactions to be genuine. He stressed the word *authenticity*."

"I think he's overestimating the demand for a seventh *Evil Elf* film."

NDAs weren't unusual in the film industry–Jennifer signed one for every movie she worked on. But handing one out for a fan film crossed into absurd territory. Vincent was all about playing the big shot movie director more than anything else.

"So you had no idea we were coming here to film? Didn't you find that a bit odd?" she asked.

"Not really, Vincent wanted it to be a surprise. He said that we could call our families after we arrived. Besides, I've done a few of these kinda films before. These youngsters are always acting like they're making the next Marvel movie or something." He laughed. "Besides, I trust the guy. I've met him a few times now at cons. He's always getting me to sign a bunch of photos and merchandise. Hell, he's basically paid for Emma's college fund by this point."

Jennifer nodded, then cast a look over her shoulder at Tinseltown. Even from this distance, the silhouetted tip of the Christmas tree Ferris wheel stood stark against the darkening sky.

"Can you believe how much the park has changed since we've been back here?"

"It makes me feel old," Douglas admitted. "Seeing all the once bright and colorful buildings now dull and decrepit is a bit depressing. I can't believe it closed less than two years ago. Goes to show that if you don't take care of yourself, or if no one takes care of you, you'll wear down fast."

"I love you, Dougie, but you're being a total bummer."

He laughed. "You're right. Sorry."

Jennifer's stomach growled, reminding her how long it'd been since she'd eaten anything substantial. On every production she'd worked on, they served breakfast, lunch, and dinner free of charge. Typically, studios would hire a couple of food trucks for the entire shoot. The best catering experience she ever had was on *Our Broken Hour*, where they laid out a lavish spread of freshly prepared food throughout the day. Crispy bacon and leek quiches, creamy mac and cheese, bite-sized tacos filled with fresh beef, cheese, and guacamole. And the desserts–oh, the desserts! There were rich chocolate tarts, fluffy éclairs filled with vanilla cream, and colorful macarons in every flavor you could imagine. The thought of it made Jennifer's mouth water; she used to have her assistant load up her plate with every available item. She doubted she would get anything close to that on this ramshackle production.

Right on cue, Vincent and Michael emerged from one of the gazebos carrying a few packs of hot dogs, a bag of buns, and roasting sticks.

Jennifer stared in horror as Michael handed out paper plates.

"What's wrong, Ms. Daisy?" Christy asked, peering at Jennifer through the flickering fire. "Not used to preparing your own food without a private chef?"

"I wouldn't say this is food, and I'm just not six years old at summer camp. What's next–s'mores for dessert, holding hands, and singing Kumbaya around the fire?"

"Sure, I can hold your hand if you want," Johnny chimed in, appearing behind Jennifer with wet hair and a towel slung over his shoulder. "Oh, sweet, hot dogs." He reached out, grabbing a roasting stick and hot dog from Vincent before settling into a chair, thankfully far enough away from Jennifer.

Michael handed everyone else buns and hot dogs skewered on long sticks. When he reached Jennifer, she shrunk back from the pinkish meat.

"Do you have anything else?"

"Sure," Michael said. "Let me start up my grill and I'll prepare a fresh lobster for you."

Vincent shot his brother a look, and Michael turned away. "I'm afraid this is all we have. We're working with a tight budget, so we've had to stretch what we've got." He stressed the word *budget*, a subtle reminder of how Jennifer's huge fee had consumed most of their funds.

With a heavy sigh, she accepted her fate.

"This is pretty fun," Luna said, as she stuck her cold, precooked hot dog over the fire to warm it up. "Reminds me of when I used to take my daughter camping."

"Me too," Douglas said, his face brightening as he thought of his own children. "Although I'd somehow always burn the hot dogs. Then I'd have to get in my car and drive around looking for the nearest McDonald's."

"There's no fast food places anywhere near here, so don't burn your dog. I'm not sharing," Thomas said.

As if on cue, Douglas's hot dog burst into flames. He yanked it out of the fire and started comically blowing on it. Everyone laughed; even Jennifer smiled. Succumbing to her stomach's continued growls, she picked up her roasting stick and began rotating her hot dog over the fire.

She meticulously charred the meat to make sure it heated evenly before placing it in her bun. Taking a cautious bite, she had to admit it was surprisingly delicious.

"So, how did everyone find their first day of filming?" Vincent asked as he settled into his seat.

"Easy," Johnny said, taking a big bite of his hot dog. "I slipped right back into character, like no time had passed at all."

Douglas rolled his eyes.

"It was tough–I haven't acted in years." Thomas said. "But I think having to pretend to care about everyone's problems while I cut their hair has helped me a hell of a lot. I couldn't have imagined a camera on me again. I thought my acting days were over."

"I felt the exact same way," Luna confessed. "When Vincent first approached me, I initially said no. The truth is, I was nervous. It's been decades since my last film, and honestly, I wasn't sure if I still had what it took." She turned her hot dog over in the fire. "Acting is like playing a sport or learning another language; if you don't practice, you lose your skill. But my daughter encouraged me to take the chance. This was my last shot to see if I still had it. Because if I didn't say yes now, then when?"

The others nodded in silent agreement. Luna was lost in the firelight, almost as if she was imagining how her life might have unfolded had she stayed in Hollywood to pursue her dreams.

Jennifer let out a tired yawn, feeling the weight of her exhaustion. As the others kept talking, she quietly slipped away and shuffled toward the bus. She collapsed onto her bunk, which, like the lawn chairs, offered little support and comfort. But her fatigue won out, and within moments, she was asleep.

* * *

Jennifer woke suddenly. For a second, she wondered where she was–that was until she heard Johnny snoring beside her. The bus. Right.

Convincing herself that Johnny was what woke her, Jennifer pulled the thin blanket up higher. But then came a pounding across the metal roof, like someone was sprinting from one end to the other. She tilted her head back, peering through the rusted holes above. Stars twinkled down at her.

Then–darkness. Something passed over the openings, blocking the sky. Her pulse quickened. An animal? Maybe. But what kind of animal moved like that? And what even lived out here? Coyotes? Foxes?

The others were still fast asleep. Slowly she sat up and peered out the window. After some time, her eyes landed on a figure in the distance. Standing. Watching. Whoever it was had a white face, but their features were distorted by the dark.

Her breath caught. She looked around the bus and found Thomas asleep in the bunk by her feet. She called to him in a low voice, but he simply grunted and turned over. Turning back to the window, the face was gone.

CHAPTER 14

The morning sun speared through cavity-ridden holes at the top of the bus and onto Jennifer's face. She groaned and threw up a hand to block its glare. Heat pressed in from every direction. The metal bus had turned into a stifling oven. After a few sluggish turns to escape the light, she gave in and sat up. The bus was empty. No one had bothered to wake her for breakfast. She fumbled for her phone. Nine in the morning. No signal. And the battery was hanging on at a desperate 5 percent.

Jennifer winced, her back aching from the uncomfortable bunk. She stretched, the joints in her body popping and protesting, before she slipped into some comfortable sweatpants and a plain black T-shirt. With a resigned sigh, she stepped out of the bus and into the blinding daylight.

She headed for the largest gazebo and found everyone already seated and eating. Douglas raised his spoon mid-bite.

"Morning, Sleeping Beauty," he said. "Breakfast is on that table."

Her eyes drifted to the pitiful spread. She couldn't help but think of her time on *Our Broken Hour* again. Every morning, a magnificent breakfast buffet was laid out and regularly topped up with warm buttery croissants, freshly toasted bagels with cream cheese, eggs benedict drenched in creamy hollandaise sauce, moist blueberry muffins, and a colorful pile of fresh fruit. But here sat two cereal dispensers, offering a choice between stale Cornflakes or Lucky Charms. Alongside the dispenser was a sad, half-melted bucket of ice containing a single opened carton of milk. With a sigh, she skipped breakfast and opted for another cup of gritty, lukewarm coffee. As she stirred the mixture, she reminded herself this was her final day of filming. By tonight, she would be back in LA, where real coffee awaits.

She spotted an empty seat next to Douglas and Christy and took it.

"Morning," Jennifer said.

Christy stood and left without a word or any acknowledgment.

"She hates me," Jennifer said, turning to Douglas.

"No, she doesn't."

Jennifer arched an eyebrow at him.

"Okay, yeah, kind of."

"Why are you so friendly with her, anyway?" Jennifer asked. "Actually, how are you friendly with everyone here?"

"Because I've actually spoken to them and spent time with them. Both on set and at various conventions over the years. Have you ever done that?"

Jennifer shook her head. "You know you're the only cast member I talk to from the whole franchise."

"I would be flattered, but that's only because *I* made the effort. If I hadn't insisted on badgering you with conversations between takes, we probably wouldn't be friends now." He softened his expression. "Look, I know you're not the most, uh..."

"Choose your words carefully, Dougie."

"...sociable person, but it might help you to be a little friendlier. And that's coming from a friend. Get to know your costars. Ask them questions about their lives and families. Who knows? You might make a new friend. This can be a lonely job, and actually putting yourself out there might make even that coffee a little more bearable."

"I doubt it," Jennifer grimaced, setting the cup down. "But message received. I'll try to take your advice on board."

Her thoughts drifted back to last night. "Say, Dougie...you know how you were a bit of a prankster on set?"

"Remember on *Evil Elf IV* when I kept sneaking that whoopee cushion on the director's chair? Man, he got so mad." He laughed, nearly spilling milk from his mouth.

"Yes, yes, it was hilarious. Well, are you pulling any pranks on *this* set?"

"Nah, I like to think I've gotten more mature in my old age." A mischievous smile crept across his face. "Unless you're planning one of course. Please tell me it's targeted at Johnny. If so, count me in."

"So...that wasn't you messing around last night?"

"What?"

"Forget it. It's nothing."

Douglas shrugged and went back to his soggy cereal.

Jennifer exited the gazebo. Thankfully, the slight morning breeze offered some relief from the oppressive heat. Cupping a hand over her eyes, she spotted Vincent talking animatedly to his brother. His hands waved frantically as he described some elaborate scene he was planning to film that day.

"Morning," she said, as she approached them. She was feeling a lot more positive knowing this was her last day.

"Good morning Ms. Hawkins," Vincent beamed. "I trust you slept well?"

She opened her mouth to complain about her bunk, but reconsidered; it wasn't worth it. She wouldn't have to put up with the bus again tonight. "Yep, fine thanks. I wanted to ask, do you have somewhere I can charge my phone?"

"Sure, we've got a generator. Leave it with us and I'll give it back to you later."

She handed him the phone, but as she turned to leave Vincent spoke again. "Actually, while you're here, I wanted to let you know that there's been a slight change of plans. We're moving your death scene from this morning to later tonight."

"What? Why?" Jennifer demanded. Though she was initially annoyed at her character being killed off, she had mostly come to terms with it. Especially after enduring the unorthodox filming conditions. All she could think about was getting home and taking a shower–assuming the hot water hadn't been shut off again. She knew how death scenes had a way of dragging on. The last thing she wanted was to spend another hour on set, not with that long drive back to LA still ahead of her.

Vincent scanned around before leaning in, his voice dropping to a whisper. "I want to shoot Johnny's death scene today. Don't get me wrong, he's fantastic...but I think it would serve the film better."

Translation: Johnny's diva behavior was bringing production to a standstill. If they kept pausing the shoot to accommodate his endless revisions, they'd be stuck filming for weeks.

Jennifer sighed, but nodded. She could see Vincent's point-anyone could, even the nearby fiberglass Santa with bullet holes for eyes. And sure, her shooting day was going to be longer than she had hoped, but on the bright side she wouldn't have to deal with Johnny for the entire day. It was almost balancing out.

"Great," Vincent said. "If you'd like to find Thomas, he'll get you ready. We'll be shooting in an hour."

* * *

Jennifer found Thomas applying Luna's makeup.

"Oh, sorry. I didn't mean to interrupt," Jennifer said, turning to leave.

"It's okay," Thomas said, carefully applying a touch of glittery eyeshadow. "We're almost done here."

"Isn't this exciting?" Luna said, her eyes sparkling as she caught Jennifer's reflection in the mirror.

"What?" Jennifer asked.

"This," Luna said, gesturing to her perfectly styled wig and makeup. "Getting pampered by a professional like this."

"Professional? Where?" Jennifer shot Thomas a sly smile.

"Oh honey, if you think I'm anything less than a miracle worker, then you're beyond saving. I've seen birds' nests more put-together than your hair right now."

Jennifer glanced over Luna's shoulder and caught sight of her own reflection for the first time that morning. Thomas was right; she was rocking serious bedhead. "Okay, I'm sorry."

"That's what I thought," Thomas smiled before returning to touch up Luna's face.

"Although I guess you're probably used to all of this," Luna said, pausing as Thomas applied red lipstick. "But for me, this is a full-on spa session. I haven't had a beauty treatment in years. No point spending all that money at the salon when your grandkids are just going to pull on your hair and touch your face with their sticky fingers."

"So, what do you think?" Thomas said, stepping back.

Luna tilted her face from side to side, beaming at her reflection. Thomas had outdone himself once again. Her smoky eyeshadow only made her eyes brighter, and the slight silvery glitter glimmered under the mirror lights.

"Oh my God, I love it," she exclaimed, squeezing Thomas's arm. "You're a true artist, Thomas."

He gave a playful bow. "It's nice to see *someone* appreciate my talents."

Jennifer rolled her eyes. "I said I'm sorry, okay?"

"Your throne awaits," Thomas said, nodding toward the chair as Luna rose and headed for the clothes rack.

Jennifer sat as Thomas pinned the polaroid of 1985 Jennifer again at the corner of the mirror. He then picked up a brush and got started on her hair.

"Ouch," Jennifer said as her head was tugged back by the forceful brushing. "Watch what you're doing back there."

"I have less than an hour to perform a miracle. So please keep your complaints to a minimum, thank you."

"I don't envy you, I only have to wear a wig," Luna said, grabbing her oversized, black leather jacket from the rack. "Though I'd argue this jacket might outdo your Christmas sweater for the title of the most impractical piece of clothing ever worn in the desert."

"Hey, I'd be happy to swap. I was so jealous of your costume back in the day," Jennifer said in-between deep breaths as Thomas worked through her knots. "So much cooler than the stuff I was forced to wear."

In the film they starred in together, Jennifer was thankfully spared from wearing the Christmas sweater from the first film. Instead, she was dressed in rather plain clothes to represent the average suburban girl: a white T-shirt tucked into high-waisted blue "mom" jeans. It was the quintessential "final girl" look of the time–neither too provocative nor too nerdy. Though this wardrobe was a step up from her previous ensemble, Jennifer couldn't help but envy Luna's edgier wardrobe.

"Yes, I remember how you kept trying to steal my leather jacket all the time," Luna said, a hint of a smile at the corners of her mouth. "Now I kind of wish you had. Wearing this thing in the godforsaken heat is unbearable."

"Like I said, I'd happily trade." Jennifer instinctively scratched at her neck at the sight of the Christmas sweater hanging on the rack.

"Yeah right, no deal," Luna giggled. "But hey, at least you only have to wear it until the end of this morning. Then you can burn the thing...or sell it back to Vincent with an improved *eau de Jennifer*." Her French imitation was flawless.

"Actually, it turns out that I'll have to wear it a little longer. Vincent rescheduled today's shoot to bring Johnny's death scene forward."

"Oh, thank God," Thomas said, looking up to the heavens and holding the hairbrush between his hands like a holy relic.

"Thomas," Luna scolded, though Jennifer spotted a mischievous glint in her eyes. Back in the day, whenever Luna flashed that sly expression during their scenes, Jennifer had a habit of ruining the take by grinning back.

"Oh, come on," Thomas said, grabbing the bottle of foundation. "We're all thinking it."

"I hope we can watch his death scene," Jennifer said hungrily.

"You two are awful," Luna exclaimed, fighting a smile.

"I wonder how they'll do it," Jennifer said.

"No idea, but I hope it's slow, painful, and bloody," Thomas said. "Vincent's kept everyone's death scenes a secret, I guess he wanted to keep up an element of surprise. One thing's for sure, when this movie's out, you better believe I'll be there with a bowl of popcorn, replaying his death scene over and over."

Jennifer and Luna's eyes met before erupting into laughter.

"What's so funny?" Johnny asked, appearing at the entrance of the gazebo.

"It's nothing," Thomas said, "We were just lamenting how your acting brilliance tends to overshadow everyone else."

"Yeah, laugh it up," Johnny said. "Are you ready for me yet? I need to get into costume. Vincent had a breakthrough last night and decided that he wants to kick off the movie with a bang.

He's making my death scene the biggest shocker by offing the most iconic legacy character right off the bat. He was saving it for the great Jen Hawkins here, but he figured my scene would be more impactful."

"Gee, that's great Johnny," Jennifer said, glancing down and desperately avoiding eye contact with Luna.

"It's a real honor, you know?" Johnny went on. "Vincent said the first death is the most memorable. And I guess after seeing how rusty you guys were yesterday, he decided that I'd be a better choice. I mean, let's face it, who could do it better?"

Jennifer peeked up and caught Luna's smirk. That was all it took for the two of them to burst into laughter.

"Weirdos," Johnny muttered before strutting out of the gazebo.

CHAPTER 15

Within an hour, Thomas had worked his magic, transforming Jennifer back into a "final girl" ready for the camera. Granted, she was a sixty-year-old "final girl" in an outrageously itchy and hideous Christmas sweater, with hair teased to the high heavens–but still, a "final girl" nonetheless.

Douglas and Christy were deep in conversation in the shade of the bus when Jennifer and Luna approached.

"Hey," Jennifer said before noticing that Christy was holding her phone along with a comically tiny microphone.

With a heavy sigh, Christy tapped her screen and turned toward Jennifer. "Can't you see we are in the middle of an interview?"

Jennifer was taken aback. "Sorry, I didn't realize."

"Of course you didn't," Christy sighed again. She turned back to Douglas. "Let's continue this in the catering gazebo?"

"Sure," Douglas replied, flashing Jennifer an apologetic smile before following Christy.

"I can't seem to stop pissing her off," Jennifer said, turning to Luna.

"Yep, with her, you're going to have to try a bit harder," Luna teased, lightly nudging Jennifer with her elbow.

"It's because I didn't do her stupid podcast," Jennifer said, rolling her eyes. "Can you believe that?"

"I actually sat for an interview with Christy," Luna said. "It was pretty cool; I felt like a celebrity. I hadn't done one before, so it was fun to reminisce about old times."

"When?"

"The first day," Luna replied. "When you barged in on us and demanded that I fetch you an iced skinny hazelnut latte."

Jennifer winced. "Oh, is that what was going on? Jesus, I'm so sorry about that, by the way."

Luna waved her off. "It's fine. It had been a long time since we last saw each other."

"Thirty-seven years, to be exact," Jennifer said, lowering her eyes to the ground.

"Like I said, a long time."

Their eyes met for a moment, and something old yet familiar stirred in Jennifer's chest.

A high-pitched squeal pierced the air. They turned to find Vincent fumbling with a megaphone. "We begin shooting in five minutes."

Jennifer and Luna exchanged a glance, the moment now broken.

* * *

They all passed through the gated entrance again, stepping onto the bleached Gumdrop Road that wound through the park. Jennifer tilted her head up to take in the towering Ferris wheel ahead, its green skeleton stark against the clouded sky. She was grateful for the clouds, which provided a welcome respite from the sun's relentless glare. The group made their way back through Reindeer Park.

Jennifer glanced over at Michael and saw a large black duffel bag slung over his shoulder.

"What's inside?" she asked.

"Special effects stuff. Props, fake blood, that kind of thing," Michael replied.

When they arrived at their destination, Vincent turned to the cast.

"I've tweaked the script so that we will be filming Johnny's death scene first. The reason for this change is because, as Johnny has pointed out *repeatedly*, everyone will be eagerly anticipating his long-awaited return as Calvin. And so, we want to really shock the audience by spending the appropriate amount of time on his death scene."

"Yeah, we talked about it, and we agreed that my character was too smart to be killed off as easily as the rest of you," Johnny said without an ounce of irony. "It made more sense for Calvin to take on the little fucker himself and go out heroically. Very Shakespearean, right, Vincent?"

"Right you are, Johnny," Vincent turned to the rest of the group. "While we film this, I want the rest of you to carry on down the road toward Elf Village and practice your lines. Michael and I will be there as soon as we are finished here."

"Oh, I was hoping we could stay and watch," Douglas pouted. It was clear he was already picturing Johnny's death scene–and enjoying every second of it.

Vincent shook his head. "No, sorry, gang. This will be a closed set."

"Why?" Jennifer asked Vincent. She was also curious to watch, not just because she wanted to see Johnny suffer–even if it was all pretend–but because she wanted to see a death scene before filming her own later that day. She hadn't filmed one herself as her character's death in *Our Broken Hour* was off-screen. While her films had a massive body count, she had personally never acted out a death scene, nor had she stuck around long enough to witness her costars'. Thinking back, Jennifer regretted her habit of slipping away rather than staying to learn from others–although the fake blood had been too much for her to stomach even if she'd wanted to.

"Because the actor playing Plucky doesn't *want* you to meet him yet," Vincent said. "We both agreed that it's best to keep you all in suspense. So that when you do finally meet Plucky, it feels more authentic."

"Yeah, I guess that makes sense. Didn't they do that in the *It* movie?" Christy asked.

Vincent nodded. "Bill Skarsgård, who played Pennywise, kept his distance from the kid actors because he wanted their reactions to be real and pure. It was the exact same on the set of *Scream*. Roger Jackson hid from the other actors while performing his menacing on-set calls, so they were genuinely freaked out. Even Anthony Hopkins didn't meet Jodie Foster before filming their scene together in *Silence of the Lambs*. That was real fear on her face when she spoke to Hannibal Lecter, and she won an Oscar for that. Not to mention on the set of–"

Thomas held up a hand. "Okay, Vincent. We get it. If it's good enough for Jodie Foster, it's good enough for us."

"Thank you," Vincent said. "Okay, Johnny if you'd like to follow me. For the rest of you, we'll see you soon over in Elf Village."

Vincent, Johnny, and Michael set off toward the old barn where they used to keep the reindeer.

"I guess we should continue on the Gumdrop Road to Elf Village then?" Christy said. Everyone else turned toward the opposite end of the park and began walking.

"You guys go ahead. I'm going to go to the bathroom and meet up with you," Jennifer said.

"We'll wait," Douglas said.

"No, don't be silly," Jennifer said. "Rehearse your scenes. I won't get lost. I know this place like the back of my hand."

Jennifer turned and headed back toward the park's entrance, but as the group moved ahead, she veered off toward the barn. Jennifer couldn't care less about this method acting bullshit. Who cared about this Plucky-guy building himself up to be some ominous scary villain? At sixty, Jennifer was a seasoned actress with a wealth of experience working with actors in every genre. The idea that she needed to be shielded from the villain for authenticity was laughable. She knew fear intimately–how to evoke it, how to embody it, and how to make it real for audiences. She didn't need rehearsals in isolation; she could summon terror at will, even if that meant facing down a candy-cane-wielding malevolent Christmas elf wearing a ridiculous sweater.

She clasped her hand around the bells on her sweater to silence them and snuck around to the back so she would be out of sight. Searching for any gaps in the wood, she soon found a small hole and pressed her face up against it. It was pretty dark inside, but enough slivers of light filtered through the rafters to reveal Vincent and Michael, their cameras pointed at Johnny.

Vincent called out action.

"Hey, Plucky," Johnny called out. "Get your scrawny ass out here. You may scare everyone else, but not me."

Vincent and Michael exchanged a glance, one that almost certainly meant Johnny was going off-script again. As Johnny continued to shout and taunt, Jennifer spied a tangle of Christmas lights uncoiling from the wooden rafters, right above Johnny. Plucky descended the string of lights and dropped to the floor. With a start, Johnny spun around to find the elf staring up at him. The actor playing Plucky was shrouded in shadow, but she could make out that he was gripping a sharpened reindeer antler–one of his signature weapons in the films.

"Have you been naughty? Or nice?" Plucky asked. It was his signature catchphrase, uttered to every one of his victims. But this time, it sounded different. Douglas had delivered it playfully with a hint of camp. Yet this new actor's rendition carried a sinister undertone. His voice was deeper, slower, resonating from the depths of his throat, adding a chilling intensity to the familiar line.

Johnny stuttered, forgetting his lines once again. He turned to Vincent and Michael, who nodded at him to continue, Vincent's free hand motioning a rolling gesture.

"I'll take that as naughty," Plucky sneered, stepping forward and slashing the sharpened antler into Johnny's abdomen. The blade sliced from chest to navel, cutting through flesh like a hot knife through butter. Johnny's stomach ruptured, spilling intestines onto the floor in a steaming heap. Wide-eyed, he stared at his insides, now outside.

Jennifer had to admit, for a fan film, the effects were remarkable. Coming from the '80s, a time when practical effects were the norm, she appreciated the rarity of such craftsmanship in today's CGI-dominated era.

But what impressed her even more was Johnny's acting; he looked legitimately horrified and in shock. He dropped to his knees, scooping up his slippery entrails to shove them back inside. He gazed up at Plucky one last time, consciousness slipping away as he collapsed face-first into his own innards.

Jennifer knew the "intestines" were nothing more than sausages and corn syrup, but the realism was disgustingly effective. Even through the small crack, the scene's grotesque authenticity made her feel faint.

From inside the barn, Vincent called, "Cut."

CHAPTER 16

Not wanting to get caught by Vincent, Jennifer hurried away from the barn. The last thing she wanted was to get another lecture about the wonders of keeping secrets.

Much like the entrance into Reindeer Park, there was an open gate leading into the next area, the metal bars painted in peeling red and white. Above it was a large green wooden sign that read "Welcome to Elf Village."

Jennifer glanced back, to make sure Vincent hadn't spotted her, before stepping onto the Gumdrop Road and entering under the sign.

The path widened to a large open area of Elf Village. Memories flooded Jennifer–bittersweet and vivid. She recalled the colorful banners and bunting that once stretched overhead and bright little elves that smiled, welcoming visitors to this magical place. Now, only tattered strips hung limp from rusted poles.

Dotted around were tiny fiberglass houses, their windows once aglow with warm lights, creating an illusion of elf inhabitants bustling within. Years ago, wooden standees of elves waved or held Christmas presents, but their vibrant colors had long faded. Now, there were no lights inside the houses, and many of the elves lay toppled over. The sun had bleached most of the paint away, leaving them ghostly remnants of their former selves.

As Jennifer stepped farther into the park, she passed by what used to be a bakery. A large plastic gingerbread man hung above an empty doorframe and Jennifer swore she could almost smell the aroma of freshly baked gingerbread drifting from within. But as she peeked inside, she found that the room was almost bare save for empty chairs, a few cake stands displaying some plastic puddings, and tables covered in dust.

Up ahead she spied the group standing in a circle, reading from their scripts as they prepared for their upcoming scenes.

"We thought you'd gotten lost," Douglas said.

"I took the scenic route."

They all rehearsed their next scene for a few minutes until Vincent arrived.

"How did Johnny's scene go?" Christy asked.

"Perfect," Vincent said, his joy barely contained.

"Sorry I missed it," Douglas said under his breath.

"Michael has taken Johnny back to camp; he's dropping him off at the closest town to get a ride back," Vincent said. "In the meantime, let's continue filming. To set the scene, your characters are unaware that Johnny has snuck off and been killed by Plucky. I'd like to get some B-roll of you all having fun and playing around in this part of the park. I'll have music playing over this scene, so don't worry about what you say, I just want to capture your reactions. Do whatever feels natural."

"When are we filming my death scene?" Jennifer asked.

"Later," Vincent said. Before Jennifer could press for more details, he raised the megaphone to his mouth and called out, "Action."

The actors wandered aimlessly, their movements awkward as Vincent circled them with his DSLR camera. Vincent had directed them to have "fun," but how could you possibly do that in an abandoned theme park? Then Douglas's voice cut through the awkward silence.

"No way," he exclaimed, dashing forward.

The group shared a quick glance before following him to three carnival booths. There was the Snowball Toss, a game where players hurled foam balls at metal targets shaped like penguins and elves. Next was Santa's Snack, a game where players toss beanbags into the open mouth of a fiberglass Santa Claus. The Santa figure, though faded and torn, still smiled, its eyes inviting players to take a shot. Finally, there was Elf Fishin', where players used plastic poles to catch floating fish. The water was long gone, leaving only the cracked, empty basin and a few forlorn plastic fish scattered at its base. The back shelves of the booths held a few remaining prizes: a lonely plush polar bear with a missing eye, a couple of plastic elves, and several penguin dolls. Yet compared to the rest of the park, this area seemed pretty well preserved.

Douglas grabbed a foam ball from the counter and tossed it up in the air. "I'm the undefeated champ at this carnival game," he declared proudly. "I've won my kids hundreds of prizes playing this." He turned to Jennifer with a grin. "Want a game?"

"No, I'm good, thanks," Jennifer replied, stroking her right wrist with her other hand.

"Aw, scared?" Douglas teased with a playful smirk.

Jennifer wasn't scared, but her wrist had been twinging all day. She had no desire to explain the arthritis that would make her wince with every throw of the ball.

"I'll take you on, champ," Christy said, snatching the ball from midair as Douglas tossed it up.

"You're on." Douglas's smile widened. "Thomas, rack 'em up."

Thomas moved behind the counter, setting up the metal targets, while Christy gathered a handful of loose balls from the floor. With the targets in place, Douglas took the first shot, but his ball sailed wide.

"What happened, champ?" Christy teased.

"Just warming up," Douglas replied, shaking his arms and preparing for his next throw.

Christy stepped up and hit a penguin with precision. She raised her index and middle fingers together and blew out imaginary smoke with a dramatic flair.

Douglas threw his next ball. It hit a penguin with a satisfying dink. "Oh yeah, baby. That is how it's done," he said before breaking into the robot.

"Oh my God, Dougie," Jennifer said, hiding her face in secondhand embarrassment. "You do know Vincent is capturing all your dad dancing right now, right?"

Vincent circled around them, not saying anything but continuing to film.

"I hope so because I'm on fire," Douglas said, shifting into the hammer dance with even more enthusiasm.

Jennifer heard Luna's giggle and couldn't help but smile. She had missed that sound.

While Douglas danced, he heard a metallic dink from behind him. He spun around to find that Christy had knocked down another target.

With a renewed determination, Douglas threw his ball but missed again. Without wasting a second, Christy threw her final ball and knocked down another target for the win. Douglas stared wide-eyed in shock.

"Look at me," she said with a grin, pointing to her eyes. "I'm the champion now."

"Rematch," Douglas demanded.

"No way. Who's next to get their ass whooped?" Christy cracked her knuckles. She turned to Jennifer and swiftly threw a foam ball at her, which Jennifer caught reflexively.

"Oh no, I'm good," Jennifer replied coolly, tossing the ball back.

"Come on, it's only a game," she said, sending the ball back with a sharper throw.

Jennifer caught it again, but this time it sent a sharp jolt through her wrist. She masked the reaction, refusing to give Christy the satisfaction. "I'm not interested," Jennifer said, flinging the ball back.

Christy caught the ball and rolled it in her hands. "Yeah, I figured. You're never one to get involved, are you? Acting like these things are beneath you?"

Jennifer stiffened, she knew this was about Christy's damn podcast again. Everyone was staring at her now, including the camera, awaiting her reaction. Then, with some strength behind it, Christy threw the ball at Jennifer, but it was intercepted by Luna, who caught it in midair.

"I'll take you on," Luna said.

Christy's surprise flickered before she regained her composure. "Go ahead," she challenged. "Take your best shot."

As Luna walked up to the counter, gratitude and unease twisted in Jennifer's chest. She was glad Luna had stepped in, but the possibility of her screwing it up–and giving Christy even more to gloat about–gnawed at her. Jennifer turned away, unwilling to watch.

Then came a sharp *dink*. She spun around. A target had tipped over.

"Nice shot," Christy conceded. She threw her ball and successfully knocked one down as well.

Luna, unfazed, picked up her next ball and threw, hitting her target dead-on. Christy followed, matching Luna's success. The game was neck and neck. Luna stepped up for her final throw.

Jennifer held her breath as the ball sailed through the air and knocked over a penguin. A quiet, "Yes," slipped from her lips.

Christy's confidence faltered as she prepared for her last throw. She released the ball, but it veered off course, missing the target by inches and hitting the back wall with a thud.

"We have a new champion," Douglas declared.

"Rematch," Christy demanded.

"Sorry, I retire undefeated," Luna said with a playful grin, glancing over at Jennifer, who, in turn, shot her a thankful smile.

With tensions now eased, Douglas, Thomas, and Christy continued to play the carnival games, while Jennifer and Luna stood a little behind them, watching.

"Thanks for that, by the way," Jennifer leaned over and whispered.

"Don't mention it," Luna replied. "Christy was being annoying. She needed to be taken down a few pegs."

"How are you so good at that game?" Jennifer asked. "Is that why you left acting? To pursue a pitching career?"

"When my daughter was born, we didn't have much money. Especially not for any toys. So when the fair rolled in, I'd win her a whole sack full of prizes until I was turned away."

Jennifer sized up Luna's petite frame and smiled at the image of her heaving a giant sack of toys over her shoulder.

"But let me ask you something," Luna began. "Why didn't you want to play? Your aim can't be that bad."

Jennifer cast a quick eye toward the others, then dropped her voice to a whisper. "For the past year, I've been getting random sharp pains in my wrists. I think it might be arthritis. My mom had it when she was my age."

"Can I see?" Luna asked.

Jennifer hesitated, then extended her right arm. Luna's touch was gentle, reassuring, her fingers gliding over the delicate skin of Jennifer's wrist. A warmth spread through Jennifer.

"Don't worry, I'm a school nurse. I went to college and everything." Luna winked.

Jennifer was strangely proud of Luna. She remembered how Luna talked about her struggle deciding between acting and going to college. Nursing had never even come up. Still, it made sense. There was a calmness to her. Something in her voice, the way their beach conversations stretched on after long shoots–she had a way of pulling Jennifer back into alignment.

Even now, with Luna gently turning her wrist, the tension was gone. The ache had faded.

"So, what's the diagnosis, doc?" Jennifer asked. "Does it need to come off?"

Luna smiled. "It doesn't appear to be too severe at the moment. You'll be fine. But some reflexology could ease the pain–and I'd probably cut down on those cigarettes. It did me a world of good when I moved back to Texas."

Luna then gently used the base of her fingertips to massage Jennifer's wrist. It felt amazing, and Jennifer was finally feeling a bit more relaxed, despite hearing the loud cheers from the rest of the group as they knocked down more pins.

"Do you want to sneak off?" Jennifer asked, nodding over her shoulder.

Luna glanced toward Vincent, who was engrossed in filming their three costars. "Do you think we're allowed?" Her eyes sparkled.

"Vincent did direct us to have fun, didn't he?" Jennifer said. "We'll just be following the director's orders."

Luna grinned. "Even after all these years, you're still trying to get me into trouble."

Jennifer headed off, calling over her shoulder, "Well, are you coming?"

Luna hesitated for a beat before following.

CHAPTER 17

Jennifer and Luna strolled through the park, the distant shouts of their group echoing faintly. They walked in silence for a while, taking in the empty gift shops and restaurants: The Jingle Bell Bazaar, Saint Nick-Nacks, and Kris Kringle's Kitchen.

Luna wandered over to the front of one shop lined with giant fiberglass stockings. "Santa's Stocking Stuffers? I'm not sure about that one."

Jennifer giggled. "Let's go." She put her hands over Luna's shoulders and pushed her into the store.

The room was set up like an oversized living room, like Luna and Jennifer were the animated mice in a Christmas movie. At one end, a giant armchair sagged, the bottom kicked in at one end, and, at the other, there was an ornate fireplace still lined with giant stockings. Beside it stood a crooked Christmas tree with warped cardboard box presents. The display tables were either flipped over or stripped bare, save for a few scattered remnants–a cracked ornament, a torn Christmas card, a shattered crystal candy cane.

They came across an oversized TV set, with two round holes where the rotating dials would have been and a speaker at the bottom.

"How the hell has this survived?" Jennifer asked as she wiped the dust off the screen with her sleeve. She was reminded of her mom's old TV set and how, as a little girl, she would sit in front of it for hours. "I'm surprised it wasn't stolen."

"I guess maybe there were some things people couldn't be bothered to steal," Luna said.

"No fucking way." Jennifer picked something up off the floor, turned it over in her hand, and read the words *Evil Elf*. It was a DVD case, dusty and faded, but the text was still legible.

Luna peered over Jennifer's shoulder. "What the hell is that doing out here? Think it's Vincent's?"

Jennifer shook her head. "No, I'd say it's been here for a while. I imagine some fans snuck in to watch the movie where it was filmed. They probably used this TV to watch it."

"Can I see?" Luna asked.

Jennifer handed the DVD over and Luna turned it over in her hands, reading the synopsis in her best Hollywood voiceover impression.

A group of misfit teens, each harboring hate for the holiday season, decide to break into the most bitchin' Christmas theme park in the desert. What starts as a night of fun soon turns into a nightmare when they discover the park's dark secret: Santa's wickedest elf, Plucky. He's armed with all the weapons in the workshop and is out to cross the naughtiest teens off Santa's list. They're about to find out Christmas has a whole new meaning...and it's killer.

"Hey, if this acting gig doesn't work out for you, maybe you should try voiceovers for commercials instead?" Jennifer joked.

"Are you saying I only have a face for radio?" Luna teased.

Jennifer's eyes met Luna's, shining green beneath smoky eye shadow. "Absolutely not," she replied, turning away. "Anyway, let's carry on."

The two exited the hut and continued their walk along the dusty path. "I don't really know what they were thinking. Building a Christmas-themed amusement park in the Nevada desert is crazy."

"I think it's brilliant," Luna said.

"You're kidding."

"Growing up in the South, I used to watch holiday specials like *Charlie Brown* and *Rudolph* and always wanted that classic white Christmas. Bringing that nostalgic, timeless spirit to somewhere like this is amazing."

"If you say so," Jennifer said, not entirely convinced.

"You're from Chester, Connecticut, right? You wouldn't get it. I bet every single one of your Christmases came straight out of a Rankin/Bass special."

"How the hell do you remember where I'm from?" Jennifer was secretly flattered that, after all this time, Luna remembered those little details.

"I remember a lot of things."

They continued walking in silence until Luna pointed to a two-story structure shaped almost like a lighthouse. It had a spiraling slide that twisted round like a helter-skelter carnival ride. Above the entrance, a sign read "Penguins' Ice Slide."

Luna turned to Jennifer with a wide grin.

"You've got to be joking," Jennifer exclaimed, staring up at the terrifyingly tall platform.

"Didn't you ever go on these as a kid?" Luna asked. "The wind rushing through your hair, like you were about to blast off into space?"

"Yes, that's exactly why I never went on one. Besides, who made you the rule breaker now?"

"Oh, please, come on."

"I'm kinda afraid of heights," Jennifer admitted, putting it mildly.

"Well, I'm not going to force you," Luna said. "But I'm going for a ride."

Luna stepped through the entrance. Jennifer's anxiety spiked as Luna began to climb the creaky steps. When Luna disappeared from view for a few moments, Jennifer was about to call out, but then her face appeared at the top.

"I'm not going up after you if you chicken out," Jennifer shouted.

Luna stuck her tongue out before settling down at the edge of the slide. She hesitated for a split second and then pushed off. Luna's laughter echoed as she spiraled down the slide, her hands thrown up in the air and the red hair of her wig streaming behind her. She landed at the bottom with a soft thud, her rear end hitting the dirt with a dusty puff.

Jennifer rushed over, afraid that Luna may have hurt herself.

"That was awesome," Luna exclaimed, still laughing.

"You're insane," Jennifer said, unable to suppress a smile.

"I'm going again," Luna said, getting to her feet.

"You defied death once, let's not tempt fate again shall we? Besides, if your wig comes off, Thomas will definitely kill you."

"Maybe I'd be safer if someone came down with me."

Jennifer had to admit that it did seem fun. But when her eyes traced the towering rickety structure, her stomach dropped like a stone. A soft touch brushed her hand as Luna's fingers gently intertwined with hers.

"You look innocent, but really you're the devil," Jennifer said, smirking despite herself.

"I'll take that as a yes?"

Jennifer rolled her eyes. "Fine, but just one ride."

"Deal," Luna beamed, her grin widening.

Hand in hand, Luna led Jennifer through the entryway and up the stairs. The wooden steps groaned and creaked beneath them, so Jennifer clutched the railing with her free hand. When they finally reached the top, she made the mistake of peeking over the edge. She tightened her grip on Luna's hand, as if a sudden gust might blow her away. They were only twenty feet up, but to Jennifer, it was as if the ground had dropped away.

As Jennifer's anxiety surged, Luna's hand gently stroked hers, the motion steady and calming.

"Want to be the big spoon or little spoon?" Luna asked.

"What?"

"Want to sit in front of me as we go down, or behind?"

Jennifer hesitated, then motioned to her face wryly. "Behind. I can't risk damaging all this work."

"I thought you said it was all diet and exercise," Luna teased, raising an eyebrow.

Jennifer huffed dramatically. "Alright, I'm leaving."

"Oh, shut up and sit. Come on," Luna said, before sitting down and patting the edge of the slide behind her.

With a reluctant sigh, Jennifer sat behind Luna, straddling her legs around Luna's. Her hands wrapped lightly around Luna's waist, their closeness making her heart skip a little.

"Ready?" Luna asked, turning her head slightly, her green eyes sparking with mischief.

"No," Jennifer replied.

Luna pushed off, and in an instant, they were hurtling down the slide. Jennifer squeezed her eyes shut as the wind roared past them. They spun and whirled, picking up speed with every twist. Luna's laughter was infectious, and soon Jennifer found herself laughing too. Holding tightly onto Luna, Jennifer buried her face in the back of her neck, feeling a mix of exhilaration and relief. Time slowed as they screamed and laughed together.

When they reached the bottom, their momentum carried them into the dirt in a tangled heap, still clutching each other. The laughter that had started with the thrill of the ride now spilled out in hysterics. They lay there for a moment, struggling to catch their breath between fits of laughter. As the giggles faded, their eyes met–cheeks flushed, hearts still racing. A quiet settled over them, warm and easy, as they remained side by side on the ground. Jennifer's hand still rested on Luna's waist. The laughter had melted into a comfortable silence, and neither of them was in any hurry to break it.

A soft crunching footstep broke the silence. Startled, they shot up to find Vincent looming over them, his camera pointed at their stunned faces.

"Were you filming us?" Jennifer demanded.

"Yes," Vincent said. "There's nothing worse in horror movies than when the connections between the characters don't feel genuine. This is the real heart of the film. So please don't let me stop you, keep going."

The spell between them was broken. Neither spoke, and after a few seconds, the director lowered the camera with a heavy sigh.

"Maybe now's a good time for a break?" he suggested.

* * *

Vincent led Jennifer and Luna back to the rest of the group. Michael had returned, now wearing a black T-shirt in place of the white one he'd had on earlier. She was envious; she would have loved to have a change of clothes. He was holding the same cooler that had been in the catering gazebo. Lunch time. Well, a man's version of lunch anyway. Inside, there were some protein and nut bars, beef jerky, some overripe bananas, and a half-opened pack of water bottles.

Jennifer grabbed a water, a nut bar, and a banana, and finished the bottle almost instantly. She then took a seat on the floor next to Douglas and began peeling her banana.

"You missed all the fun," Douglas said, between bites of a half-melted chocolate protein bar. "We played Santa's Snack after you left, and I became world champion."

"World champion, you say?" Jennifer said, taking a bite of her banana.

"Yep, although you don't need to ask the others–they'll only lie out of embarrassment at how much I whooped their asses," Douglas whispered.

"I trust there was plenty more dad dancing?"

"Of course. I can't believe you missed it."

They shared a smile before eating their food in comfortable silence. After a few moments, Jennifer turned to Douglas to ask him a question that had been on her mind since she found out about her death scene.

"Could I get your advice on something?"

"You want *my* advice?" Douglas sounded surprised. "You've never once asked for my advice in all our films together."

"Well, today I feel a bit out of my depth. This will be my first death scene on film–well, second if you count my car exploding in *Our Broken Hour*. Though, I wasn't even on set for it–they fired me long before that."

"Ah, I remember watching all that on TV–my wife was obsessed with that show. She hated when they killed Lucinda off. She still thinks your character somehow survived and is in a sun lounger on a beach somewhere."

"Ugh, I wish. Lucinda's about as dead as that guinea-pig mullet Johnny had on his head."

"I'll make sure to let Linda know," Douglas laughed. "I can see why you've come to the master. After killing Plucky five times, he's finally gonna get ya."

"Six, actually," Jennifer corrected with a playful smile.

"Huh?"

"I've killed you six times."

Douglas started counting on his fingers. "You choked me out with Christmas lights the first time. The second film took place in Vegas, so of course you crushed me with a slot machine, and then after coming back from the dead you finished me off by drowning me in the Bellagio fountain."

"–and in the third one I threw you off those cliffs in Santa Cruz and into the sea."

"The water was absolutely freezing, *and* I had to pretend I was getting eaten by sharks."

Jennifer nodded, trying to suppress a smile. "And the fourth one?"

"*A Cajun Christmas* was shot in New Orleans, so you ran me over with a Mardi Gras parade float."

"That was fun driving that huge thing," Jennifer said, recalling that day on set. "And then in the fifth one I believe I pushed you off the Empire State Building?"

Douglas nodded. "Thankfully that was filmed on a soundstage, but you pushed me so hard I almost missed the crash mat entirely. That's only five."

"You died twice in Vegas. But, seriously, how did you prepare for those death scenes?" Jennifer asked, genuinely curious.

"That's right... Luckily, because those kills were all so ridiculous, it was mostly about the props and the visuals, and I guess it helped that I had a mask on. But what I can say is that, in terms of my reactions, there are two ways to approach a death scene. One is to go quietly, with a little gasp and you're done."

"And the other?"

Douglas grinned. "The other is to go out kicking and screaming. Thrash around, scream your lungs out. In horror movies, people remember the deaths more than anything. Take *A Nightmare on Elm Street*, when Tina crawled on the ceiling as Freddy slashed her stomach. A memorable death scene can immortalize any actor."

"So you're basically saying ham it up?"

"Absolutely. Have fun with it. This isn't *Hamlet*. You're being killed by a guy in a cheap rubber elf mask."

Jennifer mulled this over as Vincent walked over.

"Okay, Ms. Hawkins, are you ready?" he asked.

"Ready as I'll ever be."

"Excellent," Vincent said, before turning toward Douglas. "Sorry Douglas, like before, this is going to be a closed set. But Michael will continue to film with the rest of you."

"No problem," Douglas said. "Good luck Jenny, knock 'em dead. Or should I say, knock yourself dead?"

Jennifer rolled her eyes as Douglas laughed at his own joke. She walked away, glancing over at Luna, who gave her a smile and a thumbs-up. Even in these awful conditions, saying goodbye to her would be difficult.

CHAPTER 18

Vincent guided Jennifer away from the group, steering her toward a large brick building crowned with a garish sign: The Jolly Elf's Eatery & Jamboree. Above the entrance, a large 3D elf loomed large, painted in bright, slightly faded colors. He held an oversized chef's hat over his head with one hand, and an "okay" gesture with the other. Back in the day, he tipped his hat to welcome guests.

"Right, so in this scene, Rebecca Sommers has broken away from the group and finds herself lost. That's when she stumbles into this restaurant–and bam, she runs into Plucky. Then, well..." Vincent dragged his thumb across his neck.

"So, how's he going to do it? Kill me, I mean."

"It's going to be a surprise," he said, his voice buzzing with excitement.

"But don't I have to know?" Jennifer asked. "So I can prepare?"

Vincent shook his head. "I want your reaction to be genuine. We're striving for *authenticity*. Especially since you've never done a death scene before. It'll be a rare performance to capture on camera." He stared off slightly as he said this.

"But don't we need to practice the choreography at least?" Although nearly all of her fight scenes in the *Evil Elf* movies were done with stunt performers, she still rehearsed every action sequence with Douglas so they could film the close-ups.

"Don't worry about any of that," Vincent assured her. "We'll feel the scene as we go–just do what feels natural. We'll handle all the practical effects afterward. Sound good?"

Before Jennifer could protest, Vincent pressed on. "Once you step through those doors, stay in character. I'll be filming the whole time, plus we've set up GoPros around the restaurant to catch every angle."

Noticing her hesitation, Vincent rested a hand on her shoulder. "Relax–you're a pro. You've got this. Just be natural."

With that, Vincent hoisted the Steadicam onto his shoulder and hurried through the door, closing it behind him. After a few moments, she heard him yell, "Action."

Jennifer took a deep breath, slipped into character and stepped into the scene.

The inside used to be a Christmas-themed Chuck E. Cheese–arcade games, personal pizzas, and a mechanical elf band that performed dinner shows. Now, however, the band sat hidden beneath dust-covered sheets. The space was silent, holding only the echoes of squealing children darting through the aisles. Chairs and tables lay toppled, the arcade games stood dark and broken, and murals that once showed cheerful elves skating on icy ponds were now buried beneath layers of graffiti.

GoPros were mounted around the room, their lenses fixed and unblinking. Vincent stood quietly in the corner, his camera trained on Jennifer. Unsure of what to do, she edged closer to the band stage, hand reaching for one of the dusty sheets. Before she could pull it away, a sudden burst of music shattered the silence. The once-jolly tune emerged twisted and warped from hidden speakers, the melody cracked and dragging.

"Well, hello there, Santa's little helpers," a chirpy voice crackled. "The band's about ready to play, so grab your cocoa and get set for a yuletide spectacle packed with some holly, jolly, jingle jams. Are you ready?"

The question hung in the silence.

"Come on now, I said, *are you ready?*"

Silence again.

"That's more like it. Let's get this party started. Put your hands together and give a big ol' cheer for the one, the only, the Jolly Elf Jamboree!"

A spotlight flicked on, casting its light over the stage as the sheets slid off to reveal the mechanical elf band. The troupe was frozen in place. It was evident that vandals had defaced several of the band members over the years. Some had scorched faces, others were melted and disfigured. Various areas of the bodies were stripped away, exposing the warped metal framework and wires beneath.

As if belatedly remembering their purpose, the mechanical elves jerked into motion. Their rusted joints creaked and groaned as they launched into a clunky rendition of "Rudolph the Red-Nosed Reindeer," accompanied by high-pitched, almost chipmunk-like voices.

Jennifer searched the stage, noticing one motionless elf. Its back was turned and its head was slumped into its chest. Aha, the new Plucky.

Now that she could fully envision how unsettling the scene could be, Jennifer leaned into it. Moving in closer, she climbed onto the stage and studied the elf. In her mind, the moment played out with cinematic clarity–the music fading as her character approached, the tension thick, and then a sudden blast of sound that would jolt the audience, sending popcorn flying.

Jennifer entangled herself with the jamboree, the elves singing and dancing all around her. The sound was so loud that it made it even easier for her to ignore the cameras. Edging closer to the motionless elf, she extended her hand, fingertips brushing against its cold shoulder. Taking a deep breath, she spun him around. But instead of finding Plucky, she was met with yet another dilapidated mechanical elf. Jennifer froze. Her mind raced, scrambling to decide her next move, all the while the unsettling creature stared back. Its face was stripped of its "skin," exposing a tangle of gears and wires beneath, and his two bright, bulbous eyes bored into her.

Suddenly, one of the dancing elves broke formation and lunged at her. She let out a startled scream, stumbling backward, and crashing off the stage. Though the drop wasn't far, the impact knocked the breath from her lungs. Gasping, she looked up as the elf jerkily emerged from the others. With stiff, unnatural movements, it grasped its plastic face and peeled it away–revealing another mask underneath: Plucky's.

As he advanced out of the shadows and into the spotlight, Jennifer could finally see him up close. He was a stark departure from the original movies.

Plucky's original rubber mask had a cheerful latex smile that lifted his cherubic rosy cheeks. Douglas also wore pointed prosthetic ears that poked out from beneath a green hat, topped with a gleaming golden bell. His emerald velvet suit was buttoned up over a red-and-white striped shirt, paired with curly, shiny shoes. The filmmakers had improvised the costume on a tight budget, never imagining it would lead to five sequels. They were also unaware of how Plucky's peppy appearance would be loved by the fans–making it a costume they could never really change.

But before her stood a very different Plucky. His once-vibrant attire had faded to near-rags. The golden bell on his hat had oxidized and rusted, now a sickly blend of green and orange. The rubber mask was weathered and cracked, and the delicate edges of the latex mouth were torn and crudely glued shut, forming a sinister, lopsided smirk. His once-rosy cheeks had faded to a sickly, yellowed hue. What disturbed her most were the actor's eyes. Where Douglas's bright blue eyes had sparkled through the mask, this actor's were dull and murky, casting a clouded, unsettling gaze.

The band of mechanical elves continued to play and Plucky's dirty, gloved fingers danced in the air like a proud conductor of his very own orchestra. He paused, tilting his head to one side, expectantly, as if waiting for Jennifer to respond. Jennifer stole a glance at Vincent, who remained focused on filming. She took a steadying breath and composed herself.

"Plucky," she shouted. "I killed you. What are you doing here?"

The elf peered down at her from the stage. "Silly girl," he sneered. "Haven't you realized now that you *can't* kill me? I will always come back. I will never leave you."

He slid off the stage and crept toward her. The original Plucky had a musical rhythm to his movements, but this new actor had only heaviness in his steps.

"For thirty-three long years, I have waited to ask you one question."

He lurched forward and grabbed Jennifer's wrist, squeezing hard. She yelped. In the rare fight scenes she'd done with Douglas, he had never been this rough. Vincent circled behind Plucky on the stage, still filming. His face was stoic, almost vacant.

Plucky was now face-to-face with Jennifer. Up close, the rubber mask was visibly flaking, the cheap material worn and cracked with age. The stench of his stale breath seeped through, nauseating her.

"Have you been naughty?" he hissed. "Or knifed?"

She stared into his cold eyes, then at his left fist that clenched a candy cane shiv. He raised it up high, the stage light capturing its sharpened edge. Jennifer winced and let out a scream–it felt natural. And with that, his fist began its sharp descent.

"Cut!"

CHAPTER 19

The music abruptly stopped and the room fell silent. Plucky released his grip, and Jennifer pulled her hand back, rubbing her aching wrist as she remained on the ground.

"What are you playing at, you asshole?" she demanded. "You're being too rough."

The actor only stared at her in silence before snapping his head toward Vincent. He stormed over, and they began talking in hushed whispers. Though she couldn't make out what they were saying, the anger radiating from the other actor was unmistakable. Vincent turned toward Jennifer, smiled, and raised a finger before ushering Plucky to the far side of the room and into the shadows. After what looked like a heated exchange, Plucky's actor slammed open the emergency exit doors and stormed out.

Vincent then ran over and offered a hand to Jennifer.

"What was that about?" she said after being pulled onto her feet.

"It's nothing. He's a little annoyed that I've decided to switch things up at the last minute."

"Well, is he coming back? We have a scene to finish."

"You see, that's the thing. As I watched you guys, I had a feeling something wasn't quite right." He placed his camera onto a table.

"What do you mean wasn't right? You wrote it."

"Yes, I did," Vincent said. "But even the greatest filmmakers don't always stick to their scripts. If you see something not working, then you must change it for the sake of the movie. In this case, I wasn't feeling it."

"We can do another take if you didn't like what I did? I mean, you did tell me to improvise."

"No, it's not that. I mean, I don't think this is where your character would die. It didn't feel right. It's all wrong. I'm going to have to change it."

Jennifer pinched the bridge of her nose. "Vincent. You need to kill me. I need to get home today. Do you understand me?"

"Yes, yes, I will, but not like this. The audience wouldn't accept it," he said, rubbing his chin.

Jennifer sighed. She picked up an upturned chair and slumped into it. "I think you're taking this little fan film too seriously. I mean, you've got the blood, you've got the elf, you've got the screaming, even this itchy-ass Christmas sweater–who cares about making it perfect?" She was fully aware of the campiness of the franchise, and it was something that the past filmmakers hadn't shied from.

Vincent's head whipped toward her, a vein bulging in his neck. "I care. Fans of the *Evil Elf* franchise care. This isn't some little throwaway movie. We are making the most important fan film in history. Trust me, everyone will remember this movie, even if you and the others don't."

His neck vein continued to pulse. "It's frustrating that you don't even understand *why* it's important, or care. It seems like you only want to say your lines and go back to LA. I wish you had at least a *bit* of passion for what we're trying to do out here." Vincent turned away, throwing the sheet back over the elves. Jennifer could hear him muttering under his breath.

Vincent certainly wasn't the first hot-headed director Jennifer had worked with–one of those guys making schlock but still thinking of themselves as the next Tarantino. He was young, overly passionate, and probably in way over his head–or *up* his own ass.

Jennifer let Vincent have a few moments, before walking over to him. "I'm just saying, don't be so hard on yourself, kid. People barely remember the first movie. *Anything* you do will probably get better exposure and reception–especially now with the internet. You have to stop putting this franchise on a pedestal. I mean, I thought that scene was going great... Well, apart from Plucky trying to dislocate my wrist." She touched her wrist before glancing toward the door where Plucky had exited. "And it was the most scared I've ever been on set. I barely had to act. Also, that mask was terrifying and positively hideous. Who made that?"

"You didn't recognize it? That was the original Plucky mask. The OG. The one Douglas wore in the first movie. It was found under the bed of the old prop master when he died, and his daughter sold it at auction. I bought it for $5,000, and I'm now using a piece of film history to make film history."

The pulse in his neck eased and his smile returned. Vincent was back to his geeky self.

"Seriously? $5,000?" Her mouth dropped open. "The things kids waste their money on these days."

Vincent's face slipped again slightly, before recovering with a smile. "At least the fans will appreciate it," he said, before turning and grabbing his camera.

"Wait," Jennifer said. "So, what are we doing with my death scene?"

"I don't know. I just know that now is not the right time."

"When is the right time, Vincent?"

"You're *the* 'final girl,' Ms. Hawkins. We can't rush your death scene. It's too important. While I have a think on what to do, why don't you rejoin the group?" Without waiting for a response, he walked out of the restaurant.

Standing alone in the large room, Jennifer muttered, "If he walks away from me before I'm finished one more time, I'll make sure he gets his own close-up by shoving that camera so far up..."

She took a deep breath, let it out slowly, and followed him out.

* * *

As Jennifer stepped outside, she spotted the group up ahead wrapping up a scene with Michael. When they finished, Vincent grabbed his megaphone.

"That's a wrap for today, everyone. We created some magic out here. Let's all head back to base camp."

Douglas spotted Jennifer and approached her. "So, how did it go?"

"It didn't."

"What do you mean?" he asked, puzzled.

"Partway through the scene, Vincent called cut. He said it 'didn't feel right.' Whatever that means."

"So you saw him then? Plucky, I mean. What was he like? Vincent still won't let me meet him."

"He was..." Jennifer hesitated, recalling the image of his aged yellow mask and those unsettling dark eyes. "Let's just say he wasn't you."

When Douglas raised his eyebrow, she continued. "He gave me the creeps to be honest. Sure, you played it a little creepy too, but there was a campy fun that you brought into it. This new guy played it far too straight."

Douglas stared straight ahead.

"Does this whole thing bother you at all?" she asked. "Like, you *are* Plucky." She considered Douglas now. He was in a pretty generic costume, and Jennifer couldn't help but wonder what Vincent was planning for his character. She couldn't make any sense of it.

"I'm hardly the only one who's ever played him. I don't *own* the character. Unlike you–no one else could be Rebecca Sommers. It's part of the tradition of slashers; passing the torch, or, in this case, the candy cane shiv. And let's face it, I'm getting too old."

As they passed through the decrepit Elf Village and the ruins of Reindeer Park, a dull throb stirred in Jennifer's wrist. She gripped it, willing the sensation to fade.

"That's not all, though," Jennifer said. "He was also a little rough with me."

"What?" Douglas stopped. "Did he hurt you? Where's Vincent? As director, it's his responsibility to ensure the cast's safety. This isn't right."

"It's okay, really. Please don't worry about it."

"Well, I'm at least going to find that actor and give him what for."

"I appreciate your concern, but I'm fine. Really. Forget I said anything."

Douglas didn't look entirely convinced, but nodded anyway.

The group made their way back through the entrance gates and to the parking lot. Jennifer was itching to wash off the day's makeup and grime, but she shivered at the thought of those icy showers. If she hurried, she hoped to snag at least a hint of hot water before the others drained it all. Knowing better than to ask for fresh towels, she grabbed the one she'd used the night before from her bunk, along with a set of comfortable clothes, and headed back into the park to use the showers.

In the shower room, Jennifer began unpacking her toiletries. As she began scrubbing her face clean under the faucet, she heard the door creak open. She snatched up her towel, rubbed her eyes clear, and found Luna standing in the doorway. Her silvery hair was bundled up into a claw clip, leaving a few face-framing locks, and her leathers had been swapped for a loose robe with billowing sleeves and a pair of crocs.

"Sorry, I seem to have a habit of scaring you," Luna said, rearranging her towel over her arm awkwardly.

Jennifer breathed a sigh of relief. "Oh no, sorry–I thought you were Johnny for a second."

"Wow. I'll try not to take that as an insult." Luna walked over to the sink next to Jennifer and started unpacking her stuff. "Besides, Michael dropped him off in the closest town to get an Uber back home, remember?"

"Thank God." Relief washed over Jennifer. "By the way, I want to tell you a secret." She turned to Luna while her eyes flickered toward the bathroom entrance. "I watched his death scene earlier today."

"Like hell you did," Luna said, her mouth dropping in disbelief.

Jennifer grinned. "I snuck off to watch it."

"Oh man, you should've brought me with you. So, how was it?"

"Awesome," Jennifer said, locking eyes with Luna before they both erupted into laughter. "But honestly, as much as I hate to admit it, his acting at the end was pretty impressive."

"You're kidding! I don't believe you for a second."

"Well, believe it," Jennifer said. "Despite all his bullshit, he really delivered in his final scene."

"Whaddaya know, maybe he'll have another trophy soon to display between his Razzie and XXXcellence awards."

The pipes in the shower room rattled and shook, the sound echoing through the space.

"I don't know about you," Luna said, "but the thing I'm looking forward to most after this is a hot shower."

"Amen to that."

"The showers are freakin' freezing. This movie better be good, that's all I'm saying."

Jennifer winced, knowing that she hogged all the hot water for herself yesterday, and, even worse, she was already planning to do it again today.

"There was some hot water at the start yesterday. Why don't you have the first shower?" Jennifer offered.

"No, you were here first, so you should go first."

"No, I insist. I hogged it all yesterday."

"I can't," Luna said, shaking her head.

"Look, if we keep arguing about this, Christy or someone else will show up and grab all the hot water for themselves."

"Oh no, we can't have that." After a pause, Luna added, "You know, there are, like, six shower heads in there."

"Right..." Jennifer said, unsure where Luna was heading.

"We could share the hot water? I totally understand if that makes you uncomfortable. I thought, like–when we filmed back then–we'd do it all the time after being in the ocean."

"No, it's not that," Jennifer said, struggling to find the right words. "It's just..." She hesitated, grappling with her thoughts. In truth, it had been a very long time since they'd seen each other naked. And even though she knew she was in pretty good shape thanks to working out and hot yoga, there was the undeniable fact that her body had changed significantly over those forty years.

But then again, what did it matter? And would it be even weirder to say no? And is it weird to think about this so deeply?

"Sure," Jennifer said. "Sharing the hot water sounds like a good plan."

They turned away from each other, undressed, and wrapped towels around themselves in silence. Heading into the shower area, they went to opposite ends of the room and hung up their towels.

"Ready?" Jennifer said, her hand poised over the button. She kept herself from glancing over at Luna.

"Ready."

They both pressed their buttons at the same time. The pipes groaned and rattled before warm water cascaded from the showerheads. Jennifer sighed as the heat enveloped her, savoring the moment. But she knew the hot water wouldn't last forever, so she squeezed a generous amount of shampoo into her hand and began vigorously working it into her hair, determined to wash out the ungodly amounts of hair spray.

"Damn," Luna said.

"You okay?" Jennifer called over the sound of running water.

"I forgot my shampoo."

"You can borrow mine."

Jennifer slid the shampoo bottle across the wet tiles toward Luna. Their eyes met before Jennifer had turned away. Then, as if on cue, the warm water turned ice cold. Both women screamed and scrambled for their towels.

After drying off and getting dressed, Jennifer and Luna stepped outside to find that it was now dark. Jennifer had lost all sense of time. As they made their way back toward the safety of the path, Jennifer couldn't shake the thought of scorpions and snakes skulking on the ground below their feet. She stayed close to Luna, their arms lightly brushing against each other. Once again, being this close to Luna calmed Jennifer's nerves and her anxiety drifted away.

"I take it you're staying for another day, then?" Luna's voice was soft, almost hesitant.

"It looks like it."

"I'm glad."

Jennifer raised her eyebrow at Luna.

"I mean..." Luna continued, her voice faltering as she searched for the right words. "I know you're eager to get home, that this production isn't exactly what you're used to. But selfishly...I'm glad you're here."

Jennifer smiled, but kept her eyes focused on the floor. "So am I."

They walked in silence for the rest of the journey, their pinky fingers entwined.

CHAPTER 20

When they arrived back at base camp, the fire pit was crackling warmly, and everyone had gathered around it. Jennifer found a few empty chairs next to Thomas and she and Luna settled in. They warmed their hands and smiled to themselves, the glow of the fire illuminating their wet hair and clean faces.

Thomas stared at Jennifer and Luna. "If you two have used up all the hot water, then so help me, I'll make sure your makeup ends up looking like a toddler's art project tomorrow."

The women shared a glance but said nothing.

Thankfully, Michael provided a distraction by bringing a metal grate out of one of the gazebos and setting it up over the fire. Vincent came up behind him holding a large pot.

"So, what feast do you have in store for us tonight?" Jennifer asked hesitantly.

"We're having a good ol' fashioned campfire chili," Vincent announced.

"Oh good, something warming–but how did you keep it all refrigerated?" Christy asked.

Vincent answered by cracking open a can of storebought chili and dumped it into the pot. This was followed by three more cans of chili, each one landing with a wet thud. Ordinarily, Jennifer might have questioned this "meal," but tonight she didn't have the energy for complaints. Besides, she was starving, and the rich aroma of tomatoes and chili simmering over the fire was a comforting relief after the long and exhausting day.

The cast and crew sat in comfortable silence, listening to the campfire crackle and a metal entrance sign creak as it swung in the gentle breeze. Michael poked the fire with a stick, sending a shower of sparks upward.

"While we're all here, mind if I record some interviews?" Christy asked Vincent. "It'll help promote the movie once it's out."

We've only just got comfortable, Jennifer thought. But Vincent and his brother exchanged a glance, then nodded.

Without hesitation, Christy pulled her phone from the pocket of her hoodie, plugged a mic cable into the aux port, and held up the small microphone. She tapped the screen to start recording and raised the mic.

"So, what was it like on set for the first movie–like, where were you at in your careers?" She asked this without making any eye contact, but Jennifer knew the question was meant for her. Christy was clearly fishing for something to use on her podcast. Instead of answering, Jennifer let the silence linger, the crackling fire filling the pause, until Douglas broke it.

"Well, for me, I was mainly restricted to character roles," he began. "There wasn't a lot of work out there for a–well, guy like me. So, when I got the call for *Evil Elf*, I couldn't believe it. A villain. In a horror movie. It was a big deal. I mean, never in my whole life had I been seen as an intimidating person, but when the prop artist gave me that candy cane shiv for the first time..." He smiled faintly at the memory. "I felt powerful."

Douglas's smile faded as he gazed into the flames. "But then I read the script and I got on set. And well...I found I had to rein in my expectations." He turned to Vincent apologetically.

"Don't get me wrong: yes, I was given this iconic role–and I am so grateful it's become this cult favorite for fans like you. And honestly, the absurdity of it did let me showcase my range as an actor–and I guess I do have it to thank for some relatively steady work..."

He turned his head back to the fire. "But honestly, we all know it, the films were silly. And as the series went on, each one trying to out-crazy the last, I started to hate what they were doing to my character. By the time I was asked to reprise Plucky for the sixth film, I knew it was time to walk away."

He forced a smile to lighten the tone. "But hey, playing Plucky paid my bills, it's what got me on the map. And, let's face it, no one would be interested in me at the conventions if I didn't bring the mask or say the lines." He turned back to the fire, his face cast in flickering shadows, and fell silent.

"That's not true, Doug. People are there to see *you*." Luna had said this with such conviction that Jennifer almost believed her.

But like Douglas, Jennifer understood the harsh truth about Hollywood. She recognized his quiet acceptance of the industry's unspoken rules. The fans, the managers, the studios–they never really saw *you*. They only saw the character you played, especially if that character came from the blood-soaked world of horror. And as you got older, the roles dried up. So you either clung to your old characters, squeezing out every drop of relevance, or you faded into the background, stuck playing forgettable supporting parts. It was hard enough for actresses like her–but for someone like Douglas, it could be even worse.

Christy posed another question. "So, if you didn't want to come back to *Evil Elf* before, why now?"

Douglas leaned back, considering. He was calm and collected, composed and unhurried.

Jennifer had always hated interviews and was aware that she had a bad habit of rushing through each question, throwing out a jumble of words that never seemed to satisfy the interviewer. More often than not, she was met with confused smiles or stiff, uncomfortable thank-yous. She just wanted them over and done with.

"I always said I'd return to the franchise only if the tone shifted or if Plucky was taken in a different direction–maybe a darker or more sophisticated direction," Douglas said, nodding toward Vincent. "And when this kid pitched his idea to me, I loved it." He took a deep breath. "But I'll admit, I was a little disappointed when Vincent told me I wasn't playing Plucky. I guess I should probably be glad I'm not stuck playing a stereotype or some cheesy character. But honestly, I'm not sure who I'm supposed to be in this movie. Like, what's my role here? Who do I represent?"

He poked at the glowing kindling with a stick, his movements slow, almost absent. "Then again, I guess a sixty-five-year-old elf isn't exactly what you'd call intimidating."

Jennifer had never heard Douglas be so vulnerable. He was the kind of person who could laugh off anything with a quick joke and an easy smile. But now, the worry lines etched into his face told a different story.

Silence hung in the air, broken only by the crackle of the fire that sent embers up into the night air. Vincent shifted awkwardly in his chair before speaking.

"You do know that no one could replace you, right?" he said. "I knew I wanted you in the movie–and I promise, what we have coming up will be a landmark moment, for the movie and your career." Vincent switched his focus from Douglas and into the fire. "Something no one will ever forget."

Douglas smiled faintly and nodded to himself.

With that, Vincent stood up and accepted a stack of paper bowls from Michael, but Jennifer couldn't ignore the quick glance he exchanged with his brother.

"And hey, at least we get to see your gorgeous face this time, instead of hiding behind that God-awful rubber mask," Thomas said, cutting the tension.

"That's the nicest thing you've said to me all day," Douglas broke out in a smile.

Vincent stirred and scooped the chili into the bowls with a large ladle, the steam curling into the cool night air. Jennifer eyed the paper bowls warily. But despite being storebought, the chili was surprisingly delicious. It was a simple comfort, warming her from the inside. The group ate in silence, and the chili was gone within a few minutes.

With everyone's bellies now full, Christy tried her luck again. She shifted her gaze to Jennifer. "What about you, Jennifer?"

"What about me?" Jennifer asked as she scraped her paper bowl clean.

"What's it like to be back at the place where it all began?"

Jennifer's eyes dropped to Christy's mic, which was pointed directly at her. Around the campfire, the others waited, their faces shadowed but expectant. Christy's sly smirk told Jennifer she was determined to get her exclusive–no matter what.

Jennifer didn't want to give Christy the satisfaction. She even considered getting up and heading to the bus. But then she felt Luna's light touch on her arm. She turned. Luna was leaning in, her green eyes wide, genuinely curious–waiting to hear her answer.

Jennifer sighed. "Okay well, what was it like on set for the first time? I mean, honestly, it was a little scary, but exciting. This was my first proper acting role, and I had no idea what to expect. Moving from a small town in Connecticut to LA at twenty, I was already overwhelmed. Then I was brought out here to Tinseltown, and I couldn't believe it–they'd actually built a Christmas-themed amusement park in the middle of the Nevada desert."

She glanced back toward the park, her eyes tracing the faint outline of the Ferris wheel silhouetted against the moonlit sky. "Back then, the whole park was lit up. The star at the top of the Ferris wheel used to shine so brightly. It was beautiful, in a sort of cheesy, over-the-top way."

Christy leaned in. "And the owners were totally cool with you filming a horror movie at their family-friendly theme park?"

Jennifer smiled, shaking her head. "Absolutely not. But even in the '80s, the park was struggling. Money was tight, and we offered easy cash. As soon as the park closed for the night, we'd move in, shoot our little movie, and make sure we were packed up before they opened in the morning. In many ways, the first film's shoot was very similar to this one. It was also low-budget, fast-paced, and had a small creative team. When the film was released, the owners were so horrified by the violence that they publicly disavowed it and refused to let the sequel be filmed there. That's why the producers went in a different direction and started using a new location for each subsequent movie."

"They were idiots," Vincent blurted. The sudden outburst made everyone turn to him in surprise. "If they'd only embraced it, maybe this park wouldn't be dead. Hell, they should've rebranded it as an *Evil Elf* amusement park to fully capitalize on the movie's success."

"You mean like Disneyland?" Thomas asked, raising an eyebrow.

Douglas smirked. "So instead of getting a picture with Mickey Mouse, you'd pose with Plucky the Elf?"

"And instead of Mickey waffles, you'd get Plucky pancakes," Thomas added, laughing.

"Would that make Jennifer a Disney-type princess then?" Luna asked with a smile.

"Yeah," Jennifer said, playing along, "instead of sitting on my ass on the convention circuit, I could've been wandering this park for the past few decades in a tiara, signing autograph booklets."

The group burst into laughter, except for Vincent, whose expression remained deadly serious.

"So, Vincent," Christy began, "as the biggest *Evil Elf* fan here, why do you think it resonates so much with horror fans?"

Vincent rolled his eyes as if the answer was obvious. "It's a masterclass in filmmaking. Like I was saying to Jennifer, the setting for a movie is so important." He turned in his chair to face the park. "Christmas brings back childhood memories of wonder and joy–a magic that feels harder to hold onto as adults. By blending classic Christmas spirit with horror, *Evil Elf* turns holiday lights, cheerful decorations, and festive sounds into something eerie and tense. It gives those familiar holiday symbols an edge. And so we got a fresh, suspenseful twist on both holiday and horror genres."

"I wonder if this movie will inspire those same feelings in new and old fans when it's released," Christy mused.

"Maybe this will be the beginning of a new chapter?" Luna said. "What if this movie changes our lives–even more than the originals did? Can you imagine if it takes off and leads to other opportunities?"

Luna's green eyes were wide and hopeful. For a moment, Jennifer glimpsed the twenty-two-year-old girl she first met–so full of hope and optimism about a promising acting career. Even now, all these years later, Jennifer could still see that flame burning in her, not yet extinguished by life's inevitable disappointments. Jennifer caught the hopeful expressions mirrored on the others' faces: a silent wish that this film could be their second–or maybe their last–chance to revive their Hollywood dreams.

But deep down, Jennifer knew the truth. This was just a fan film, destined to be seen only by the most devoted *Evil Elf* fans, and even they would likely forget it soon after. It would be swallowed up in the endless sea of other fan projects on YouTube.

Still, as she turned back to Luna, she found she couldn't be the one to stamp out her flame. "If I know the fans–and I think I do–they'll be begging for a sequel."

"Hell yeah," Thomas exclaimed, grinning.

Luna beamed and squeezed Jennifer's knee.

"That means a lot, Jennifer." Vincent said, absolutely beaming. "Honestly, out of everyone, I didn't expect those words to come from you."

With that, he clapped his hands on his knees and stood up. "Well, on that positive note, we're calling it a night. Keep up that spirit because we have a big day ahead of us tomorrow, possibly the most important day of filming yet. So, please don't stay up too late."

He and Michael then said their goodnights before disappearing toward their gazebos.

The moment they were out of earshot, Thomas grinned and pulled a whiskey bottle from the pocket of his sweater. "Now that Mom and Dad are asleep, who's up for some fun?"

CHAPTER 21

"I'll grab some plastic cups from the gazebo," Christy said and walked off.

"What about the rest of you?" Thomas shook the bottle.

"Count me in," Douglas said.

"Thanks, but I don't drink," Luna said.

Thomas turned to Jennifer. "How about you?"

Jennifer stared at the golden liquid sloshing around in the glass bottle and licked her dry lips. "For the love of God, yes."

Christy reappeared, and handed a stack of cups to Thomas. He poured a generous amount into each one, which Christy distributed to everyone except Luna.

"Let's play, 'Never Have I Ever,' " Thomas suggested with a sly grin.

"What are we, twenty-year-olds at a frat party?" Jennifer groaned.

"Got a better idea?" Christy asked.

"Yeah, it's called 'Just Drinking.' Allow me to demonstrate," Jennifer said, raising her cup to her lips.

Thomas held up a finger. "If you want to drink, you've got to answer some questions first."

Jennifer sighed but dropped her cup.

"Never have I ever pranked a costar," Thomas said, glancing over at Douglas, who rolled his eyes as he took a sip of his drink. "I knew it was you, you son of a bitch."

All eyes turned to Douglas, who shrugged, feigning innocence. Then, with a sly smile, he said, "I guess it's safe to come clean now that the statute of limitations has passed. Fine–I admit it. I was the one behind it."

"I knew it," Thomas exclaimed, jumping up with a wide grin.

"What did you do?" Christy asked.

"This bastard hid one of those fart machines during one of my big scenes and kept triggering it. It ended up in the bloopers, and some fans still ask if it was me."

"That is hilarious," Luna laughed.

"To be fair," Douglas said, holding up his hands. "Plucky is very mischievous, and I was only getting into character."

"Yeah, yeah, this shoot isn't over yet, so I may still get my payback," Thomas said. "You know what they say, 'Revenge is a dish best served cold.' "

"Your turn," Christy said, nodding toward Douglas.

Douglas tapped his chin thoughtfully before smirking. "Never have I ever started a food fight on set."

Christy rolled her eyes and drank.

"Wait, what?" Luna asked.

"Douglas bet me ten dollars I couldn't hit our director in the back of the head with a piece of cheese. Naturally, I did, and before I knew it, I'd started a full-on food war. The producers were not amused that we wasted a day of catering."

Jennifer didn't recall that at all. But then again, she always took her lunch alone, far away from the chaos of the cast.

"Oh, and Douglas, you still owe me that money by the way," Christy added.

"I still don't think you hit him. You missed by a couple of inches," Douglas said, holding his index finger and thumb close together.

As the group laughed and argued about the details of the food fight, Jennifer stared down at the cup in her hands, wondering when she'd finally get to take another sip.

"Alright, Christy, your turn," Douglas said.

"Don't try to change the subject, I still want my money," Christy said with a grin. "Okay, let me think. Never have I ever..." She paused, tapping her cup thoughtfully before her gaze landed on Jennifer. "Slept with a coworker?"

Douglas didn't drink, Thomas took a large gulp, and Jennifer took a quick sip. Luna watched from the side.

"Hey, I saw that," Christy said, smiling at Jennifer. "So, come on, who was it?"

"That's not how the game's played," Jennifer said.

"Aw, come on. We're all friends here. If you don't share, it'll only make us speculate. Maybe that person is even on this set."

Jennifer and Luna's eyes met–just for a second–before they both looked away.

It was only now that Jennifer realized that Christy, still staring expectantly, was wearing her podcast's merchandise. A hooded sweatshirt with "The Horror Haven" embroidered on it with red stitching. As her eyes lowered, she could see that Christy was still holding onto her microphone.

"I'm going to bed," Jennifer announced, downing the last of her drink and placing her cup down.

"Wait," Christy began, "Sorry, I didn't mean to make you uncomfortable."

"It's fine. It's late and I'm tired. Goodnight, everyone," Jennifer said, walking away.

* * *

When Jennifer climbed onto the bus, Johnny's bunk was cleared of his belongings. She let out a silent sigh, relieved she wouldn't have to deal with him ever again–unless, of course, Vincent had some grand plan for a film premiere that involved the entire cast.

Not wanting to get caught with her bare ass out, Jennifer hurried into her pajamas. As she settled into her bunk and pulled the covers up, the bus rocked slightly as someone else came aboard. She raised her head to see Luna placing her belongings on the vacant bunk next to Jennifer.

"Mind if I sleep here? Douglas snores like a freight train."

"Sure. But it's a small bus, it won't make much of a difference."

"It'll make a difference."

Luna unzipped her bag and pulled out her pajamas. Jennifer turned to face the wall, offering Luna some privacy. Despite herself, Jennifer's eyes drifted back just long enough to catch Luna slipping into Garfield pajamas. There was something endearing about seeing a woman in her sixties wearing cartoon cat PJs. It brought back a memory of Luna on set, always grabbing the newspaper and heading straight for the funny pages to read the adventures of that lasagna-loving cat. It was a comforting reminder that, despite how much time had passed, some things never changed.

Luna settled into her bunk as Jennifer turned to face her, propping her cheek on her hand, her elbow sinking into the mattress.

"It's almost like old times," Luna said.

"Even though you had your own trailer, you always crept into mine," Jennifer smiled at the memory.

"Well, yours was way bigger."

"Do you remember how we'd stay up all night, talking about our futures?"

Luna nodded, a smile on her lips. "We were going to be major Hollywood actresses in big movies. We were gonna have mansions in Beverly Hills and long display cabinets large enough to hold all our Oscars."

"Don't forget about our Grammys."

"Of course," Luna said, chuckling. "I think we also planned on snagging a couple of Tonys?"

Jennifer's smile softened as the memory lingered, but it gradually faded. "Our grand plans didn't exactly pan out. Even Johnny has more awards than we do."

"I might not have made it, but you did," Luna said, her voice sincere.

Jennifer laughed. "Yeah, right."

"You're an actress in Hollywood, aren't you?"

"Barely," Jennifer said. "I spend more time in convention halls than I do on sets these days. I don't have a Beverly Hills mansion, but what I do have is a crappy apartment on the outskirts of the city. You've accomplished more than I ever did."

"No, I haven't."

"At least you have a family–got married, had children. You got a degree, became a nurse, and got up and did something with your life. I have nothing to show for my time in Hollywood except for five crappy C-tier horror movies, a short stint in a soap opera, and countless direct-to-DVD movies that hardly anyone has seen." She rolled onto her back. "And I still stay, clinging on."

"I never had a husband."

"But your daughter?"

"Lily wasn't exactly planned," Luna said. "When I went back home to take care of my dad, I was his full-time caretaker. It was...hard." Her throat tightened.

"You don't have to explain anything to me."

"It's okay, I want to," Luna said. She took a deep breath before continuing. "Acting was my only escape, and without it, I spiraled. One night, I went out, got drunk, and hooked up with a random guy. Nine months later, Lily was born. When my father passed away, I couldn't go back to my old life or the lights, the fame, or the ounce of glamour I experienced in my short time in Hollywood. I had a daughter to care for, and LA isn't a place for a kid. Who would look after her while I went to auditions? And if I did land a role, who would care for her while I worked fifteen-hour days?"

"I had no idea," Jennifer said, pausing to consider. "I could've helped you. I would have cared for you both."

"You always said you hated kids. Besides, after how we left things, I wasn't sure you'd ever want to see me again."

Jennifer opened her mouth to speak, but the bus gave a jolt and their costars clambered onboard, loud and unsteady. They swayed to their bunks and collapsed onto them. Douglas was out the moment his head hit the pillow, snoring almost instantly. Thomas smacked him with another pillow.

Luna and Jennifer exchanged small smiles before turning away from each other. Jennifer stared up at the metal roof, her mind racing with memories from a lifetime ago. As her thoughts gradually faded, she drifted off to sleep, soundtracked by Douglas's snoring.

* * *

Jennifer jolted awake. That sound again–heavy footsteps pounding the roof, metal creaking under some weight. She held her breath, listening. Above her, the stars vanished one by one as something moved over the rusted holes in the ceiling. Something up there was peering down through the gaps, right at her. Her mind flashed back to the night before–that pale face. It had been real.

She reached over to Luna's bunk beside her and shook her by the shoulder. She groaned and turned away.

The stomping had stopped. Jennifer peeked out of the window. There was a small red light. It was moving. Floating around the bus like a firefly.

Her eyes flickered to Douglas, who was snoring soundly in his bunk.

"Luna," Jennifer whispered, shaking her again. "Wake up."

Luna stirred.

"There's something outside."

Luna groaned, rubbing her eyes.

Jennifer pointed at the window. Luna sat up and looked at the red light floating and dancing in the dark.

"Maybe Vincent's playing with that stupid drone of his again?" Luna suggested.

Jennifer nodded, but that didn't explain the footsteps on the roof. Or that white face from last night.

"Get in with me," Luna whispered, scooting closer to the wall, flipping over, and lifting up the blanket.

Jennifer's eyes flicked to the window once more. The red light was gone. Her gaze darted back to her bunk and then back to Luna. Around them, a soft chorus of snores filled the dark.

Quietly, she slid in. It felt strange at first. Familiar, too. She lay stiffly until Luna reached back and guided Jennifer's arm around her waist so they were spooning.

"You're big spoon again," Luna muttered.

The footsteps, the red light, the pale face–it all melted away as Jennifer exhaled and let herself drift off, holding Luna close.

CHAPTER 22

A hand touched Jennifer's shoulder. "Good morning."

Jennifer groaned, burying her face in the pillow.

"I was wondering if you'd like to grab some breakfast together?" Luna said softly.

Jennifer peeked out from the pillow.

* * *

Inside the catering gazebo, Vincent and Michael had already laid out the morning's meager offerings. There were the two cereal dispensers, a plate of stale croissants, and a paper bowl holding a banana and an apple. Jennifer opened the cooler to find that the ice had long since melted, leaving only the same half-empty carton of milk in a small pool of water.

Jennifer was relieved to find some powdered milk next to the instant coffee, and she made some for both herself and Luna.

"Banana or apple?" Luna asked, holding up the two choices.

"Surprise me."

Luna handed over the banana before settling into a chair.

Jennifer apprehensively settled on another sagging lawn chair. "You'd think they could've splurged on at least *one* comfortable piece of furniture." She shifted around, trying to get comfortable.

"You only have to put up with it for one more day," Luna said, as she struggled to slice her apple with a plastic knife.

"Unless of course Vincent gets another stroke of inspiration and rewrites the script for the hundredth time," Jennifer sighed. "Just watch, I'll still be filming here until Christmas."

Luna smiled. "Do you know how he's going to kill off your character yet?"

"He hasn't told me, and he probably won't until the last minute," Jennifer said, taking a bite of her banana.

"When that happens, will I see you again before you head back to California? It's just that...Johnny left without so much as a goodbye," Luna said, her eyes fixed on the apple.

Jennifer couldn't figure out how Luna was managing it, but she was now deftly peeling the apple with the flimsy plastic knife. "I won't go right away," Jennifer said.

"Promise?" Luna said, glancing up.

"Promise."

In stumbled Thomas, Douglas, and Christy, each one clearly nursing a hangover.

"I'm never drinking again," Douglas groaned, heading straight for the coffee.

Noticing the bags under their heavy eyes, Jennifer was glad she'd quit the game when she did. It also had given her the chance to have a quiet conversation with Luna, just the two of them. Jennifer couldn't shake the thought of what Luna had shared the night before–the sacrifices she'd made to care for her father and raise her daughter alone. Her eyes drifted to

Luna, who had expertly peeled her entire apple and now held it up like a trophy, a childlike grin lighting up her face. Jennifer smiled and clapped softly.

* * *

After breakfast, Thomas got the whole cast ready in the hair and makeup gazebo. This time, he was noticeably quieter, wincing at the harsh whirring of the diesel engine outside and the relentless roar of the hairdryer.

"You have no one to blame but yourself," Jennifer said, as Thomas brushed her hair back.

"Thank you for the life lesson, Mr. Rogers," Thomas groaned.

Despite his raging hangover, Thomas worked his magic yet again. As she pulled on her Christmas sweater from the rack, Jennifer caught her reflection in the mirror. She was grateful that today would be the last time she wore this jingling woolen monstrosity–but a small part of her would miss seeing herself like this. Maybe she'd ask Vincent if she could ceremoniously burn it once shooting wrapped? Then again, he'd probably insist it was a collector's item.

Once Thomas had finished getting everyone ready, they gathered outside the park's front gate as Vincent outlined the day's plan. Standing in the center of their circle, he unfurled a map for everyone to see and announced that the day's shoot would take place in Elf Village.

"Ah man, I was kind of hoping we'd film in Toy Town," Christy said, pointing to another colorful area on the map.

"Don't worry, we will," Vincent assured her, folding the map away. "But we need to wrap up a few extra scenes first."

With that, the group set off, making their way through the park: up the uneven Gumdrop Road, through Reindeer Park, and arriving at Elf Village.

"Jennifer and Luna, could I grab you both for the next scene please?" Vincent asked. "As for Christy, Thomas, and Douglas, you can start rehearsing page thirty."

"What are we shooting?" Jennifer asked.

"Inspiration struck and I wrote a new scene last night. Come with me and I'll show you," Vincent replied cryptically, then turned and walked away with Michael.

Jennifer and Luna exchanged a curious glance before following them.

* * *

Vincent led Jennifer and Luna under the entranceway and through the switchbacks of the line to a water ride called Jingle Bell Creek. At the very front of the line was a tall wooden totem pole of elves all piled up on top of each other, beckoning guests onto their ride.

"You've got to be kidding me," Jennifer said, staring down at a boat bobbing in murky brown liquid.

"This must have been built in the '80s," Luna exclaimed.

"Try the '70s," Vincent stated matter-of-factly.

"Are you sure this is safe?" Jennifer asked.

"Absolutely," Vincent said confidently. "Michael tried it out this morning. A little bumpy, but she works fine. Nothing to worry about."

"That's easy for you to say," Jennifer retorted. "You don't have to ride in this death trap. How is this thing even still operational?"

"Back in the day they built things to last," Vincent said, tapping the control panel. "Look how long Disney's It's a Small World has lasted. And remember, this park only closed its doors a year and a half ago; you'd be surprised to learn how much stuff is still operational here."

"*How* can it still run though? Doesn't this ride need electricity to work?" Luna asked.

"Most of this place is still connected to the main grid," Vincent explained. "They never shut it off."

"Don't rides need like...constant maintenance or something?" Jennifer asked, still not entirely convinced.

"Ordinarily, yes," Vincent said. "But that's only because rides at places like Disney and Universal have thousands of visitors every day, so they're constantly running around the clock. Trust me, it's perfectly fine."

Jennifer peeked over into the water below, where a single brown bubble rose to the surface and burst.

"Screw it, let's get this over with," Luna said, climbing into the small boat. It wobbled precariously in the water. For a split second, Jennifer feared Luna would topple into the sludge, but Luna steadied herself. Once she was balanced, she extended a hand to Jennifer.

"What's wrong? Scared of a little kid's ride?" Luna teased.

"Yes, actually," Jennifer admitted. Still, she reluctantly took Luna's hand and carefully climbed aboard. Once they were seated, Vincent pressed a button on the control panel, and the safety bar clanked into place over their laps.

"At the front of the boat, you'll see a GoPro mounted there," Vincent said, pointing to the small camera on the bow. "Other cameras are mounted inside, and I'll also be filming with my drone. Once you pass through those curtains, it's action time. So please don't stop acting until you're back outside and I call cut." He bent down and pressed a button on the front of the camera, a red light blinked on to indicate that it was recording.

"How are we supposed to act?" Jennifer asked.

"Pretend you're having the time of your life, just like yesterday," Vincent said, before his face dropped. "And then, well, stop." Without elaborating further, he turned and walked back to the control panel.

"You know how to control this thing, right?" Luna asked, eyeing Vincent warily.

He shrugged. "I interned at Six Flags one summer. Only caused four accidents on Skull Mountain."

The two women stared at him in horror until he broke into a grin. "Kidding, only one."

Before they could respond, Vincent yanked down a lever. There was a loud grinding noise as the boat jolted forward. It lurched toward the black curtain. Jennifer imagined a series of rusty gears grinding beneath the water, yanking on a worn-out chain. She tried not to imagine that chain snapping.

"Don't forget to smile for the ride camera at the very end, ladies," Vincent called after them with a wave. *He seems to be enjoying this way too much.*

As they bobbed toward the black curtains, a faint, warped melody drifted through. The music, emanating from aging, tinny speakers sounded suspiciously like "It's a Small World," but the tune seemed even more grating and repetitive.

It's a snowy land with twinkling light,
so bring all your friends, with their cheers so bright.
Gather round, boys and girls, and your parents too,
because in Jingle Bell Creek, we welcome you!

"This song is going to be stuck in our heads until the day we die, isn't it?" Jennifer groaned, as the song looped for the second time. Luna nodded, laughing in agreement.

The tattered black fabric washed over them as the boat drifted into a snowy village scene. On either side were both wooden and mechanical elves. Most of the robotic elves were frozen in place, broken down by neglect and vandalism. A few still whirred to life, spinning on their platforms as if ice skating or standing atop rooftops, waving and dancing. Even over the grating melody, Jennifer could hear the gears grinding as the elves moved jerkily. Their stilted motions and unblinking eyes gave Jennifer the creeps.

"This is amazing," Luna said, taking in the broken and battered festive scenes.

"You're weird," Jennifer said with a smile, watching Luna's face glow under the fairy lights.

As the boat rocked along the water, various Christmas scenes bobbed by. Luna gazed in awe, while Jennifer feigned the same as they drifted through the snowy displays.

She slid her hand across the seat until it brushed against Luna's. Luna caught Jennifer's eye, then lowered her gaze to their fingers. A gentle squeeze from Luna was met with a quiet smile. The simple touch kindled a warmth inside Jennifer that had long been dormant. Time seemed to pause, and even the elves' melody softened into something unexpectedly sweet.

But the spell was broken by the whirring of Vincent's drone, which zipped through the curtains and hovered overhead. Jennifer became acutely aware of its lens that swiveled to capture their every move. Before her, the camera fixed to the front of the boat silently recorded the scene.

She started to withdraw her hand, but Luna's grip tightened, drawing it back into hers.

Jennifer turned back to Luna who squeezed her hand reassuringly. Soon enough, she ignored the cameras, their penetrating lenses, the whirring of the drone, and the thought of capsizing into the mysterious water below. Her worries melted away, freeing her mind to be entertained by the comically malfunctioning elves and their clumsy attempts at dancing and singing.

As the boat meandered through the twists and turns of the ride, Jennifer and Luna pointed out their choices for the weirdest-looking elves. One was perched atop a gingerbread house, its left eye missing, others were fighting over a giant candy cane, and one wore a grass skirt and lei, shaking his hips manically.

But out of the corner of her eye, Jennifer caught sight of one that stood apart. It stood perfectly still, its back turned to them. Remembering yesterday's scene in the restaurant, Jennifer squeezed Luna's hand to silently warn her.

As the boat approached, the elf spun around, holding out an oversized present. Another mechanical elf. The tension dissolved instantly as the women giggled.

Then, from the large box, Plucky emerged. He jumped out and stood on the bank. The colored lights dimmed around them. He was mostly shrouded in shadow, with the rusted bell on his hat–the only part of him that caught any light–glinting as it swayed. His silhouette remained still for a few moments before he danced in place. His movements were energetic but rigid.

Jennifer reluctantly released Luna's hand, slipping into her role.

Plucky grabbed one of the nearby wooden cutout trees, wrenching it from its base before swinging it toward the women. The brittle wood shattered on impact against the boat, sending splinters flying. They raised their arms to shield their faces.

The close call shook Jennifer, but she kept up her terrified façade as the mysterious actor scrambled across the rooftops to grab another cardboard tree. With a heavy throw, he launched it at them. Jennifer and Luna ducked as it flew overhead, splashing into the murky water behind them.

That was the last straw. Jennifer didn't care if it meant redoing the entire scene. She had had enough of this actor's unprofessional and dangerous behavior. "Hey, watch it," she shouted.

The elf paid no attention, now ripping the head off a mechanical elf. It popped off easily, spilling entrails of machinery and wires. With the force of a shot put throw, he hurled the dismembered head. Jennifer and Luna barely ducked in time as it hurtled past them, missing them by mere inches.

"I said fucking watch–" Jennifer began, turning back, only to find the actor had vanished.

She and Luna exchanged bewildered glances before scanning their surroundings, but he had seemingly evaporated. The boat continued its journey for a few moments until it violently halted with a grinding noise that reverberated through the space. Jennifer and Luna lurched forward in their seats, and the safety bar across their laps was the only thing keeping them from falling onto the front of the boat.

The music stopped and the lights went out. In the darkness, the fluorescent paint on the buildings and elves cast a faint glow, barely illuminating the space.

Jennifer and Luna exchanged uncertain glances, unsure whether this was part of the plan or a genuine breakdown of the ride.

"Haha, very funny, guys," Luna attempted to joke, though her voice betrayed a hint of fear. "You can knock it off now."

Despite the darkness, Jennifer could still see the red light and hear the soft hum of the drone overhead.

"Vincent, you little shit," Jennifer shouted up the drone, knowing he was watching them live from outside. "If you're messing with us, I swear, as soon as I'm off this boat, I'm gonna ring your scrawny little neck."

But the drone made no motion indicating that the person on the other end heard them, continuing to hover above them. Jennifer shook the lap bar, but it stubbornly remained locked in place.

"What now?" Luna whispered.

She couldn't see Luna clearly, only a faint green fluorescent glow reflecting the side of her face, but Jennifer could hear a tremor in her voice. It tugged at Jennifer's heart, and she hated that they were so helpless.

A loud thud echoed through the room, and the boat lurched, jolting both women in their seats. Plucky stood on the bow, looming above them, his figure half-swallowed by the dark. The mechanical elves were silent. The only sound was the harsh, heavy breathing behind Plucky's mask.

In the dim light, Jennifer could make out the glint of a long, sharp object held high–a candy cane shiv, his signature weapon. He laughed, that same chilling, throaty sound she'd heard in the barn with Johnny.

Plucky stepped forward, driving his arm down in a stabbing motion. Both women raised their hands to protect themselves, the sharp tip of the shiv hovering inches from their skin, stopping just short. The drone buzzed around them, capturing every tense, breathless moment.

Jennifer leaned forward as far as her restraint allowed, swiping at Plucky and catching the cuff of his trousers. "Back off," she hissed, "you're getting too close."

Plucky froze mid-motion, his jovial façade vanishing as he stared down at Jennifer's hand gripping his leg. For a moment, the room was still–then, without warning, he stabbed at her with the candy cane shiv, the sharp edge pricking her hand.

Jennifer cried out and recoiled, clutching her hand to her chest. When she looked up, Plucky had vanished. The lights flickered back on, the boat lurched forward, and the music resumed–as if nothing had happened.

It's a snowy land with twinkling light,
so bring all your friends, with their cheers so bright.
Gather round, boys and girls, and your parents too,
because in Jingle Bell Creek, we welcome you!

Both Jennifer and Luna scanned the area frantically, eyes locking on every mechanical elf in case Plucky was hiding in plain sight. But he was gone–vanished.

Jennifer turned her focus to her hand. A thin cut, bleeding afresh after she wiped it clean.

* * *

The boat glided through the curtains as they reached the end of the ride, they squinted as they were hit by the blinding sun. The moment the boat shuddered to a stop and the safety bar jerked up, Jennifer and Luna scrambled off the boat.

"Ladies, that was fantastic work," Vincent said, as the drone flew out from behind them before landing softly in his palm.

Jennifer stormed up to Vincent, until they were almost nose to nose. "Where is that fucker?"

"Who?" he asked, taking a cautious step back.

"You know damn well who," she snapped, stepping forward to close the gap. "The bastard who's playing Plucky. Bring him here so I can shove his candy cane so far up his ass his breath will smell like peppermint for a week."

Hearing the commotion, Douglas, Thomas, and Christy halted the scene they were filming with Michael and rushed over.

"Jenny, are you okay?" Douglas asked.

"No, Dougie, I am not okay," Jennifer said, raising her hand to reveal a thin trickle of blood. "The actor playing your character stabbed me."

"Ms. Hawkins, on behalf of Plucky, I am so sorry," Vincent said. "He is very passionate and method in his craft. I'm afraid he got a little carried away in the scene. That's all."

"Vincent," Douglas said, turning to the director, his voice steady but firm. "In all five movies I played Plucky, not once did I ever injure a costar during a scene. This isn't right. Please tell me where he is and let me talk to him. From one actor to another."

Vincent held up his hands. "I'm sorry, but he's insisted he shouldn't meet everyone right now, and, as the director, I agree. But rest assured I will speak with him myself. This won't happen again."

"You know what? I'm done," Jennifer said, throwing up her hands in defeat. "I quit."

"What?" Vincent's eyes went wide.

"I quit," Jennifer repeated. "As in, we're through here. Get me back to LA right now."

"No, please," Vincent stammered, his earlier bravado crumbling into a desperate whine. "We'll film your death scene very, very soon, and then you'll be done. After that Michael can drive you back home."

"No," Jennifer said firmly. She wasn't going to negotiate.

"But if you leave now, the whole movie will be ruined. We can't finish it without you," Vincent pleaded. When Jennifer remained unmoved, he shifted gears. "At least think of your costars. Your friends. If you walk away now, the film will be unfinished, and all their hard work will be for nothing. They're depending on you."

Jennifer's jaw clenched; she felt suffocated. Trapped and cornered, she flinched when Luna gently took her hand–but any feeling of reassurance was quickly extinguished under the weight of everyone's stares. Christy's eyes lingered on their joined hands, probably already weaving this moment into the next episode of her podcast. Heat flamed across Jennifer's cheeks. Without thinking, she yanked her hand away, catching the faintest flash of hurt in Luna's eyes before turning away.

"I don't care. Give me my money and take me home," Jennifer demanded.

"Money?" she heard Christy whisper to Thomas.

Vincent let out a long sigh, his shoulders slumping. "Fine. Michael will take you back to camp and fix up that cut." He paused, choosing his words. "It was a pleasure working with you, Ms. Hawkins."

With a curt nod to his brother, Vincent turned and stormed off.

Michael stepped forward, extending his arm to guide her back to the parking lot. Jennifer hesitated, casting one last glance at her costars. Thomas shook his head, Christy rolled her eyes, and Douglas, though looking a little hurt, gave her a small, encouraging wave. Jennifer couldn't bring herself to look at Luna. Without a word, she turned away and followed Michael.

As she walked away, Jennifer could feel their eyes on her back. She turned her hand over and wiped away the small pinprick of blood. It didn't return.

CHAPTER 23

Jennifer and Michael walked in silence as they exited Elf Village, passing through Reindeer Park and onto the Gumdrop Road that led to the parking lot. Guilt gnawed at Jennifer. The image of everyone's disappointed faces replaying in her mind, but it was Luna's hurt and rejected expression that cut the deepest. Jennifer turned her hand over, the tiny mark was barely visible now.

When they reached the parking lot, Michael broke the silence. "I'll grab the first aid kit," he said, already running toward one of the gazebos.

"Don't worry about it," she said, waving it off. Then, as an afterthought, she added, "Before I forget, can you bring me my phone?"

"Your phone?"

"Yes, Vincent gave it to you to charge, remember?"

Michael stared at her blankly for a moment before nodding. "Oh, right. Yeah, of course. I'll go grab it for you."

For the first time since yesterday, she craved a cigarette. Reconnecting with Luna had made her forget all about her habit–but now it hit her full force. Her throat was dry, scratchy, and aching for a drag.

Jennifer headed into the catering gazebo to grab a bottle of water. She opened the cooler swimming in melted ice and grabbed a bottle. The water was warm but still quenched her desperate thirst. When she finally got home, she promised herself she would make a pitcher of frozen margaritas, sink into her bed, and do nothing all day but drink herself silly.

She downed the bottle, then opened another one before stepping back outside. Jennifer climbed onto the bus and started packing her things, grabbing clothes and stuffing them into her suitcases. She struggled to zip them up, wondering how she had fit everything in there in the first place. After sitting on top and squashing the contents, she got the zipper on the last case to close. With her luggage packed and ready to go, Jennifer's eyes settled on Luna's bunk across from her; her Garfield pajamas were bundled into a heap at the foot of the bed. A small smile tugged at Jennifer's lips as a memory from thirty-nine years ago surfaced. She could still picture the heap of their clothes, tangled in a careless knot on the floor of her trailer. The windows were wide open, welcoming the sounds of the ocean waves and the scent of salt in the air, while they lay draped over each other. Luna traced slow circles on Jennifer's back while Jennifer kissed the curve of her shoulder. It was a moment of rare happiness, a time when everything felt right for her.

But the memory was interrupted by Luna's hurt face, and the smile vanished. Just like their last night together, Jennifer wouldn't get to say goodbye. She picked up the pajamas and neatly folded them–one last excuse to feel closer to Luna.

After placing the pajamas onto Luna's bed, Jennifer dragged her heavy bags off the bus and plopped them down beside Michael's car.

How long does it take to grab a phone? While she waited, Jennifer took one last stroll around the parking lot, walking behind the gazebos.

Jennifer took a final moment to look at the Tinseltown amusement park, knowing this was the last time she'd see it. She wasn't one for nostalgia–moving on to the next project was just part of the job. It was best not to get too sentimental or comfortable at any location; you never knew when a show might be canceled or when you'd be fired.

But as she took in the park with its towering Ferris wheel, something shifted inside her–like the bittersweet feeling on the last day of school, when only the good times remain. Memories flooded in: laughing with Thomas in the makeup gazebo, Douglas's goofy dance moves after winning the carnival game, flying down the slide with Luna between her legs, late-night talks in the bunks.

She turned her hand over. The cut had faded; maybe she had overreacted. It wouldn't be the first time.

As she walked past the firepit, she thought back to that first night they all sat around the campfire. Luna and Thomas had spoken about this being their last chance to recapture something they had lost long ago. In many ways, without intending to, Jennifer had also rediscovered something she thought she had long lost.

As she considered this, her foot caught on something and she stumbled forward. She caught herself before she fell flat on her face, but her hands and knees scraped on the gravel.

She cried out, wincing as sharp stones bit into her palms. She looked behind her at the heavy black sack that lay sprawled. To her surprise, a head rested at the opening. It was Johnny's. His blank face stared back at her.

Jennifer had seen her fair share of prosthetic body parts over her years on horror movie sets. It was an art form with which she had long harbored an uneasy fascination, always sneaking into the prop tents for a closer look before they were covered in fake blood. Even though the *Evil Elf* movies were often criticized for their writing and acting, the effects had always been top-tier, rivaling some of the bigger horror franchises. The studio pumped money into the effects more than anything else. And it worked to some extent: the film's artists set a new standard for gore, and the effects helped popularize the slasher genre.

As she stared at Johnny's prosthetic head, it was clear Vincent kept that tradition going. It was disturbingly lifelike—one eye drooped, gazing off to the left, the other fixed on Jennifer. She mused that the fake head did a better job at emoting than Johnny himself. She wondered if Vincent had also made a prosthetic head of her for her death scene. A scene she now realized she would never film. Which was a shame... Jennifer had actually been looking forward to the challenge.

She picked up the prop, turning it in her hands to take in the insane level of detail. It was heavier than she expected. Bending her knees slightly, she hoisted it up to peek underneath. The fake blood, a deep shade of maroon, dripped onto her lips and caught the tip of her tongue. Jennifer had endured copious liters of fake blood dumped on her over her "illustrious" career. So much so, that the sickeningly sweet taste of cornstarch mixed with red food dye was forever stained on her tongue. But this fake blood didn't taste sweet at all. In fact, it had a salty copper taste and the constancy of congealed jelly. It was then that she noticed that the prosthetic head didn't have Johnny's mullet, but rather his real balding gray hair. As she turned the head back around, more of the sticky substance oozed over her wrists. Johnny's one good eye stared straight at her, then his other lazy eye began to turn, rotating itself to stare at her. With both eyes now fixed on Jennifer, she almost didn't notice when a small scorpion crawled out of his left nostril. Startled, she tossed the head away from her where it fell with a heavy thud to the ground. The head rolled a couple of times before Johnny's glazed eyes stared straight up at Jennifer.

"Holy fucking shit," Jennifer scrambled away, her breath coming in ragged gasps. She staggered to her feet before doubling over, retching.

"This can't be real," she muttered, wiping her mouth with a trembling hand. She had to get help. Her phone. Her hands flew to her pockets–empty. Panic flared, until she remembered: Michael had it.

She edged around the bag, forcing herself to keep her eyes forward. "Michael," she shouted, her voice cracking. "Where are you?" she spun in frantic circles, her eyes wide.

A hand clamped down on her shoulder, and she nearly jumped out of her skin. She whirled around, her heart pounding, to see Michael's surprised face.

"What's wrong? Are you okay?"

She couldn't answer right away, her breath still ragged and catching up with her. "Do you have my phone?"

"What's wrong?"

"It's Johnny."

"What about Johnny?"

"He's fucking dead," she blurted, her voice trembling.

Michael stared at her as if she was a babbling madwoman. "No, Johnny went home yesterday."

"He's fucking dead. I tripped over his goddamn head."

Michael's eyes widened, and he took a step back. "What are you talking about?"

"His head was in that bag right over there. You need to call the police, the FBI, I don't fucking know, just call anyone."

"Okay, okay, calm down," Michael said, more to himself than to Jennifer. "Go on the bus, barricade the door shut. I'll go get help."

"Wait. What about the others? We have to warn them."

"Don't worry, I'll radio Vincent," Michael said, pushing the first aid kit to Jennifer's chest.

Before she could respond, he spun on his heels and hurried away. Hesitating between following him or obeying his orders, she turned toward the bus instead. Alone now, anxiety tightened its grip as the possibility of a killer lurking nearby–maybe even watching her right now–settled in. The thought quickened her steps. As she reached the bus door and pushed it open, a chilling realization stopped her cold: Vincent had said Michael personally drove Johnny to the nearest town for a ride back to the airport.

A wave of dread surged through her, followed by a sudden, sharp sting at her neck–quick and precise, like a bee sting. She slapped her hand to the spot, but met only bare skin.

Her vision blurred, she gripped the bus railing for support before her legs gave way, sending her crashing onto the ground. She didn't feel the impact–her entire body was numb. She could only stare helplessly up at the empty sky as a blurred face appeared above her.

"I'm sorry, Ms. Hawkins."

Those were the last words she heard before everything went black.

CHAPTER 24

Jennifer stirred. Her eyes fluttered open to a haze of shapes and shadows. Her body was numb, but the surface beneath her was unmistakably hard. She ran her hands along it–rough wood, scattered straw. The air reeked of dry rot and musk.

As her mind unfurled, fragmented memories floated to the surface and pieced themselves together. She recalled her frantic plea to Michael for help, the sharp pinprick in her neck, and then darkness.

She rolled onto her back, blinking to clear her vision. Above her, wooden timbers stretched across a dilapidated roof, riddled with gaping holes. Through the gaps, stars glittered in the night sky. The last thing she remembered was that it was still daylight. How much time had passed? Hours? Days?

She groaned as she sat up, her head pounding as her vision fluttered in and out of focus. She had experienced some serious hangovers in her time, but this took the cake. When the world eventually stopped spinning, she found herself inside an old barn, trapped in a pen made of roughly hewn boards, a gate closed before her. Despite it being nighttime, faint light filtered through the gaps in the weathered slats, casting slivers across her face. Taking in her surroundings, Jennifer's eyes settled on a sign hanging overhead. The words danced and floated. She squeezed her eyes shut, counted to ten, and reopened them. The words steadied enough for her to read: Rudolph. Her body was still a little numb, but she grabbed the wooden slats for support and hoisted herself up.

It dawned on her–this was where Johnny's death scene had been filmed. No–this was where Johnny had been murdered.

The image of his severed head floated back into her mind, and a wave of nausea overtook her. She gripped the side of the pen.

As she tried to steady herself, her eyes fell on something attached to a beam. Jennifer squinted. *Was that a camera?*

Jennifer clutched her throbbing head, struggling to make sense of the bizarre scene unfolding before her. As her thoughts settled, she heard music drifting in from outside, along with something else. *Was that laughter?*

She stumbled to the gate and fumbled with the latch. The room spun around her, and she hooked her elbow over the gate to steady herself. As her vision cleared, she made her way to the barn doors, noticing the light seeping in from beneath. A pulsing glow of red, green, and white lights. Utterly drained, she barely had the strength to drag her feet. Summoning the last of her energy, she pushed against the heavy barn door. It groaned on its rusted hinges, opening just enough for her to squeeze through.

Once outside, she found the source of the illumination, trails of candy cane street lamps were now alight. Most of the bulbs flickered or were out completely, but a few cast a scattered glow.

She discovered the source of the music, the reindeer carousel. Although they seemed lifeless earlier, the reindeer rose and fell with each rotation almost as if they were galloping around a pillar lined with lights and mirrors, all while an out-of-tune melody of "Rudolph the Red-Nosed Reindeer" filled the air.

Douglas and Christy came into view, each riding a reindeer and giggling like children as the carousel spun. Luna and Thomas stood off to the side, watching.

"Careful, you're going to break it before I get a turn," Thomas called out.

"I don't weigh that much, you bastard," Douglas shouted back.

Jennifer tried to call out, but her throat was dry and raspy. She hurried toward them, or at least tried to; one of her legs dragged limply behind the other. As she got closer, she tried calling out again. Luna turned, her expression lifted from mild amusement to delight.

"Jennifer?" Luna gasped, rushing over and meeting Jennifer halfway.

"What are you doing here, Jenny?" Douglas said, sliding off the reindeer. "I thought you went home!"

Jennifer tried to steady herself as the group circled around her. She panted, her mind whirling with decapitated heads and bounding reindeer. Luna hovered her hand behind Jennifer's back but hesitated, pulling it away before making contact.

"Don't tell me you missed us that much?" Thomas teased.

Jennifer's head pounded again. "Where are Vincent and Michael?"

"We've wrapped the daylight scenes, now we're moving on to the nighttime shots," Douglas explained. "Vincent told us to wait here while they go set up and prepare."

"No thanks to you," Christy interjected. "Vincent was close to shutting down production after his main star walked out. So, why'd you come back? Did Vincent offer you more money to stay?"

"Who cares?" Thomas said, smiling at Jennifer. "The important thing is she's back to help us finish the movie. And just in time, too, because I seriously need to touch up your hair and makeup." Thomas took in Jennifer's disheveled appearance. "I've got my kit right here; with a little luck, I might be able to salvage your hair before Vincent returns to roll cameras."

"How soon will Vincent and Michael be back?" Jennifer said, ducking out of Thomas's comb's reach.

Douglas shrugged. "No idea. We've been riding the carousel while we waited."

"Isn't it incredible?" Christy exclaimed. "Who would have thought this old thing could still work?"

"Vincent mentioned that most of the park was still connected to the power grid," Douglas said. "But even so, they built things to last back–"

"–We have to get out of here," Jennifer interrupted.

"What do you mean?" Luna asked.

"I mean, we need to go, now," Jennifer insisted.

"Leave? Where?" Luna pressed.

"Anywhere," Jennifer snapped. "I don't care, as long as it's away from here. The parking lot. We need to grab a car and drive to the nearest police station."

"What the hell are you talking about?" Christy asked.

"I saw Johnny," Jennifer said.

"Johnny?" Douglas said. "But he went home."

Jennifer shook her head. "No, he didn't. I found his body back at camp. Those little fuckers cut him up into pieces and hid him in a bag."

"Hold up a second," Thomas said, shaking his head. "Are you telling us that Johnny was murdered? That you actually saw his body?"

"It was probably a bag of Vincent's props, Jenny," Douglas reasoned.

"I literally held his head in my hands. He's fucking dead," Jennifer snapped. "I'll explain everything later, but for now we have to go."

They all stared at Jennifer in stunned silence, the only sound coming from the carousel playing "Rudolph the Red-Nosed Reindeer."

Then, abruptly, the group burst into laughter.

Jennifer blinked in disbelief as Douglas doubled over into a fit of giggles. The only one who didn't join in was Luna, her eyes fixed on Jennifer.

"You had us going for a second there, girl," Thomas laughed.

"Did you put her up to this?" Christy asked, turning to Douglas.

Douglas held up his hand. "Don't look at me. I'm not involved. Although, if it was about a dead Johnny, I wish I was."

"I'm not joking," Jennifer pleaded.

"Wait," Thomas said, his laughter dying down. "This isn't part of a scene, is it? Vincent did mention there would be a lot of improv coming up."

Christy spun around and spotted a GoPro mounted on a street lamp. "Hey, Vincent," she called out to it. "We weren't ready. Can we redo that?"

"Okay, let's reset," Thomas said, taking a deep breath and shaking off the laughter. "Jennifer, say that line again. And this time, no laughing from anyone."

"That means you, Douglas," Christy smiled.

"No promises," Douglas said, wiping away a tear.

They all stared at Jennifer expectedly, waiting for her to repeat the line.

"Guys, I'm serious," Jennifer said, her words spilling out. "Johnny is dead. I saw it myself. Out there." She flung an arm behind her. "In the parking lot."

"Uh, oh no," Thomas said, scrambling to find a reaction. "I mean, what the hell? That's awful," He was floundering and turned to the others to help save him.

"Oh, Jesus," Douglas stammered, jumping in. "Was it Plucky?"

Jennifer stared at them in disbelief and growing frustration. "Yes, it was fucking Plucky. I saw him do it with my own two fucking eyes. He sliced his belly open."

"Jeepers, that's fucked up," Christy said.

"Jeepers?" Thomas laughed, turning to Christy. "Really? Did you turn into a Scooby-Doo character or something?"

"Screw you," Christy shot back smiling, "Like you did any better. Want to throw in a few more 'oh's and 'um's while you're at it?"

"Guys, guys," Douglas interjected, waving his hands dramatically. "You both sucked, okay? Let's redo the scene."

"Where's our director? We need something to work with here," Thomas said.

"Yeah, where is he?" Christy asked, looking around.

Jennifer ignored the group and spoke only to Luna. "You believe me, don't you?"

Luna studied Jennifer, her eyes bouncing between Jennifer's face and her trembling hands. After a pause, she turned to the group. "Guys, I think we should listen–"

She was interrupted by a crackle that cut through the air, followed by a high-pitched, sustained beep. The cast clutched their ears and scanned the area for the source. It came from a speaker mounted atop a tall pole, painted in a swirl of red and white to match the candy cane street lamps.

The piercing static gradually faded, and a muffled voice came through the speaker. "Sorry about that, these things haven't been used in a long time."

"Is that Vincent?" Christy asked.

"Hi cast, I am speaking to you through the park's PA system. These were used to pump Christmas music around the park, report lost children, and, of course, let folks know when Tinseltown was about to close. Cool, right? Anyway, quick heads-up, I want to remind you all not to stare directly at the cameras; it breaks the illusion and ruins the shot. I know you're all pros, but just a friendly reminder. Oh, and huge shout-out to Ms. Hawkins for coming through to wrap up the movie. We seriously appreciate it, and honestly, the film wouldn't be the same without you. So, let's give her a big round of applause."

Thomas and Douglas began clapping and Christy rolled her eyes. All the while, Luna kept her eyes locked on Jennifer.

"You have to be kidding!" Jennifer exclaimed.

"So, we've filmed a lot of the shots we need, and we are now in the final act of the movie. Like in the previous entries, you're being hunted by Plucky, and it's your goal to escape. Like I've already mentioned, there is no script for this part: it's all improv. So do what feels natural to your character in the moment. We're striving for *authenticity*. Got it? Awesome. Now, let's finish this movie. And...*action.*"

"Action?" Christy said. "What the hell do you mean 'action'? You have to give us more than that."

Vincent didn't reply, and the crackling of the PA system abruptly ceased.

"So, what now?" Thomas said.

They stood in silence, exchanging bewildered glances. "Rudolf the Red-Nosed Reindeer" continued to play from the carousel's speakers. Then another noise broke through: the familiar buzz of Vincent's drone as it zipped past them toward the barn.

"Wait, who's that?" Luna asked, pointing to a dark figure that stood on the roof.

Douglas squinted. "Is that Plucky?"

Despite the shadows, Jennifer could make out his distinctive hat, its bell rattling in the breeze. In one hand, he held something aloft–its outline jagged and gleaming faintly in the low light.

"What's he doing?" Thomas asked, focusing in on the elf by shielding his eyes from the glow of the candy-cane-shaped lamps.

Plucky lifted the object and aimed it at them.

"Uh, guys," Jennifer said, edging backward.

"I'm guessing we're supposed to be acting now?" Christy said quietly.

"Vincent did say 'action,' after all," Douglas said.

"But I haven't even touched up everyone's hair and makeup yet," Thomas said. "No offense, but you all look awful."

"Please listen to me," Jennifer urged. "We need to go now."

"You're right, Rebecca," Thomas said with a wink. "This doesn't seem right."

They still thought it was part of the movie. Jennifer turned to Luna in desperation, holding out her hand. Luna stared reluctantly. "Please?" Jennifer pleaded, her voice trembling.

A sudden swish sliced through the air, followed by Luna's sharp cry as she crumpled to the ground. She clutched her leg, and Jennifer's heart lurched at the sight of the bolt jutting from her calf.

The rest of the group stared dumbfounded. Their eyes darted from the bolt embedded in Luna's leg to the figure on the barn roof. Plucky was now fully visible, holding a crossbow, and calmly loading another shot.

Knowing they had only seconds before Plucky had another bolt ready, Jennifer's heart raced. "Douglas," she screamed, her voice cutting through the panic.

Douglas turned, bewildered.

"Help me," Jennifer pleaded.

Snapping into action, Douglas grabbed one of Luna's arms. Together, they dragged her out of the open and behind the spinning carousel.

Plucky's next bolt whistled through the air, burying itself into the dirt inches from Thomas's foot. "Fuck," he yelled, before diving for cover behind the carousel with the others.

"Do you still see him?" Douglas asked, his voice tense.

Jennifer peeked out from behind the carousel, but the rising and falling fiberglass reindeer made it difficult to get a clear view. "I can't be sure," she replied, her voice shaky. "But I think he's gone."

The carousel's music stopped, as the wheel ground to a halt.

The speaker crackled back to life. *"Cut."* Vincent's voice boomed, brimming with enthusiasm. "Wow, that was awesome. Incredible acting, everyone–I really believed that. Take five, okay? We'll set up for the next scene."

The speaker cut off with a crackle, leaving the group staring at each other in horror.

CHAPTER 25

"Oh my fucking God." Christy kept repeating, her makeup now blue and black streaks down her face. "We're going to die."

"Can you shut up for a second?" Jennifer snapped. "We need to get this fucking arrow out of Luna's leg." She took Luna's hand. "Luna, what do I need to do?"

"Why are you asking me?" Luna gasped, wincing.

"Because you're a nurse."

"School nurse," Luna corrected through clenched teeth. "I deal with scraped knees and period cramps, not arrows in the leg."

"You went to college, you can do this."

Luna breathed through the pain. "We need to keep it in there. That's the only way." She ignored the cast's concerned expressions. "But we need to secure it–to minimize disrupting the wound further. Wrap a strip of cloth around the arrow."

"Use my jacket," Thomas said, yanking off his lime green bomber jacket, revealing the basketball jersey underneath. He swiftly began tearing the lining into strips with his teeth.

Jennifer took each strip from Thomas and bound them around Luna's leg. She worked swiftly to stem the bleeding while wrapping it around the bolt. She put the rest of the torn cloth in her pocket, knowing she would likely need to replace the bandages with fresh ones soon.

Jennifer turned to the group, her voice sharp. "Why didn't any of you listen to me? None of this would have happened if we got the hell out of here when I said."

"How were we supposed to know you were serious about finding a goddamn severed head?" Christy shot back.

"Stop arguing," Douglas snapped. "We need to get Luna to a hospital before she bleeds out."

"You're right," Jennifer said. "Thomas, grab her left arm, I'll take the other."

They lifted Luna together. She gasped, struggling with the sudden movement.

"It's okay, we've got you," Jennifer reassured her. "Let's head toward the parking lot."

Moving as fast as they could carry her, they fled toward the south gate out of Reindeer Park, but as they approached, Jennifer's heart sank. The gate, which had been open since they arrived, was now locked. Two thick metal chains were tightly coiled around the bars, securing them shut.

"No," Christy cried, shaking the gate in frustration.

Thomas carefully let go of Luna before gently pushing Christy aside. He inspected the lock before pulling on it with all his strength, but it didn't budge an inch.

"Now what?" Christy asked.

Jennifer stared up at the massive gate. The narrow gaps between the bars were spaced too tightly for anyone to fit. The bars were vertical with no footholds, almost impossible to climb. Not that it mattered; none of them were below the age of fifty or fit enough to climb to the top. Besides, even if one of them was physically able, the top was curled over and lined with razor-sharp points.

"There must be another way out!" Christy exclaimed.

"I'm going to check around the perimeter. There must be a section missing that we could squeeze through," Thomas said before darting off.

"If he doesn't find a gap, then what?" Luna asked.

Douglas dug into his back pocket and pulled out the map of the park. He unfolded it and stepped under one of the candy cane lamps.

"According to this map, there are only three ways out of this area. This route is a dead end." He gestured toward the locked gate ahead. "The other potential path is to cut through that gate on the right." He pointed past the carousel. "It leads to the center of the park, where we can then head south toward the exit."

"I'm not sure, but it looks like that gate might also be locked," Christy interjected.

"If that's the case, we're left with one option." Douglas traced his finger along the Gumdrop Road to Elf Village on the map. "We'll have to navigate through here, circling the park until we reach Toy Town. From there, we can loop back to the entrance and find our way to the cars."

"That's if those gates are open too," Jennifer said.

"Well, we better hope they are. Otherwise we are stuck in this area of the park with no food, no water, and no way to call anyone," Douglas said, folding up the map and putting it into his pocket.

"Wait," Christy said, "You actually think that Vincent and Michael would keep us locked up in here?"

"Look around you, that's exactly what they've done," Jennifer said.

Christy shook her head, struggling to process the situation. "No, this has to be a prank or part of the film. They wouldn't bring us here just to trap us in a theme park and kill us, would they?"

"A prank?" Jennifer snapped. "They killed Johnny, and look what they did to Luna." She gestured to Luna's bandaged leg. "That bastard shot her with a crossbow while Vincent filmed the whole thing."

Thomas came running back, panting hard, and leaned against the lamppost to catch his breath.

"Well, did you find anything?" Jennifer asked.

He shook his head. "No. The bars are rusty but still strong. I didn't find any missing sections."

"What about the other two gates?" Douglas pressed.

"Locked up tight," Thomas replied.

"Well, what now?" Christy asked.

They exchanged uneasy glances, but no one offered up solutions.

Jennifer swore under her breath before gazing hopelessly up at the night sky. Suddenly, a shiny object caught her eye, glinting above her. Dangling from the Jolly Rail Ride was a key threaded through green tinsel.

"Look, there," Jennifer exclaimed, pointing upward.

"Is that a key?" Douglas said.

"It appears to be," Christy said, squinting at the glimmering object. "But what does it unlock?"

"Hopefully one of these gate chains," Thomas said. "The question is–who's going to go get it?"

"I would, but I'm terrified of heights," Jennifer said, crossing her arms.

"That's convenient," Christy muttered under her breath.

Jennifer spun around to face her. "Excuse me?"

"Are you sure it's not just because you don't want to ruin your nails?" Christy said, turning to her.

"What the fuck's your problem?"

"Everybody, stop fighting!" Douglas shouted. The cast fell silent. "I'll go. I've had plenty of experience being thrown off big heights." He directed a faint smile at Jennifer.

"I'm not sure you should go, Douglas. This is obviously a trap, like a *Saw* rip-off," Luna said.

"I know, but it's our only lead on how to get out of here. Just promise someone will catch me if I fall. Please?"

"We'll be right under you, don't worry," Jennifer squeezed his arm.

Douglas nodded, hesitation flickering across his face. He approached the steps leading up to the Jolly Rail Ride and began his ascent. Each worn, wooden plank creaked beneath his feet. He put a hand on the wooden railing to steady himself as he neared the top, but it splintered under his grip and crashed to the ground. Arms flailing, Douglas teetered before snapping back to balance at the last second.

The group collectively gasped.

"I'm fine," Douglas shouted back, although his tone wasn't so sure. He cautiously regained his footing and continued up the stairs until he reached the platform. Here, park staff assisted guests into pedal sleighs, which they rode along the railed path through Reindeer Park, circling back to this platform at the end.

"Maybe I can use one of these to peddle to the key," Douglas called down.

He tentatively stepped onto the lead sleigh. It wobbled precariously and Jennifer feared for a moment that it would fall off the rail. When it didn't, he stepped fully onboard and sat. Placing his feet on the pedals, he began to cycle his legs. The pedals were stiff, but with some effort the sleigh cart inched forward along the track. Douglas didn't look down at them as the sleigh left the platform and grinded forward. But only a few feet into the journey, his sleigh slowed and stopped.

"Why have you stopped?" Christy shouted up.

"The pedals aren't working, it's like they're jammed," Douglas shouted back. "I've got to go by foot."

"Are you insane?" Jennifer cried out.

"No choice if you want that key," Douglas said. "Besides, I've done way riskier stunts than this."

"Yes, but you were wearing a harness when you did those," Jennifer reminded him.

Douglas carefully stood up, the sleigh wobbling slightly. He peeked over the edge to the long, fifteen-foot drop below. He paused a moment before climbing out onto the front of the sleigh and placed a foot on the rail.

"Be careful," Thomas shouted.

"Well, I was going to cartwheel, but now that you've reminded me to be careful, I definitely will, thank you!" Douglas shouted back.

Douglas hesitated, eyes darting between the rail and the ground below. He drew a slow breath, then placed one foot in front of the other. Arms stretched out for balance, he moved like a tightrope walker. The rail wasn't razor-thin, but thin enough that his size seven shoes barely stayed planted, toes nearly slipping over the edge.

"You can do it, Dougie!" Luna shouted.

"Come on, man, you've got this," Thomas called up to him.

Douglas froze mid-step. "Guys, I know you mean well, but seriously, please shut up."

He continued walking along the rail until he made it to the key. He carefully sat straddling the rail, his legs hanging over the sides. He reached down, grabbed the tinsel, and yanked hard, attempting to snap it, but the material refused to yield. After failing to pull the key free, Douglas began trying to untie the knot.

"Why did I have to bite my nails, today of all days?" Douglas groaned as he struggled with the knot. "My wife always said that it was my worst habit. I should have listened to her."

"Come on, you're almost there," Thomas said, rubbing his hands together.

Douglas shot him a pointed glare.

"Sorry." Thomas mimed zipping his lips shut.

Everyone stared up, feeling helpless as Douglas struggled with the stubborn knot. Beads of sweat appeared on his forehead and swam down his face. The group remained silent, not wanting to distract him.

Then, Jennifer detected another sound, a faint but unmistakable squeaking noise. "Do you guys hear that?"

"Hear what?" Luna replied.

Jennifer pressed a finger to her lips. The squeaking grew louder.

"What is that?" Thomas said.

Jennifer's gaze shot up to the rail, tracing it to where the sleigh cart was moving again, heading straight toward Douglas.

"Uh, Dougie?" Jennifer said.

"What did I say about talking to me while I'm concentrating?" Douglas said.

"I don't want to alarm you, but your sleigh is heading straight toward you."

"What?" Douglas snapped, stopping his task to peer down at them.

They all pointed frantically ahead, and Douglas's eyes shot up to see the sleigh cart heading straight at him, until it crawled to a halt about twenty feet away. Douglas squinted at the driver.

A drone whirred into view, hovering between Douglas and the sleigh. Its lens contracted and expanded as it recorded him, before zipping away to capture a wide shot.

A nearby speaker crackled to life; the sudden noise nearly causing Douglas to lose his balance on the rail.

"Okay, Douglas," Vincent's voice came from the speaker. "In this scene, your character is being chased by Plucky. You need to untie that key and drop it to your friends. Time is running out, and your character is feeling the pressure to get to safety before Plucky catches up to him."

"What are you talking about, you bastard?" Douglas shouted, his feet swinging erratically to steady himself.

"As for the rest of you, I want to see big reactions," Vincent continued. "You're all scared for your friend, but you also need him to drop the key down to you. Got it? Okay, and action."

With those words, the sleigh lurched forward again. Douglas winced at the squeak of its wheels as it came closer, revealing the ominous silhouette of Plucky in the driver's seat.

"Get up, Dougie," Jennifer shouted.

"You need to get moving," Thomas yelled.

"Hang on, I've almost got it," Douglas said, his focus locked on the key.

"Forget the damn key," Jennifer shouted.

"Almost there," Douglas called back.

Jennifer's eyes darted between her friend and the swiftly approaching sleigh. If he didn't move soon, the cart would crush his fingers and knock him off the rail.

"I got it." Douglas said. The knot came loose and the key fell. Thomas grabbed it before it hit the ground.

"Now run," Jennifer shouted.

Douglas got to his feet and walked quickly along the narrow rail, but the sleigh was gaining on him. The squeak of the pedals grew louder, accompanied by the drone's incessant whir as it circled overhead.

"You can run, but there's no escaping the naughty list, Dougie," Plucky taunted behind him.

Douglas's steps quickened. When he risked a glance back, his foot slid on the slick metal. He stumbled, nearly toppling over the edge, but caught the rail at the last second.

"Enjoying your trip? Send me a postcard next time, will ya?" Plucky cackled.

Gripping the rail, Douglas's eyes squeezed shut. Above him, the drone buzzed like a circling vulture. The sleigh was closing in fast.

"Get back up!" Jennifer yelled.

He was frozen with fear, his fingers gripping the rail in a desperate, white-knuckled hold.

Jennifer scanned the area for something to distract Plucky. She considered throwing a rock at him, but she hesitated–her aim was shaky at best, and the thought of accidentally hitting Douglas stopped her.

With no other option, she turned to Luna. "I'm going to put you down for a moment, okay?"

Luna nodded, and Jennifer carefully lowered her to the ground. She faced the rest of the group.

"Everyone, join hands like this." Jennifer thrust her arms out.

"What are you–" Christy began.

"Just do it," Jennifer snapped.

Christy and Thomas followed suit, linking their arms to form a makeshift safety net.

"Dougie, jump," Jennifer called up to him.

"What?" he yelled back.

"Trust me and let go!"

Douglas turned his head to find Plucky leaning forward in his seat, pedaling furiously. The elf's mask obscured the actor's true expression, but Douglas had worn it long enough to recognize the malevolent grin hidden beneath its rubbery façade.

With a deep breath, Douglas released his grip on the rail just as the sleigh threatened to crush his fingers. He fell through the air and into the waiting arms of the group. Though he was slight, the impact sent them all crashing to the ground.

The speakers crackled to life, "And cut. Great work, Douglas. Although I'd say that your acting was a little over-the-top toward the end there. Otherwise, great work. We've got that scene in the can, let's move on to the next one."

When the speakers fell silent, Jennifer's eyes shot to the rail.

Plucky and the drone had vanished.

CHAPTER 26

"Is everyone okay?" Thomas asked as he helped Christy to her feet.

"I think so," Christy replied, brushing herself down.

"I think I broke my wrist." Douglas winced as he sat up. He lifted his arm, and his hand dangled at an unnatural angle. "Well, that's not good."

"Holy shit," Jennifer exclaimed.

"Maybe it's the adrenaline, but I don't feel it too bad–yet, anyway," Douglas said, eyeing his broken wrist. "As soon as that wears off, it's going to hurt like hell."

"Show me," Luna said, hobbling over and leaning over Douglas's wrist. She grabbed some of the extra fabric strips from Jennifer and began wrapping his wrist to immobilize it.

Jennifer marched over the speaker. She glared up at the small camera attached to the pole. "Vincent, we're done with your sick games. Let us out."

They waited a moment for Vincent to respond, but the speaker remained silent.

"Do you hear me?" Jennifer shouted, her frustration boiling over. "The movie's over."

But still there was no response.

"Asshole," she screamed, her voice echoing through the still air.

"Well, what now?" Christy asked.

"Now we use this to open a gate and get the hell out of here," Thomas said, holding up the key.

"But the real question is, which gate does this key open?" Douglas asked.

Thomas rushed to the south gate that led directly back to the parking lot and jammed the key into the top lock. It didn't budge. He cursed under his breath, fumbling for the second lock beneath it, but it too resisted. He gave the gate a shove, then took off toward the west train station gate. He slid the key in, wiggled it, tried again–but it still didn't unlock.

With only one gate left, Thomas ran north, passing the now motionless reindeer carousel. He reached the final lock, slid the key in, and whispered a prayer.

He turned it. The lock popped open. Relief flooded through him. He turned and waved. "Over here!"

Christy broke into a run, while Jennifer and Douglas stayed behind to help Luna. With their arms wrapped around her waist, they made their way across the park.

Jennifer peered into the murky void of the path leading into Elf Village. The feeble glow of a few sputtering lamps cast long, jittery shadows across the ground. "You can't be serious," she said, the park's layout flashing in her mind. "That route will drag us around the whole park. We've got to find another way–"

"There is no other route," Thomas snapped. "Haven't you been paying attention? We have no other choice."

"But Luna can't walk that far," Jennifer said.

"So what do you suggest?" Christy demanded. "We just sit here, trapped in this place?"

"Maybe we wait," Douglas suggested. "They're basically herding us wherever they want. I don't want to walk into whatever else they have planned. Someone will come and find us eventually."

"Who?" Christy cut in sharply. "No one knows we're here. Our families and friends think we're off shooting for a week, and this place has been abandoned for over a year. By the time anyone realizes we're missing, who knows how long it'll take for them to find us out here in the middle of nowhere?"

"She's right," Luna said through gritted teeth, trying to avoid putting pressure on her leg. "We've got no food, no water, and no one knows where we are. We need to keep moving."

"But your leg?" Jennifer protested.

"As long as I don't put too much pressure on it, I'll be fine," Luna said, trying to sound more confident than she felt.

"You've always been a lousy liar," Jennifer said.

"Maybe that's why I never made it as an actress." Luna forced a weak smile.

"Then it's settled," Thomas said. "We continue on. But stick together and pay attention. You see that little fucker around, let us know."

The group exchanged uneasy glances before Thomas and Christy pushed open the gate, its rusty hinges whining in protest. Ahead, the path led into Elf Village.

* * *

Although they had been in this themed area a few hours ago, it now appeared warped, obscured by darkness. The streetlamps cast harsh shadows from the cartoon standees of elves and snowmen, stretching their shapes. Christy flinched beside Jennifer more than once.

"Will you calm down?" Jennifer hissed. "You're freaking me out."

"Excuse me for being scared," Christy whispered back, her voice trembling. "They could be hiding, waiting to jump out at us."

"I've met hundreds of freaks like Vincent over the years. I can handle them," Jennifer said.

"It's not Vincent and Michael I'm afraid of," Christy whispered. "I'm more concerned about the pissed-off elf with the crossbow."

Jennifer's eyes dropped to Luna's leg before scanning the buildings around them. Her heart raced with the thought that he could be hiding anywhere, even in plain sight. She scrutinized every elf standee they passed, searching for any sign of movement.

A nearby speaker crackled to life, breaking the silence and making the group freeze in their tracks.

"Hi cast," Vincent's voice boomed over the speaker. "So, you've rolled into Elf Village, and guess what? The only way out is through the entrance to Toy Town, but you're surprised to find that it's locked too. Don't freak out though, because like before, the keys to get out are hidden around here. You'll find one in the Snow Globe Maze. Just remember to show us that nervousness, alright? And remember to use your characters' names please. Cool? Now, let's continue making some movie magic. Action."

The static from the speaker cut out, plunging them back into silence.

"For someone who's so intent on creating something authentic and original, you really have used the most basic MacGuffin ever. Finding keys? Fuck you," Douglas shouted at the speaker.

"What are we going to do?" Christy asked.

"We have no choice but to go and retrieve the key," Thomas said.

"Are you crazy?" Jennifer said. "That's exactly what he wants. I say we don't play into his sick game."

"So you're suggesting we just stay here?" Christy said. "In case you haven't been paying attention, we are stuck. Nobody is coming to save us."

"I'll go inside and get the key. You guys wait behind outside," Thomas said.

"You can't be serious." Jennifer said. "Have you ever even watched a horror movie? Hell, have you ever watched your own movie? The number one rule in a slasher is you don't split up."

"You're right, we should all go," Douglas said.

"What do you mean *we*?" Jennifer said, turning to Douglas and motioning toward his wrist.

Thomas shook his head. "We are most likely heading into a trap. There's no point putting us all in danger."

"Well, you can't go alone. I'll come with you," Douglas said.

"Me too," Luna said.

Jennifer turned to face Luna. "You're in no condition to walk through a maze."

"Like you said, the number one horror movie rule is don't split up," Luna replied.

"Fine, we all go. Together. Okay?" Thomas said, scanning the group.

Everyone nodded, then turned to Jennifer, who threw her hands up. "I guess I'm outnumbered."

"So, where is this Snow Globe Maze?" Christy said.

Douglas pointed to a dome-shaped building, framed by two tall, glowing, silver Christmas trees. Its exterior, decorated with paintings of elves, polar bears, and igloos, once gave a charming impression of peering into a giant whimsical snow globe. But the illusion was shattered as the artwork was bleached and peeling.

Thomas led the group to the entrance. He grasped the handle, and after a wary glance at the rest of the group, opened the door.

CHAPTER 27

They stepped inside and found a small foyer with an empty desk. Ahead were two doorways: one marked "Entrance" and the other "Exit." Both were covered with plastic flaps that hung like curtains, gently rippling as a rush of cool air flowed from behind them.

"Stay here," Jennifer said, turning to Luna.

"You want me to wait here and become an easy target for Plucky? I don't think so," Luna replied.

"Douglas will stay here with you," Jennifer said. "Keep the door closed and make sure nobody gets in."

"Fine, but remember to keep right," Luna said, "If you keep your hand on the right wall in a maze, you'll eventually find the exit."

"That doesn't sound right," Christy said, frowning.

"Every summer, my town set up these huge corn mazes," Luna explained. "Once, my daughter and I got lost until we started sticking to the right. That's how we found the exit."

Thomas nodded before taking a deep breath, parting the plastic flaps of the entrance and stepping through, with Christy following closely behind.

Jennifer released Luna, allowing Douglas to support her on his own. Luna reached out, trying to grip her fingers as they slipped from her grasp.

"I'll be back," Jennifer promised her.

"You've told me that before," Luna said.

She lingered for a second, then turned and slipped through the curtain.

Jennifer stepped onto a carpet of tattered felt. Once pristine white to replicate snow, it was now a grimy gray, marred by years of countless footsteps. Hidden wind machines created a gentle, swirling snowfall, sending flurries of white Styrofoam pellets to whirl around them. One neglected wind machine emitted a loud grating hum. The three of them ventured on and soon came to a corridor of mirrors, branching out in two different directions. Jennifer stared at her reflection, distorted by countless smudges and fingerprints. Her previously pristine hairstyle, meticulously arranged by Thomas, had become messy and wild.

Thomas peered down both directions, then turned right and made his way down a narrow hall of mirrors. "Stay alert–for the key and Plucky," he called back.

At each branch, Thomas took the right turn. As they moved deeper into the maze, the mirrors reflected distorted versions of themselves, like at a carnival funhouse. Jennifer's reflection appeared squat and wide, while Christy's stretched seven feet tall. She might have laughed if they weren't being hunted by a homicidal man in an elf costume.

The wind machines grew louder, as if someone had cranked up the dial. The gentle flurry of white pellets transformed into a full-blown snowstorm, with Styrofoam balls blasting down the narrow, mirrored alleyways and circling overhead. The intensity of the artificial blizzard made it difficult to see, as the pellets pelted their faces and clothes.

"Come on," Thomas roared over the noise. "Keep moving."

Shielding their eyes with their arms, they shuffled forward. The mirror maze twisted and shifted with every step, and the swirling blizzard left Jennifer dizzy and off-balance. Endless reflections multiplied the paths; the walls seemed to close in around her. Her palm pressed against the cold glass as her breath hitched and panic edged in. A touch on her shoulder made her jump. It was Christy. Her voice cut through the machine's roar, asking if she was okay. Jennifer nodded. They pressed on until they reached a crossroads–but Thomas had disappeared.

They called out for him, but the wind machines drowned their voices. As Christy started to turn left, Jennifer grabbed her shoulder and pointed right.

"No, he went this way," Christy said.

Jennifer didn't argue as she followed Christy down the path. She dragged Jennifer around corners in different directions until their faces unexpectedly met a glass wall.

"We've hit a dead end. We have to go back."

They turned around and tried to retrace their steps. They took a left and once again hit a dead end. Jennifer cried out, a number of the Styrofoam pellets getting in her mouth.

The women kept moving, hands skimming along the walls while the relentless artificial snow continued to beat down. Above the deafening roar of the wind machines, Jennifer made out another sound, a buzzing from above. Squinting through the swirling blizzard of plastic pellets, she spotted the drone hovering overhead, its red light like a watchful eye. She could picture Vincent recording them from his phone, laughing at the sight of them struggling to escape a children's fun maze.

Then something else caught her attention, a movement in the mirrors in front of them. Jennifer froze.

"What's the hold up?" Christy yelled, trying to push her forward.

There it was again, a flash of green. Someone was in the maze with them, watching them, stalking them. When Jennifer didn't move, Christy sighed with exasperation and pushed past her.

"Christy, wait."

But Christy was swallowed by a flurry of artificial snow.

Jennifer shouted again, sprinting forward. She caught a glimpse of Christy just ahead–then slammed face-first into a mirror. The impact sent her sprawling to the ground with a sharp yelp.

Dazed, she looked up. Plucky's reflection stretched and warped to eight feet tall. He was bearing down on an oblivious Christy. Gripped in his gloved hand was a long carving knife, similar to one used for carving ham. Jennifer tried to scream, but the howling artificial wind swallowed her voice. Plucky turned toward her, raising a finger to his cracked mask, and sliced the back of Christy's Achilles tendon. Christy screamed as she crumpled to the floor. Overhead, the drone whirled, capturing the brutal moment. Plucky lunged at Christy from behind, plunging and dragging the knife through her back.

His reflection doubled, tripled, and multiplied endlessly in the mirrors around her.

Christy's blood pooled, mixing with the swirling artificial snow. And as the pellets circulated, it became a blizzard of red and white.

Plucky's head spun toward Jennifer, and he pointed his knife directly at her, blood dripping from the sharpened blade. Jennifer willed her legs to move but found herself rooted to the spot. Multiple Pluckys stalked toward her from all directions.

Jennifer was paralyzed. The mirrored walls pressed in around her, multiplying Plucky's mask until he was everywhere. She sank to the floor and curled into herself.

Then she remembered what she'd promised Luna–that she'd come back. She wasn't going to break that promise again.

Her legs wobbled beneath her, but she forced herself upright and sprinted back the way she came. Luna's advice echoed in her mind: stick to the right. Jennifer pressed a hand to the glass and kept turning right. Red-and-white pellets lashed at her face, while reflections of Christy's mangled body chased her through the maze. She could vividly imagine Plucky chasing after her, waving his blood-tipped knife, the blade coming dangerously close to slicing her legs. Desperation and her promise to Luna fueled her forward, and she soon burst through the plastic curtains into the foyer. She collided with someone, strong hands seizing her shoulders. She screamed and struggled, but then her eyes met Thomas's face.

"Jennifer, where's Christy?"

CHAPTER 28

"Where is she?" Thomas asked again.

Jennifer's heart pounded. She cast a quick look back toward the maze she'd just escaped. She caught her reflection in the mirrors–Christy's blood was streaked across her skin. Thomas's eyes narrowed, and he made a move to go back, but she gripped his wrist and shook her head urgently. In his hand, she felt the key.

"If she's still in there, we have to go find her," he insisted, trying to pull his arm free from her grasp.

"She's dead," Jennifer said.

Luna gasped, her hands clasped to her mouth. Douglas slumped back against a wall, his legs barely holding him up, and Thomas simply stared at Jennifer.

"How?" he demanded.

"Plucky," she replied.

Thomas ran both hands over his head. "This is fucked up, man. Seriously fucked up."

"Where were you? You left us and then Christy left me."

"I'm sorry, I saw the key and grabbed it. I thought you two were right behind me, but then I turned and..."

Jennifer's gaze drifted back to the plastic curtain where a few small crimson beads rolled out from beneath. Her stomach twisted, and she stumbled outside, doubled over, and retched into the dirt.

Douglas followed her outside and placed a tentative hand on her back. "Jenny, are you okay?"

"No, I am not fucking okay, Dougie," she snapped, her voice raw from shouting over the wind machine. "None of this is okay."

Luna and Thomas stepped outside as a nearby speaker crackled to life.

"And cut." Vincent's voice blasted over the intercom. "That was awesome. Seriously, great work, everyone. Jennifer, your line at the end–'None of this is okay'–was chef's kiss. A bit cliché, but totally nailed the vibe. Douglas, though, your delivery was a little stiff. But no biggie, just make sure to bring a bit more emotion into the next scene, okay?"

Jennifer's head snapped up. "What next scene, you freak?"

"You've only got one key so far. You need *two* to open the next gate," Vincent explained calmly.

"I'm not playing this sick game any longer," Jennifer roared, her voice echoing around the dark, quiet park.

"The shoot isn't over until the director calls it a wrap. You've been in plenty of movies, Ms. Hawkins, you know this," Vincent replied. "But hey, take five, grab some water from the cooler and we'll pick this up shortly as we set the next scene."

With that, the speaker fell silent and the group turned their attention to a red cooler sitting underneath the speaker lit up by a nearby streetlamp. Thomas made his way over, lifting the lid to reveal four bottles of water inside. He tossed three of them to the others before unscrewing the cap of the last for himself.

"Wait," Jennifer interrupted, "You're not actually going to drink that, are you?"

"You're damn right I am."

"But what if they poisoned it?" Jennifer swirled her bottle, peering inside.

"Vincent wants us for his movie. And I don't think slowly dying of poisoning is cinematic enough for him."

With that, he took a long gulp from the bottle.

Despite her reservations, Jennifer couldn't help but stare as the water trickled down Thomas's chin. The dryness in her own throat intensified, her head pounding with every heartbeat.

Jennifer couldn't resist any longer. She twisted off the bottle cap and let the lukewarm water slide down her throat.

"I can't believe Christy's gone," Douglas said, turning his crumpled bottle around in his hands.

Flashes of Christy lying in a pool of her own blood and Plucky plunging the knife into her assaulted Jennifer's mind. A fresh wave of panic hit her, forcing Jennifer to bend forward, hold her head between her knees, and hyperventilate. A warm sensation tickled her back–it was Luna.

"It was my fault," Jennifer whispered.

"What do you mean?" Luna asked, her voice low.

"I saw it happen," Jennifer said, barely above a whisper. "Plucky killed Johnny. Then Christy. And both times...I just stood there."

"What could you have done? He would have killed you too if you hadn't run away."

"Still, I could have done something." Jennifer said, her voice cracking as she dropped her head into her hands. "I could have done *anything*."

The familiar crackle of the speaker sent a jolt of dread through Jennifer's body.

"Okay, cast, break time is over," Vincent's voice rang through the speaker. "We're moving on to the next scene at the Elf Jamboree restaurant. This is where you'll find the next key."

"Fuck you, asshole." Thomas stuck his middle finger up in the air.

"Come on now, Thomas," Vincent replied. "Jennifer can back me up here–it's the perfect spot. Super atmospheric. Totally gives off those *Five Nights at Freddy*'s vibes. I'm telling you, this one's gonna be all over the trailers–you're going to love it. So I want to see you all bring your A-game. And action."

The speaker silenced.

"There's no way we're going in there," Jennifer said. "He almost killed me last time. I'm not going to let him finish the job."

"I'm done being jerked around by these assholes. You guys hang tight–I'm going in to grab the key myself," Thomas declared.

"What about our rule of not breaking up?" Luna said.

"No offense, Luna, but you can barely walk," Thomas said, glancing at her leg. "Douglas has a busted wrist, and Jennifer's a wreck. Plus, I'm pretty sure I can handle a four-foot guy in an elf mask." He looked over at Douglas. "No offense."

"None taken," Douglas shrugged. "But I'm coming with you. You're gonna need backup or a distraction for Plucky."

"Fine," Thomas said. "But we're not going in defenseless again." He scanned the area and spotted one of the fallen elf standees. He lifted the corner of its base and forcefully pulled the brittle wood until it splintered. He gathered the makeshift weapons and distributed them to the group.

"It's not much, but it's better than nothing," Thomas said, swinging his long, sharpened wooden stick around like a makeshift baseball bat.

"There's a bunch of mechanical elves in there, last time he was hidden amongst them," Jennifer warned them.

"If you see anything, call for us and we'll come right back out," Douglas said.

Douglas and Jennifer exchanged a nod before he and Thomas turned and headed toward the Elf Jamboree restaurant.

"Seriously, look after yourselves in there," Luna called out as the door slammed shut behind them, leaving the women alone.

"Can you believe this is actually happening?" Jennifer finally spoke.

Luna took her hand in hers and squeezed reassuringly. "We'll get through this."

"See, you are a good actor after all. I almost believe you."

Luna smiled but grimaced, clutching her injured leg. Jennifer kneeled to examine it and saw that the makeshift bandage was soaked through with blood.

Jennifer pulled another strip of cloth from her pocket and carefully untied the blood-stained bandage. The wound in Luna's leg looked angry-red and oozing. Jennifer reached down for the half-drunk bottle of water she had saved. She doused the wound as best she could before swiftly replacing the bandage with a fresh one. Luna winced as Jennifer tightened the cloth around the wound and arrow.

Jennifer offered an apologetic smile.

"You'd make a pretty great nurse, you know," Luna grimaced.

"Well, I was on an episode of *General Hospital*, you know? So I'm pretty much a qualified medical practitioner." Jennifer glanced up at Luna and offered a reassuring smile. Luna's wig sat askew, messy and lopsided on her head.

"I'm still wearing my wig, aren't I?" Luna asked. "Thomas did too good a job keeping this thing in place." She peeled away the wig, then removed the wig cap.

"Uh that feels so good, it's so hot under there," Luna sighed as she freed and tousled her silver hair which lapped against her chest. "It was nice being a redhead again, at least for a little while."

"I actually like your hair better now," Jennifer replied. It suits you–very ethereal."

"Oh stop it." Luna rolled her eyes.

"I mean it, like a sexy Mrs. Claus," Jennifer joked. She shifted her eyes to the slide nearby. "Can you believe it was only yesterday that we rode that thing? When our biggest worry was what Vincent was gonna feed us that night?" Jennifer could still hear their laughter echoing from the day before, could almost feel Luna's warmth beside her as they held each other close. It had felt so effortless, so right–until Vincent showed up and shattered the moment.

"I haven't felt like that since–" Luna hesitated, then turned her gaze to Jennifer. "What happened?"

"What do you mean?" Jennifer said.

"That last time we were together?" Luna said. "We spent the night in your trailer, and we finally said what we'd been dancing around for months. I remember feeling so happy. It was perfect. I knew you felt it too." Her voice wavered. "But the next morning, everything changed. You disappeared. Ran away to hide in LA, dodged my calls... And then, well–I never saw you again until a few days ago."

Jennifer was silent for a moment, her fingers idly tracing patterns in the sand.

"I was scared."

"Of what?"

"Come on, Luna. We couldn't be in a relationship in Hollywood. Not openly, anyway. Not back then. We were just starting out, do you think anyone would have hired us if they knew?"

She looked ahead, replaying the memory as she spoke. "You didn't know, but that morning, my agent walked into the trailer and caught us asleep together. Later, he pulled me out of hair and makeup and totally flipped out. He told me it would be bad press if anyone found out. That no one would ever cast me as a leading lady if they knew I was a 'dyke.' He said it was career suicide."

"So, you abandoned what we had...for your career?"

"For both of our careers. We were so young, our careers were ahead of us still–I didn't know if we would last." She met Luna's eyes, weighing her words carefully. "Remember all those nights we talked about our careers, our ambitions? I couldn't throw all that away. And I knew you shouldn't either. I had to think about our futures."

"I thought we *were* each other's futures."

A part of Jennifer couldn't believe Luna's lack of perspective–she was almost naïve. Yet, as Luna stared ahead, dejected, Jennifer dropped to her knees, resting her hands gently on Luna's thighs. "At one point, I thought the same. I hate how I left–"

Jennifer froze as a whirring noise cut through the air. Both of them turned their heads to see Vincent's drone hovering above.

"No, don't stop," Vincent's voice crackled through a speaker. "This is the good stuff."

"You fucking–" Jennifer jumped to her feet and swung her stick at the drone. It nimbly avoided her. She swung again and again, but the drone continued to dodge with ease.

"Now, this is the real meat of the story," Vincent continued. "It's why I chose not to kill off your character earlier. We couldn't miss out on this drama. I had no idea about this amped-up passion between you two. But as soon as I saw it, I knew we had to explore further."

Jennifer swung again, but the drone dodged.

Vincent continued, "Fans have always speculated about a romance between your characters–there're loads of fanfics about it. But now, my movie's gonna confirm it."

Vincent taunted her as the drone continued to evade each of Jennifer's desperate swings. She was driving it away from them, so she kept up the pressure and stepped after it.

Luna called after her, but Jennifer was too focused on the drone, determined to bring it down.

After one final, exhausted swing, Jennifer's strength gave out. She collapsed to the ground, panting heavily.

"As much as I am an ally of your community, I'm a filmmaker first," Vincent said through the old speakers. "As such, I still have to stick to some codes and conventions, like the whole 'Bury Your Gays' trope. Do you know what that is?"

Neither of the women replied.

"Well, it's the idea that LGBTQ+ relationships are doomed to end tragically in movies, with one of you having to be killed off for dramatic effect. It's kinda dumb, but I can only break so many filmmaking rules without coming off as pretentious. I hope you understand."

Jennifer rose to take another swing at the drone. Again, it dodged her attack with ease. As she turned back to Luna, a chill ran through her. The drone had drawn her away. Then her stomach dropped–there, in the shadows behind Luna, something moved.

Plucky stepped into the dim glow of a streetlamp, his mangled mask catching the light. His sharpened candy cane struck every lamppost he passed–*clang...clang...clang*. The sound echoed down the empty street.

Plucky stood over Luna. She screamed as he raised his signature weapon high. The drone whizzed past Jennifer and toward Luna, its lens homing in on the unfolding scene.

"Stop!" Jennifer screamed.

Plucky paused, his attention snapping toward Jennifer.

"That's right, you little fucker," Jennifer said. "It's me you want. Come on, you've been waiting to kill the 'final girl.' Well, I'm right here."

Plucky tilted his head, giving Luna one final look before turning and stalking straight toward Jennifer.

Luna shouted out, but Plucky ignored her. His eyes stayed fixed on Jennifer, who backed away–drawing him away from Luna.

The drone wavered in the air, darting between Plucky and Luna, then whizzed back toward him.

"Whoa, hang on, Plucky–cut," Vincent's voice crackled through the speaker. "I said *cut*. This isn't in the script. I directed you to take out Luna, not Jennifer. Let's reset the scene, alright?"

"No," Plucky croaked, waving his arm, trying to swat the drone away like an annoying mosquito. "I'm moving on to the next scene. Make sure Michael's ready."

For a moment, there was silence, broken only by the faint hum of the old speaker. Then Vincent's voice crackled through, his tone wavering as though trying to convince himself. "Okay, it's fine. This could work. Continue with the scene."

Jennifer assessed her situation. She had the height advantage, but Plucky, though small, seemed solidly built under his costume. And then there was the candy cane shiv in his hand compared to her splinter of wood. Even still, she was confident she could disarm him.

However, almost as if reading her thoughts, Plucky unclipped another weapon from his leather belt–a shortened deer antler, the same one she had seen him use to slice Johnny open.

Plucky spoke, his voice slow, deep, and gravelly. "Hey Rebecca, hold on for deer life."

"Cut," Vincent said over the speaker. "Let's try that line again. Puns are a core part of Plucky's character, so put emphasis on the last part."

The actor paused, shaking out his limbs, before Vincent called out, "Okay, action."

"Hey Rebecca, hold on for *deer* life," Plucky repeated.

Jennifer continued to step backward; her only goal was increasing the gap between Luna and this murderous psycho. Plucky lifted both weapons and pointed them directly at her.

Jennifer kept her eyes fixed on Plucky, stepping backward until her foot found nothing but air. She fell and tumbled backward with a sharp cry. She landed hard on her back, the fall knocking the wind from her lungs. She found herself sprawled on the seat of a familiar wooden boat. Before she could get up, the safety bar dropped onto her lap with a mechanical clunk, locking her in place.

Jennifer lifted her head to find Plucky at the control panel, his hand pressing one of the buttons. She shoved with all of her strength against the metal bar, but it didn't budge. The cruel bastard then gripped a lever and yanked it down. The boat lurched forward, starting its slow drift toward the dark curtain ahead. Plucky waved mockingly as the tattered fabric swallowed her whole.

CHAPTER 29

It's a snowy land with twinkling light,
so bring all your friends, with their cheers so bright.
Gather round, boys and girls, and your parents too,
because in Jingle Bell Creek, we welcome you!

She struggled in the boat and pushed against the restraints. If she could lift the bar even slightly, she might be able to slip free. But it held firm, trapping her in place. Frantically, she looked around at the singing, dancing mechanical elves, searching for any sign of Plucky hiding in plain sight. Instead, her eyes landed on Michael, who was crouched on top of one of the houses with a camera on his shoulder.

"Michael," Jennifer cried out. "For the love of God, please help me."

"Please don't stare directly at the camera."

"You son of a bitch," she screamed as she thrashed around in her seat. Grabbing the metal lap restraint, she rattled it, feeling the clasp shift–just a little–under the strain. She then spied Plucky on a rooftop, holding a robotic elf and prancing around as if they were waltzing together. As he spun, she spied the crossbow slung over his back. As her boat drew nearer, he spun around and tossed his mechanical partner onto the seat beside her. Jennifer screamed as the robot convulsed and sparked, its wires writhing like entrails.

"She wanted a night to remember; too bad she won't," Plucky cackled.

With a swift motion, he hopped onto the boat and kicked the malfunctioning robot overboard, sending it splashing ahead of the boat into the water. Then he turned his attention to her. Despite his small stature–four and a half feet tall–he was a menacing presence. In his fist, he gripped the long, pointed candy cane. The boat jerked, slowed, and groaned as it hit the mechanical elf corpse sparking in the water.

Bending down, he pressed so close to her face she could smell the foul breath through the mask. "You're not a 'final girl.' " He hissed, "You're just an old, battered..." He raised the candy cane shiv, poised to drive it into her skull. "Bitch."

Jennifer grabbed the metal restraint and heaved it up; the metal bar sprang open with a click. It smacked Plucky in his shins, causing him to cry out in both pain and shock as he toppled back on the bow of the boat.

Now free from her restraints, she scrambled to her feet. The boat wobbled beneath her, and for a split second, she feared she might topple into the black sludge below. But she caught herself just in time and leapt to the bank.

As she landed, her left ankle twisted awkwardly beneath her, and a sharp cry escaped her lips. Fueled by adrenaline, she forced herself upright, though the pressure on her ankle sent waves of torment through her body. It wasn't enough to break her focus–she had to get out.

She peaked over to see Plucky scrambling to his feet, yanking the crossbow from his back. He fumbled with the string, forcing a long bolt into place.

Shit.

As she found a rhythm between running and limping, the music and lights suddenly cut out, plunging the snowy elf village into darkness–save for the faint glow of bioluminescent paint. Wooden standees of cheerful elves glowed in neon hues of green, pink, and blue, their blurred shapes flickering as Jennifer pushed past them to clear her path along the winding river. A mechanical skating elf spun wildly, nearly knocking her into the water, but she dodged its swinging arms in time.

A low whistle cut through the air as a bolt streaked past her and buried itself in a robotic elf's skull.

"Run, run Rudolph, I ain't too far behind," Plucky called in a sing-song voice. He stood on the boat's bow, drawing the string for another shot. *"Run, run, Rudolph, Plucky's gotta make it to town."*

Jennifer pushed through the pain, hobbling as fast as she could. If she kept this up, she may outrun Plucky and the boat.

How long is this goddamn ride? Jennifer thought, when the faintest glimmer of light appeared ahead–the exit.

Excited, Jennifer began dashing past the "Christmas Cabaret Chorus Line," but the elves came to life, coming together to form a kick line. As Jennifer hurried past, one mechanical leg kicked up right into her bad ankle. She cried out as she lost her balance and plunged into the black sludge below. Her entire body was engulfed in the liquid. She couldn't see; everything was dark.

She thrashed enough to break the surface but, in the process, swallowed a mouthful of the foul sludge. Gagging and spitting, she tried to rid herself of the putrid taste.

Jennifer stood up in the waist-high water. She wiped the sting from her eyes–then froze. Singing drifted toward her, not from the mechanical elves, but from Plucky, mocking her.

"Run, run, Rudolph, Plucky has to make it to town. Plucky'll make her hurry, tell her she can take the freeway down."

If she didn't move, Plucky would either put a bolt through her skull–or the boat would catch her, drag her under, and crush her.

She waded to the edge and tried to lift herself out, but her strength failed her. Exhausted and aching, she cried out in frustration.

"Run, run, Rudolph, reeling like a merry-go-round."

But the exit wasn't far. Summoning what little energy she had left, she pushed forward through the water. Each step dragged, her limbs growing heavier with every movement.

She glanced over her shoulder, where Plucky continued to perform, using a bolt as a microphone. The boat was getting closer and closer. If she didn't hurry, she would get caught underneath it. She pushed harder against the water, using her arms to propel herself forward.

Another bolt hissed past her ear and shot into the water.

"Said Santa to a girl, 'Child, what would please you most to get?' A little baby doll that can cry, sleep, drink, and wet."

The black curtains were closer now, shards of light flickering through them. She heard her name shouted in an unmistakable Yorkshire accent–Douglas's voice, joined by

Thomas's. Relief surged through her. But it didn't last. Behind her, the boat knocked against the banks. She risked a glance over her shoulder and saw the pointed tip of the bow closing in.

"And then away went Rudolph, whizzing like a Sabre jet."

Her throat was coated with the vile sludge she had swallowed, but she called out to her friends.

She had no idea if they could hear her over the sounds of the incessant song being sung by Plucky.

"Run, run, Rudolph, Plucky's gotta make it to town."

He fired another bolt–this one grazing her cheek. She gasped but kept moving.

"Santa make her hurry, tell her she can take the freeway down."

Propelling herself through the waist-high water, she burst through the tattered curtains and into the cool night air. Hands reached down and yanked her up. She hit the dry, cold ground with a thud. Thomas and Douglas were crouched over her, holding on tight.

She looked up as the boat drifted past–but Plucky was gone.

Through the ringing in her ears, she heard Vincent's voice. "And...that's a cut. I didn't plan for everything to play out like that, but hey, improvisation is all part of the filmmaking experience, right? Awesome job, Ms. Hawkins, totally believable. Everyone take five, and we'll pick up where we left off."

CHAPTER 30

"Jenny, are you okay?" Douglas asked, crouching beside her.

"What the hell happened?" Thomas asked.

Jennifer retched up more of the black sludge. "It was Plucky. I had to draw him away from Luna, then I got trapped on the boat." Her head snapped up. "Luna, where is she?"

"We thought she was with you," Douglas said.

"She was just over there," she pointed to the spot where she had left her.

"After we found the key in the restaurant, we came outside and you were both gone." Thomas said. "Then we heard your voice coming from the ride."

"Luna," Jennifer called out, her voice cracking. Douglas and Thomas joined in, their shouts echoing into the stillness. No response.

Douglas frowned, his eyes dropping. "We shouldn't have left you, Jenny. I'm really sorry."

Jennifer shook her head. "Forget that. We have to find her. Help me up, will you?"

Douglas and Thomas each took an arm and helped Jennifer to her feet. She took a step forward but yelped as she put weight on her left foot.

"What's wrong?" Douglas asked.

"I twisted my ankle as I jumped off the boat, and then a fucking elf kicked it." Jennifer winced.

"Plucky?" Douglas asked.

Jennifer shook her head. "No, it was one of those goddamn robot shits. I didn't see it coming. It was doing the fucking can-can."

"Can you put any weight on it?" Thomas asked.

Jennifer took a cautious step forward, a sharp jolt shooting up her leg. "A little," she lied, gritting her teeth.

"You can barely walk," Douglas said, "you're not going anywhere."

"We don't have time to argue. I'll be fine," Jennifer insisted. "We need to find Luna."

"No offense," Thomas said, "but what makes you think she's alive?"

"She's not dead," Jennifer replied, her tone defiant.

"But how are you so sure? Look what happened to Christy." Thomas pressed.

"Vincent said that my relationship with Luna is the meat of the movie. I bet he's taken her somewhere to use for the big climax of his magnum opus."

"Where?" Douglas asked.

Jennifer pointed at the keys in Thomas's hand. "Help me over to the gate."

Douglas steadied her waist with his arm. She took a tentative step, the strain nearly knocking the breath from her lungs. Gritting her teeth and biting her tongue, she pressed on.

Thomas inserted the keys into both locks and unhooked the chains, Douglas snatched one before it hit the floor.

"I'll hang on to this," Douglas said. "I might be able to use it as a weapon." He demonstrated by coiling the chain around his hand before making a fist. "Or it can double for a whip," Douglas added, swinging it lightly in his uninjured hand.

"It's not much, but it's something," Douglas shrugged. "Don't you hate it in horror movies when the character has a weapon right by them, but they don't pick it up? Like Laurie Strode in *Halloween*. It annoys me every time she drops the knife after stabbing Michael. If this was a real horror movie, people would be yelling at us right now to carry these chains."

"The thing is...we actually *are* in a horror movie," Jennifer said, nodding at a GoPro mounted on top of the fence.

"Exactly," Thomas said, picking up the other chain from the ground. "My character in part five was a complete dumbass, the first to be killed off. I'm not going to be making those same dumb decisions. I intend to be the first Black guy to survive an *Evil Elf* movie."

"We'll survive," Jennifer said. "We need to stick together."

They exchanged nervous glances before proceeding through the open gates to Toy Town, which was spelled out with giant building blocks.

Despite their dire situation, Jennifer couldn't help but marvel at their surroundings. True to its name, oversized toys were scattered around, creating the illusion that they had shrunk down to toy size.

The three of them passed by Lincoln Log huts that once served drinks and snacks to visitors, a towering teddy bear for photo opportunities, and a teacup-style ride where visitors once swirled around a single, tall, static drummer boy three or four people to a drum.

"Welcome to Toy Town," Vincent's voice blared from nearby speakers. "Your characters are so close to escaping Tinseltown, but it's not over yet. There's still one last key to find."

"We're not playing your sick games anymore," Jennifer shouted up at a camera mounted underneath the speaker. "Where's Luna?"

A deep sigh rang from the speaker. "Please remember her character is called *Sophie*. Now, let's keep it moving–cameras are rolling and time is ticking. For continuity's sake, we need to wrap this up before dawn breaks. The joys of shooting on location, am I right guys?"

"We're not filming another second of your movie until we see Luna," Jennifer stated firmly.

Vincent sighed again, deeper this time. "Why are actors so difficult? Allow me to give you some character motivation. Luna, a.k.a. Sophie, is being held prisoner by Plucky. She's got a serious leg wound and is bleeding out fast. If she doesn't get medical attention pronto, she's a goner. Your character, Rebecca Sommers, desperately wants to save her beloved from the big bad villain. But the only way to do that is to get the final key, which is where the elves make the toys. So, let's not hold up production any longer than we need to, okay? *Action*."

Jennifer didn't argue; she couldn't afford to waste any more time with Luna's life on the line. They scanned the area and spotted a large red barn with a wooden sign above it that read "Santa's Workshop."

With no other option, Jennifer, Douglas, and Thomas headed toward the barn, its doors ajar. Broken strings of multicolored Christmas lights dangled over the doorway, their bulbs either burst or emitting a dull flicker. Thomas grasped the heavy barn doors and pulled them open with a creak.

When they stepped inside, they found a massive glass wall to their right that separated them from a workshop. Behind the observation glass sat a dozen elf mannequins at their benches, all frozen while making their toys. Their painted smiles were eerily intact, and some were looking up at their visitors with glassy eyes that followed the group's every move. Beyond them, other elves were frozen in their work behind a conveyor belt, assembling boxed presents. Behind them were ceiling-high shelves stuffed with gifts, and over in the corner sat a tall pile of plush toys.

"Do you see the key anywhere?" Douglas asked, his eyes darting around the workshop.

"It's probably on the other side of the glass." She wiped some of the dust off the glass and peered through.

Thomas banged his fist against the glass, but it only reverberated.

Jennifer looked up–the glass wall ended several feet below the ceiling. "I think someone could climb over." She nodded toward a stack of crates piled beneath the overhead beams.

"When you say someone, you mean me, right?" Thomas said. He cast a wary eye toward the display on the other side of the glass, watching the mannequin elves as if expecting them to move.

"Well, I have a busted ankle, and Douglas has a broken wrist," Jennifer said.

"Right, because clearly, I'm the best candidate for 'bait of the day,' " Thomas said, still staring at the display. "How do I know one of those creepy-ass dolls isn't that fucker dressed up? He could be waiting to jump me the moment I step in there."

Jennifer pressed her face to the glass, eyes narrowing as she examined each mannequin's face in turn. "I don't think he's one of them."

"That's easy for you to say, I'm the one that has to jump in there," Thomas said, not looking convinced.

"What's the alternative?" Jennifer snapped. "Luna's in serious trouble. Vincent says she's still alive, but for how long? We can't waste any more time."

Thomas eyed the elves on the other side of the glass. Jennifer sighed and stepped forward. "Fine. I'll climb it myself."

Thomas threw his large, muscular arm in front of her. He took one last look at the mannequins and made his way over to the crates. Wrapping the chain around his shoulder, he hauled himself up onto a wooden beam. Carefully balancing, he made his way to the other side, then lowered himself down, his feet hitting the floor with a soft thud.

Uncoiling the chain from his shoulder, he wrapped it around his fist. He crept toward one of the dolls, paused briefly, then delivered a solid punch to the back of its head. The head popped off, smacked against the glass wall with a sharp thud, and bounced across the floor.

Thomas scrutinized the other elves, searching for any sign of movement. When none of them stirred, he grabbed the nearest mannequin and threw it hard to the wood floor. He seized another, tossing it across the room where its plastic limbs shattered into pieces. Snatching another, he launched it over the glass where it clattered near Jennifer's feet. Thomas took down the remaining elves, whacking them with his chained fist, kicking and punching them with full force until he was satisfied that none of them were Plucky.

Surrounded by the dismembered, plastic corpses of elf mannequins, the group let out a collective sigh of relief.

"That felt good," Thomas panted.

"Find the key," Jennifer said.

Thomas began searching the shelves, tossing toys and knick-knacks onto the floor in his quest for the key.

"Do you see it anywhere?" Douglas asked.

Thomas shook his head.

"Maybe try opening up the presents?" Jennifer suggested.

"Before Christmas?" Thomas mocked.

"Just do it," Jennifer insisted.

Thomas sighed and grabbed one of the wrapped presents on the unmoving conveyor belt. He tore open the wrapping to reveal a cardboard box. Opening it up, he found nothing inside.

"Try the others," she urged.

Thomas picked up another box, tore off the wrapping–and found yet another empty cardboard shell. He exhaled sharply through his nose, flung it over his shoulder, and reached for the next. Then the next. Each one, the same. But as he ripped the paper from one of the last remaining presents, something different caught his eye: a jack-in-the-box.

"Ugh, I've always hated these creepy things," Thomas exclaimed. He was about to toss it to one side when something hard and small rattled inside.

"The key," Douglas said.

"Play it then," Jennifer said.

Thomas wound the box, and it emitted the disjointed tune of "Jingle Bells." As the song reached its crescendo, he slowed the crank, bracing himself for the clown to pop out. But then...nothing.

Brow furrowed, he cranked the handle faster, but still, nothing emerged.

"I think it's busted," Thomas said, holding the box up to the group.

"Well, it's obviously in there," Jennifer said. "Try it again."

Thomas turned the crank once more. The music started up, and as it neared the final note, the lid popped open. He jerked his head back, bracing for the clown to spring out, but inside was nothing but a silver key.

"Oh," Thomas exhaled. "That wasn't so bad."

From the pile of plushies behind Thomas, Plucky burst out. An explosion of stuffed animals rained over Thomas.

Before he could respond, Plucky slashed the back of his knee with a box cutter. Thomas cried out, swinging his chain in a wide arc around him. Plucky ducked out of reach. Thomas lunged after him, but his injured leg gave out, buckling beneath him. He hit the conveyor belt hard, the impact knocking the air from his lungs. Jennifer was surprised that the conveyor belt didn't collapse like all the other decorations; she realized with horror that it was new, a part of Vincent's plan. Plucky leaned over Thomas, fiddling with the chain around his fist.

"Looks like you're all wrapped up," Plucky taunted, "Time for a little elf-inflicted pain."

Jennifer and Douglas watched helplessly as Plucky hopped to the other side of the conveyor belt and placed his filthy, gloved hand over a large red button. The elf then turned toward them and gave a playful wave.

"You son of a bitch. Leave him alone." Jennifer roared, pounding against the glass.

With Plucky distracted, Thomas slid off the conveyor belt, grabbed the free end of his chain, and whipped it toward the elf's head. But Plucky saw his reflection in the glass divider and ducked out of range. Before Thomas could pull the chain back, Plucky seized it. With a sharp yank, he dragged Thomas onto the belt. A thin, shiny lock dangled from the chain now fixed around Thomas's wrist. Plucky darted to the end of the line, coiled the chain around one of the machine's gears, and hovered his hand once again over the control panel's big red button.

Jennifer and Douglas pounded on the glass, their fists echoing through the enclosed space. Plucky turned his head toward them, and through a hole in his mask, the twisted curl of his lips formed a grotesque smile. With a decisive slam, he activated the conveyor belt. A buzzing filled the air, soon followed by the deep hum of machinery that reverberated through the wooden structure. The belt moved, coiling the chain around the gear and pulling it underneath.

Thomas struggled against the chain around his wrist, pulling with all his might, but it only got tighter.

If they didn't act fast, Thomas would be pulled under the conveyor belt. Jennifer considered climbing onto the crates and leaping over the glass into the workshop, but the thought of landing from that height on her injured ankle made her feel helpless. Desperation gripped her as she scanned the area; her gaze locked on the mannequin elf lying at her feet.

She snatched the chain from Douglas's good hand.

"What are you doing?" he asked, as Jennifer began winding the metal links around the elf's head.

On the other side of the glass, Plucky clapped his hands and bounced from foot to foot. He circled the conveyor belt, snatched a wooden nutcracker and a single nut from the shelf, and started toward Thomas.

Placing the nutcracker an inch from his face, Plucky squeezed the lever, snapping the jaws shut and shattering the nut into splinters. Thomas flinched and lunged for him, but the elf darted out of reach.

Meanwhile, the conveyor belt continued to move, tightening the chain around Thomas's wrist. There was a pop, and his arm dislodged from his shoulder. His scream echoed through the workshop. When Thomas was only inches from the end of the conveyor belt, the chain became lodged in the mechanics, and the machine shuddered to a halt. Douglas and Jennifer breathed a shared sigh of relief, but Plucky was still right there.

"I told Vincent not to cheap out on this shit," Plucky snarled, breaking character. Grunting, he booted an elf head sending it tumbling across the room–then caught sight of the camera. His voice shifted instantly into the bright, sing-song tone of the scene. "Oh goodie," he said, "more time to play." He positioned the mouth of the nutcracker over Thomas's nose and squeezed hard. There was a sickening crack as cartilage and skin crunched under the pressure. "Got your nose," he sneered.

With the chain wrapped tightly around its plastic head, Jennifer grabbed the one remaining leg of the mannequin elf and swung it with full force into the glass. The metal-reinforced head cracked the surface, spiderwebbing the glass.

Just as Plucky was about to squeeze down on Thomas's shattered nose for a second time, his head shot up, a thought occurring to him. Crouching behind Thomas, he positioned the nutcracker's gaping mouth over Thomas's crotch. As Plucky was about to squeeze the lever for another brutal snap, Jennifer didn't hesitate. She swung the mannequin elf again with all her strength, creating a cascade of glittering glass shards. Jennifer shielded her face with her arm as the debris rained down around her.

Stunned by the explosion of glass, Plucky froze. His head jerked toward one of the mounted GoPros, then slowly swiveled back to Jennifer. When she lifted the doll in warning, he took a step toward her, then stopped. After another glance at the camera, he let the nutcracker clatter to the floor. Wordlessly, he retreated to the corner of the room, knelt beside the pile of stuffed animals, and pulled open a trap door. Without a sound, he slipped through and sealed it shut behind him.

Jennifer turned her attention back to Thomas and hobbled over to him. His body lay sprawled across the conveyor belt, his dislocated arm twisted at an unnatural angle.

"Thomas?" Jennifer said softly, touching his face. When he didn't respond, she kneeled beside him, pressing two fingers to his neck and cocked her head over his open mouth. After a few tense seconds, she breathed a sigh of relief.

Thomas's hand was almost purple from the lack of circulation. Douglas retrieved the other chain and bashed the lock until it gave way. Luckily, it was much smaller than the ones on the gates.

A large puddle of blood had formed beneath Thomas, pooling from the laceration on the back of his knee. Desperate for something to stop the bleeding, Jennifer grabbed the headless elf mannequin, tore off its green leggings, and wrapped them tightly around Thomas's knee to staunch the flow.

"Come on, Thomas," she urged, giving him a slight shake. "You promised you'd survive this movie."

A low groan escaped from Thomas's lips.

"What now?" Douglas asked.

"We have the key," Jennifer said, picking up the jack-in-the-box and tipping the key into her palm. "Now we need to get him to the parking lot."

"You're not suggesting we move him, are you?"

"Do you have a better idea? Help isn't going to show up, and he's losing blood fast. If we don't get him to a hospital soon, he'll die."

"You need to work on your bedside manner, doc," Thomas groaned weakly.

"Thomas, are you okay?" Jennifer gasped.

Thomas's eyes fluttered open. "Is that a serious question?" he rasped, coughing violently. He winced, struggling to lift his head.

"Please, don't try to move so fast," Jennifer said, placing a hand on his arm.

He slumped back down, gasping. "Forget it, I'm only going to slow you down. You need to get Luna."

"We're not leaving you," Jennifer insisted.

"I never said anything about leaving me. Damn. Go save Luna and then come and get me. I'm not going anywhere."

"What about Plucky?" Jennifer asked, looking around.

"I'll be fine," replied Thomas with a grimace. "He's probably waiting for you in the next scene anyway. Vincent wants to wrap this movie up, remember?"

"Stay with him," Jennifer said, turning to Douglas.

"No," Thomas winced. "Go together. She'll need the help more than I do."

"But–"

"Go," Thomas snapped. "We don't have time for this."

Jennifer squeezed Thomas's shoulder, and Douglas helped her to her feet. As he supported her out of the barn, Jennifer glanced back at Thomas. "We'll come back for you. I promise."

"You best, bitch," Thomas groaned. "Otherwise I'm haunting your ass."

CHAPTER 31

Douglas helped Jennifer across Toy Town, propping her up as she limped. While they moved, she scoured the area for the next gate but was distracted by dozens of red lights. Deep in the darkness, cameras were pointing at them from every direction. She swore under her breath, enraged that their most vulnerable moments were being captured for some sick, disgusting nerd and his degenerate pals. They had no power, they were his playthings.

Eventually, they reached the south gate, and with a shaky hand, Jennifer inserted the key into the lock. But the key didn't turn.

"It's not working," Jennifer cried out, twisting the key desperately.

"There's another gate," Douglas said, taking the map out of his back pocket and unfolding it. "It must open this one." He pointed at a spot on the map. "It used to lead out to the train station."

"I hope you're right," Jennifer replied, "for your sake more than mine... You're the one having to drag me around." She lowered her eyes to her swollen ankle.

They made their way over to the east gate. Jennifer inserted the key, holding her breath. The lock popped open with a click. She removed the chain and swung the gate wide.

It led out onto a wooden platform, where a sign greeted them: The North Pole Express.

Vincent's voice came through a nearby speaker. "This film is taking all sorts of twists and turns that I didn't expect. Which is great, because if even *I* can't figure out where this film is going, then the audience is in for a ride."

"He does love the sound of his own voice, doesn't he?" Douglas remarked, hopping off the platform and onto the overgrown tracks. He extended his good arm to help Jennifer down, while she crouched and carefully descended.

"We are now at the grand climax of the movie. *Le finale.* And it's so poetic that it all comes down to the two of you–the franchise's first and most iconic actors. The legendary 'final girl' Rebecca Sommers and the original Plucky himself, teaming up in a way no one could ever imagine."

As they walked across the train tracks, Jennifer tried to block Vincent out, but his voice followed them through the park's speakers. "You guys have made this fanboy's dream come true. Directing my heroes is an unbelievable honor. So, thanks."

"Shut the fuck up and tell us where Luna is," Jennifer spat.

"You're excited to wrap up this masterpiece as much as me. I totally get it. If you follow me, I'll take you right to the final showdown."

A familiar whirring sound caught their attention, drawing their eyes upward. Vincent's drone hovered about seven feet above them. After a brief pause, it spun on its axis and zipped toward the other entrance of the train station, once the first stop of the North Pole Express. Jennifer and Douglas followed the drone, climbing back up off the tracks, onto the platform, and along Gumdrop Road. The drone then flew directly to the heart of the park, where the Ferris wheel stood.

As they followed the drone up the path, Jennifer clung tightly onto Douglas. They reached the foot of the Ferris wheel, its towering frame loomed over them. The once-vibrant green paint had peeled away, revealing the rusted metal beneath–like bones exposed under torn skin. At the top of the Ferris wheel hung a large yellow neon star, its faint flicker barely holding on, while the low hum of the transformer buzzed down the metal frame.

The drone overhead whizzed around, turning to face them.

"We've come to the final set piece of the movie," Vincent announced from a nearby speaker. "Let me set the scene: your characters are inches away from escape, but there's a catch–you can't leave without rescuing your dearly beloved from the clutches of Plucky."

"Where is Luna?" Jennifer demanded.

"*Sophie.*" Vincent sighed.

The drone shot upward at an incredible speed, racing to the top of the Ferris wheel, where it began circling the carriage at the very top. That's when they heard the scream.

"Luna," Jennifer gasped. She started toward the metal stairs once used for ride breakdowns, but before she could take her first step, the drone swooped down, blocking her path.

"Ah ah ah...not yet," Vincent's voice admonished her from the speaker. "The scene doesn't start until the director calls action. Come on, Ms. Hawkins, you've been in the game long enough to know that."

Jennifer craned her neck toward the carriage where Luna was trapped, picturing her curled up in pain, bleeding and afraid. Every second that passed was crucial. But the drone continued to obstruct her, faceless and unblinking. Jennifer thought about knocking it out of the way, but its four propellers spun so fast that any attempt would risk severe injury.

"Move it," Jennifer demanded, knowing Vincent was watching on the other side. Out of the corner of her eye, she saw Douglas's chain lashing out for the drone. The force didn't take the drone out, but it was enough to make it teeter side to side and provoke Vincent into displaying, at last, a hint of fluster and panic.

"No, Douglas, you need to wait back there," Vincent's voice crackled through the speaker.

"No way," Douglas said.

They heard a deep sigh from the speaker as Vincent attempted to compose himself. "Thematically, it makes more sense for Jennifer to rescue her lover by herself. If you're worried about screen time, relax. I've got more planned for you. Stay at the bottom while we get the shots we need."

"Screw this," Douglas snapped, striking at the drone–its spinning propeller slicing into the back of his hand. Douglas cried out.

"Watch the equipment," Vincent cried out as he flew the drone away.

"Come on," Douglas said, pushing past his own pain and helping Jennifer up the stairs.

"What about the chain?" Jennifer asked. It lay on the ground behind them.

"It's too much to carry it *and* you. No offense, love."

"Ugh, actors..." Vincent groaned, "All right then, *action*."

The drone swirled around them as Jennifer and Douglas climbed up the winding staircase. Despite Douglas's support, each step on Jennifer's injured foot sent sharp jolts through her body. She gritted her teeth and pushed on, step after agonizing step. The higher they climbed, the more the metal stairs wobbled, rattling with every movement.

They were only a quarter of the way up, but the world seemed so far below her. She froze and gripped the railing tightly. She breathed deeply, knowing that she was feeling the onset of vertigo, the world was tilting as her panic set in.

"Come on," Douglas urged. "Keep pushing. You've got this."

Jennifer's eyes dropped to Douglas's sweaty face, then to his hand. The skin was shredded from the drone's blades, blood running down his fingers.

He caught her gaze and forced a smile. "It's only a flesh wound. Don't worry."

If Douglas could keep going with a maimed hand and broken wrist, she could conquer her fear of heights. Closing her eyes, she recalled Luna's advice atop the slide: just count to three. She thought of Luna's comforting touch and counted quietly under her breath–one, two, three. Steadying her breath, she opened her eyes and fixed her gaze straight ahead. As long as she didn't look down, she'd be fine.

Halfway up, the stairs rattled violently beneath them, and for a moment Jennifer thought the whole stairway was about to collapse. Jennifer risked a glance down and discovered something far worse: Plucky was charging up after them.

When their eyes met, Plucky abruptly halted. He wagged his dirty, gloved index finger before sprinting up the stairs again.

Jennifer shoved aside her fear of heights and her aching ankle and propelled herself up the stairs in a desperate half-run. Reaching Luna was the only thing keeping her moving.

But Plucky was fast, and he would catch up to them soon. His ragged laughter grew louder behind them. Jennifer sensed that Douglas wasn't behind her anymore. She stopped and turned.

"Keep going," he said, "I'll handle him."

"No," Jennifer cried out.

"Come on, Jenny," Douglas said, forcing a smile. "I'm the original Plucky, remember? This imposter's got nothing on me."

Jennifer stared at him, then down the staircase–Plucky was charging upward, closing the gap fast.

"After a lifetime of playing the villain," Douglas said, "let me be the hero for once."

She hesitated.

"Go!"

Heart pounding, Jennifer turned and forced herself up the stairs, leaving Douglas behind.

* * *

Plucky slowed at the sight of his predecessor. The drone hovered nearby, zooming in to capture the moment.

"Wow. I must admit, this is an honor, sharing the screen with the great Douglas King," Plucky said, taking a small bow.

"You flatter me," Douglas replied, glancing up at where Jennifer was climbing, trying to buy her as much time as possible. "So, what the hell did you do to my mask?"

"Your mask?" Plucky said, cocking his head. "Don't you mean *our* mask?"

"You're not Plucky," Douglas said, crossing his arms. "You're just a mediocre, desperate, discount version. You can never replace the original."

"That's not true," Plucky shook his head. "Kane Hodder didn't start wearing the hockey mask until part seven, and people consider *him* to be the best Jason Vorhees. Once this movie is out, everyone will forget all about you and see me as the definitive Plucky."

"Oh yeah? And how do you reckon that?"

Plucky tilted his head. "I'll do what you could never do: kill the 'final girl.' "

Douglas's eyes snapped to Jennifer, then back to Plucky. He planted his feet firmly, widening his stance. "You're going to have to get through me first."

"If you insist," Plucky snarled.

The drone buzzed closer as Vincent's voice cracked through the speakers. "Don't stray from the lines, Plucky."

Plucky glanced at the drone and sighed heavily. He drew a large sickle out of his Santa-like sack. His laugh was raspy, thick with phlegm. "Did you know that anything can be a Christmas ornament if you put a little hook in it?"

He swung the sickle through the air, but Douglas dodged, causing the hook to slam into the metal railing with a violent clang. Plucky lunged again and the blade nicked Douglas's arm. He bit back a cry, determined not to give Plucky the satisfaction.

With nowhere to run, Douglas backed up the stairs, step by step, as Plucky lunged and slashed at him with wild swings.

* * *

Jennifer reached the top. She paused, catching her breath and counting to three. Then she rushed to the edge and peered over the railing at the carriage below. Luna lay sprawled on the floor, motionless, a wide pool of blood spreading beneath her.

"Luna," Jennifer called out.

Luna stirred, blinking as her eyes darted around. When she spotted Jennifer peering down at her, disbelief broke through the fog.

"Jennifer?" she said, groggy and unsure.

"I'm here," Jennifer said. "Hang on, I'm coming down to you."

The carriage was only a foot below the staircase. Jennifer pulled a latch which opened an escape hatch in the metal grate and lowered herself into the compartment.

As she did, the ornament swung on its hinges. She couldn't help but imagine the supports snapping, sending them plummeting to their deaths. But thankfully, the rocking gradually slowed.

"Jennifer," Luna whispered, a ghost of a smile crossing her face. "How the hell did you get up this high? You're terrified of heights."

"I am," Jennifer said, bending down to examine Luna's leg. "But I thought if I could go down that slide, then I could do this."

The rag that had helped stem the bleeding was gone, and the open wound had soaked through Luna's jeans. She couldn't risk Luna losing any more blood. Realizing she still had some strips of Thomas's torn jacket in her pocket, she pulled them out and tied them tightly around Luna's leg. She then took Luna's hand. "I'm going to get you out of here," Jennifer promised.

Her eyes caught one of Vincent's cameras mounted overhead. She swatted it off its casing where it fell to the ground below. Then, steeling herself, Jennifer turned back to the task at hand–lifting Luna up onto the staircase. With her injured ankle and Luna's lack of strength, it seemed nearly impossible. If only she had Douglas's help. *Douglas.*

She scanned the area and spotted Douglas on the staircase, retreating step by step as he evaded Plucky's relentless strikes. One hand pressed against his chest, blood soaking through his clothes from a dozen slashes. When they reached the top of the staircase, Douglas locked eyes with Jennifer, gave a sharp nod, and then charged at Plucky, catching him off-balance.

Plucky crashed against the railing but lashed out with ferocity as they grappled for control of the sickle. With a sudden shove, he tore the weapon free and hurled Douglas backward. Then, without pausing, he drove the blade into Douglas's stomach and twisted the hook with a brutal snap of his wrist.

Jennifer screamed.

Douglas staggered, the hook still embedded in his gut. He gripped the metal, blood spilling through his fingers in dark, steady streams.

Overhead, Vincent's drone hovered, whirring as it captured the grim spectacle. Below, Plucky drew his signature weapon–the candy cane shiv.

Helpless, she could only watch as Plucky gripped Douglas's neck and drove the shiv into his throat. Douglas's eyes went wide, blood spraying from his mouth.

Plucky leaned in, murmured something into his ear, then shoved him over the railing. His body crashed against the carriage, then tumbled to the ground below.

That's when the Ferris wheel's star above them blinked off, plunging everything into darkness. For a few seconds, silence held–broken only by the low groan of the star sputtering back to life, flickering and humming before its glow returned in full.

Blinking to clear her vision, Jennifer's heart skipped a beat. Plucky stood directly above the hatch. His hands were balled into fists, the bloodied shiv clenched tight. Drops of blood dripped from the shiv, through the grate, and onto the women.

Jennifer couldn't tear her eyes away. His mask was more damaged than before, and the lopsided, torn mouth leered at her with a twisted, malicious hatred. They were trapped. All he had to do was leap into their carriage.

Then came a harsh mechanical sound, and the carriage rattled. Jennifer and Luna clung to each other as the Ferris wheel lurched into motion.

CHAPTER 32

As their carriage descended, Jennifer turned to Luna, whose face was almost white. She squeezed Luna's shoulders tightly. "As soon as we reach the bottom, we're getting the hell out of here. Okay?"

Luna offered a weak smile. "I'm going to slow you down. Don't worry about me, just go."

"I'm never leaving you again."

Luna searched Jennifer's face, then nodded.

The Ferris wheel screeched, grinding to a crawl. Beneath the groan of its gears, a crackling, tinny version of "Frosty the Snowman" drifted from the battered speakers.

Jennifer peered out of the carriage; they were at the bottom. She shoved aside the gate and helped Luna to her feet. Luna cried out, her body buckling with the movement. Jennifer caught her and steadied her, ignoring the sharp pain in her own ankle as she bore the weight.

They stepped off the ride and spotted Douglas's crumpled body lying on the ground. Jennifer's heart sank deep into her stomach, but there was no time to stop–she had to keep moving. She forced herself away and raised her gaze to find Michael and Vincent waiting across from them. Michael rested the camera on his shoulder, eyes fixed on the viewfinder, while Vincent stepped away from the Ferris wheel's controls.

"That was epic," Vincent exclaimed. "Seriously, this will go down as the best final act in *Evil Elf* history."

"Are we done?" Jennifer asked, supporting Luna with one arm around her waist and the other draped over her shoulder.

"Done?"

"You've got your big finale filmed. It's over. It's a wrap."

Vincent rolled his eyes. "But the movie isn't over. I know you said you don't watch your *Evil Elf* movies, but even *you* know that the story doesn't end until you've killed Plucky." He stared off past her shoulder.

Jennifer turned to find Plucky walking down the last of the steps. He wiped the candy cane drenched in Douglas's blood on his emerald waistcoat.

"Or, in this case, until he kills you," Vincent said.

"Why are you doing this?" Jennifer said, turning back toward Vincent. "If you're such a fan, why kill your so-called heroes?"

Vincent pressed a hand to his chest, aghast. "I never killed anyone, he did." He pointed to Plucky. "I'm merely the director, an observer of the art unfolding before me."

"That's bullshit," Jennifer snapped. "You orchestrated this entire thing. You could have filmed all this without murdering anyone. But now you're just gonna get locked up for life. What has all this really achieved?"

"Authenticity," Michael uttered quietly, emotionless behind the camera.

Vincent smiled at his brother. "See? He gets it." Wandering over to Michael, Vincent laid a hand on his shoulder. "In fact, he was there when I was kicked out of film school for daring to show an *authentic* horror short. Apparently showing a cat being cut open wasn't appreciated. But it wasn't just that. I did it without corn syrup. No red dye, no bullshit. Those idiots didn't understand what I was striving for–authenticity in an industry that's lost its edge. Look at the reaction *Cannibal Holocaust* caused in 1980. They filmed real animals being slaughtered for shock value, and, while it made waves, it didn't go far enough. They stopped short of actually killing the people, too."

He continued, his voice growing more passionate. "Imagine a film where the authenticity of real violence transcends the boundaries of traditional horror. Today's horror movies are full of CGI blood and guts. We all know it's fake. Audiences have become desensitized; nothing shocks them anymore. But by using *real* violence, I can capture genuine fear. I wanted to bottle that raw, unfiltered terror. What I've done, the sacrifices we've made–they're all for the greater good of the art form. This will be the most groundbreaking, influential film in horror history."

Jennifer shook her head in disbelief.

"A director's vision is often misunderstood in its time," Vincent replied smoothly. "Take *The Shining.* When it was first released, critics tore it apart. Now, it's hailed as a masterpiece. Granted, people may not get it right away, but with time, they'll come to appreciate what we've done here."

He checked his *Evil Elf* watch–Plucky in the middle, his gloved hands pointing to four-thirty. "We should really wrap this up. The sun will be coming up soon. Michael, are you ready?"

His brother gave a thumbs-up.

"Plucky, are *you* ready?"

The actor readjusted his mask, securing it tightly before giving an "okay" signal with his hand.

"Excellent. Let's continue. Act–"

"Wait."

Vincent paused, raising an eyebrow.

"You just need me for this final scene, right?" Jennifer said. "You don't need Luna or Thomas anymore, they've served their roles. Please, get them to a hospital."

Vincent stared at her blankly for a moment before replying. "I can't do that."

"Why?" Jennifer demanded.

"We'll lose the light," Vincent said matter-of-factly. "*Action.*"

Jennifer and Luna scrambled back, tripping over something solid. The two fell in opposite directions. Jennifer hit the ground with a thud, the air punched from her lungs. When she looked down, her stomach lurched–she was sprawled across Douglas's body.

When she tore her eyes away, she saw Plucky yanking the coiled Christmas lights from the Ferris wheel's fence with a violent tug. He coiled them around his hands and pulled them tight. His head snapped toward Jennifer, and he began stalking toward her.

As Plucky advanced, a desperate Luna lunged and grabbed at his leg. Plucky kicked her squarely in the face.

Luna's nose erupted in blood as she was thrown backward, losing consciousness.

Jennifer tried to get up, but Plucky was too quick and tackled her back to the ground. He looped the Christmas lights around her neck and began tightening the wire.

Jennifer's airway constricted. She clawed at her throat but couldn't loosen the grip. Her vision blurred as her brain was starved of oxygen. With trembling fingers, she tried to swipe at his face, but she was too weak. Her fingers grazed the eyeholes of the mask, and with the last of her strength, she pulled it down.

The mask slipped off. Her vision blurred, darkness creeping in at the edges as consciousness slipped away. Just like in her movies, everything started fading to black. Then, a faint voice cut through the pounding in her ears, barely audible.

"Cut."

CHAPTER 33

The pressure on her throat eased. She sucked in painful gulps of air, coughing uncontrollably.

"What do you mean 'cut'?"

Still lying on the ground, Jennifer peeked up to see Plucky standing in front of Vincent, his arms gesturing wildly. "I was in the moment," he continued. "Was it because she slipped the mask off? They do that all the time in the *Halloween* movies. What's the big deal?"

"Did you not read the *new* script, George?" Vincent asked. "I entirely rewrote the final act."

"What new script?" George demanded.

Vincent handed him a script. George snatched it from his hand, flipping straight to the back. His fingers twitched as he scanned the page, lips moving quickly. Then his eyes widened.

"She lives?" George roared.

"I was thinking about the ending, and it just wouldn't work to kill off Rebecca Sommers. They'll be expecting that."

"But you said that the audience was expecting her to *live*."

"Right. But the more I thought about it the more I realized something. In every legacy sequel, or 're-quel' if you will, over the past ten years, they always bring back the original leads just to kill them off. Think about it. Han Solo was brought back in

The Force Awakens only to be stabbed by a lightsaber. *Terminator: Dark Fate* killed John Connor in the first five minutes. Even the 2022 *Texas Chainsaw Massacre* brought back the iconic character of Sally, only for her to be killed by Leatherface. Hell, even the *Scream* movie from 2022, a.k.a. the most self-aware movie ever, played into this trope by killing fan-favorite Dewey."

"What's your point?"

Vincent rolled his eyes like the answer was obvious. "The audience will expect Jennifer to die after all. By not killing Rebecca Sommers, we are re-subverting expectations."

George squared up to the director, rolled up the script and pressed it into Vincent's stomach. "You promised me that I would get to kill Rebecca Sommers. It was the only reason I agreed to this whole thing. How could I possibly become the definitive Plucky if I don't kill the 'final girl'?"

Vincent shrugged. "That's show business, baby. Plans change at the drop of a hat."

"Change it back," George demanded.

"Rebecca Sommers survives, and that's final. Don't forget that I am the director of this movie. An actor doesn't get to dictate the story. So stick to your lines. When I say 'jump,' you say, 'how high?' Got it?"

George stepped forward and Vincent flinched back. But then George paused briefly, before dropping his head and turning away. A satisfied smirk crept across Vincent's face. He picked up his camera and adjusted it over his shoulder.

"So, we're going to reset the scene, but this time–"

George lunged forward and rammed the sharpened point of his candy cane shiv into Vincent's thigh. He cried out and fell to the floor. Without hesitation, George pounced on him, stabbing him repeatedly with the makeshift weapon.

Michael dropped his camera, his eyes wide with horror as his brother was savagely stabbed right in front of him.

"Don't you dare fucking move," George barked, pointing the blood-soaked weapon at Michael. "Keep filming, or you're next."

Michael swallowed heavily before he brought his camera back up and continued recording.

Vincent was still alive, making horrible gurgling sounds as George rummaged through his pockets and pulled out Vincent's phone. With a few taps on the screen, the drone lifted off the ground, wobbling precariously as George took control of it.

"It's time you hit the *cutting* room floor," George sneered, as he guided the drone straight toward Vincent. He watched in terror as the furiously spinning propeller blades closed in on his face. Jennifer turned away, unable to bear the sight, but Vincent's screams still echoed in her ears, gradually fading into a gurgling, then silence.

George let the phone drop to the ground; its screen cracked from the impact. He then glanced at Jennifer, still splayed on the floor. He picked up Vincent's fallen camera and trained the lens on Vincent's corpse. "I should probably get some close-ups too."

"Why?" Jennifer croaked, her throat still tight.

"Oh, don't feel too bad for him," George said. "He always dreamed of starring in an *Evil Elf* movie, and now it's come true."

"No, why are you doing all of this?" Jennifer asked, her voice still coarse. "Do you really think you can film these murders, make a movie out of it, and not get caught?"

George gave her a quizzical look. "Of course I want everyone to know I did this. I want everyone to know that I was the one who killed Rebecca Sommers, *the* 'final girl.' I was expecting Vincent to edit this masterpiece together, but I guess that's not happening anymore," he said, kicking Vincent's lifeless body. "But rest assured, this film will be seen. Michael, you'll see to that, right?"

Michael stared in horror, his eyes darting between his brother's mangled body and George, who stood calmly beside it. He dropped his camera and bolted.

"It's tough to get good help these days," George said. He then took a step closer and hoisted the DSLR camera rig more comfortably on his right shoulder. Adjusting the zoom dial, he focused in on her face. "I can see you trying to figure it out. You're trying to place my face. I should feel insulted, but then again, you barely remembered half of the actors on this set. So, I'm hardly surprised."

Her eyes narrowed as she studied his face. "I've seen you before?"

"Let me give you a hint. We originally met during the preproduction of the sixth movie. Right before you abandoned the shoot. Abandoned me."

"Wait, you were brought in to replace Dougie?" Jennifer said, realization creeping in.

"By George, I think she's got it," he said, snapping his fingers. "I was chosen to replace the great Douglas King when he dropped out. I was so excited. Me and you were supposed to star together in *Evil Elf VI: Christmas in Space*. But then you decided you were suddenly too good for horror movies. It was supposed to be my big break. I was passed the mantle of Plucky, and so, I was supposed to carry the torch for the following movies. But there were no more sequels, were there? The movie tanked, because of you."

"The movie still got made, didn't it? You can't blame me for everyone hating it. I wasn't even in it. Blame the director, the writers, the producers, I don't know–why me?"

"Oh, because all the *other Evil Elf* movies were critically acclaimed, were they?" George spat. "No, the movie failed because audiences weren't interested in any *Evil Elf* film without Rebecca Sommers. Because of you, my film career was cut short."

He paused, looking down as he kicked at the sand. "And then, when I saw you years later at a convention, you didn't even acknowledge me. In fact, nobody did. Not a single person from that franchise has ever acknowledged my contribution to the series. I've never even been invited to a single *Evil Elf* reunion panel. Did you know that I was actually at your last convention? The one from the other day. I had my own booth, and you didn't even give me a second glance."

He shook his head. "Do you know how humiliating it is to go to a convention, and nobody visits your table? And the rare few who do approach you, it's only to tell you how much they hate your movie. Even to my face, they call me the wor–" The words caught in his throat, his eyes became wet. " 'The worse Plucky.'

"Meanwhile, I've studied you. I've seen your face when fans line up just for the chance to have you squiggle your name or snap a photo. I've seen the utter contempt you have for them. You think you're too good for it, like it's all beneath you." He spat at the ground, rounding in on Jennifer again. "I'd ***kill*** to be loved like that. And so, I have." Crying, Jennifer dragged herself away from George. She didn't make it far, only over to Vincent's body.

He paced over to her. "Do you know what it feels like to read every article and watch every ranking video of the *Evil Elf* movies and constantly see yours placed at the bottom? Of course you don't. But that's all going to change. Because I'm going to do what Plucky has never done, what not even the great Douglas King ever managed: I'm going to kill Rebecca Sommers. Then I will be the true, definitive Plucky. I will be the first one everyone talks about when they discuss the movies. Whenever someone types 'Plucky' or 'Evil Elf' into Google, I will be the first result."

With his free hand, George bent down, picked up his Plucky mask, and slipped it over his face. "Now, break time's over. Let's finish this movie." He straddled her, pointing the camera directly at her face. "Are you ready for your close-up?"

Jennifer stared up at her reflection in the lens.

"And this time, no one's here to say cut," Plucky sneered from behind the camera.

"You've forgotten two of the biggest rules of horror movies," Jennifer said.

George cocked his head.

"Don't waste time monologuing...and never leave your weapon behind." She swiftly pulled the candy cane shiv from Vincent's body and plunged it deep into Plucky's leg.

He screamed as Jennifer yanked the shiv free, then drove it in again. The camera slipped from his grasp. He stumbled back, clutching his leg. Without hesitation, Jennifer lifted her foot and kicked him square in the chest. Pain shot up her injured ankle, sharp and blinding–but she gritted her teeth and pushed through it.

Grabbing the Christmas lights, she looped them around his neck and pulled the wires taut. George gagged, desperately clawing at her face, but she wrapped the wire again, pulling it tighter.

As she squeezed, he made horrible choking, gurgling sounds. His breath came in strained, desperate gasps as he tried to suck in air. Jennifer closed her eyes as he frantically attempted to wriggle free from beneath her until he finally stopped moving. Jennifer continued to pull on the Christmas lights until all of the strength left her body and she collapsed on top of him.

After a few moments, with no signs of life beneath her, Jennifer rolled away and collapsed onto her back. Her breath came in ragged gasps, which steamed in the cold, early morning air. In the distance, she could faintly hear the tinny tune of "Frosty the Snowman."

She forced her head to turn, her vision blurry, only to see the fallen camera, its lens still fixed on her, even as she drifted toward unconsciousness.

EPILOGUE

Evil Elf: Retribution
Reviewed by Peter Morton for
HackandSlashMovies.com

It's been four months since the Tinseltown Massacre–when brothers Vincent and Michael Shepard lured six unsuspecting actors (Jennifer Hawkins, Douglas King, Thomas Barnett, Christy Serrano, Johnny Holt, Luna Watson, and Daniel Adams) to an abandoned theme park under the pretence of filming an indie horror movie. When in reality, it was a horrific snuff film.

But while the brothers orchestrated the trap, the killings themselves were carried out by George Lutz–reviving his role as Plucky, the homicidal elf he once played in *Evil Elf VI* (1992).

Vincent Shephard and Lutz paid the ultimate price for their art that night, but the whereabouts of Michael Shepard are still unknown. According to reports, he fled the final showdown, taking the raw footage with him. No one had seen or heard from him since...until last week, when a film was uploaded anonymously on a horror fan forum, entitled *Evil Elf: Retribution.*

Unsuspecting users were horrified to find that this was the actual movie. It seems Michael had edited the footage into a full feature.

The upload was purged from YouTube and every major social media platform within minutes. But if you know where to look, you can still find it in the darkest recesses of the internet...a venture I undertook myself when writing this review. Come on, I'm an online movie critic, what did you expect?

That said, the film is abhorrent. Vile. Utterly evil...and what's even worse is that it's not even entertaining.

Morally and tonally, it is a total mess. The plot makes no sense; it's preachy and reeks of pretentiousness. There are also long, overblown drone shots of the theme park, which might have been okay if they weren't appallingly filmed. The one decision I thought was mildly interesting was taking Lutz's portrayal of Plucky into a far darker and more sinister place than King's. Unfortunately, thanks to Lutz's lack of presence, his performance fell flatter than one of the elf standees he frequently hid behind.

Somehow, the Shepard brothers and Lutz did achieve something remarkable–they made a movie worse than *Evil Elf in Space*.

The only bright spot in this horrific film were the performances–half of which were scripted, and half driven by genuine fear. The writing in the scripted scenes was unbelievably sloppy, but the cast did their best to salvage it. King, in a rare appearance without his mask, was especially compelling. And I must say, it's a real shame we never saw the full range of his talent while alive.

Overall, aside from the morbid curiosity of its snuff-like elements, *Evil Elf: Retribution* is an easy skip.

One out of five stars ★

CHAPTER 34

One Year Later

Jennifer paced backstage at the convention center where, only a year ago, she was bored out of her mind and barely scraping by. Beyond the door, muffled sounds of excitement echoed: squeals, shouts, and cheers from, by the sounds of it, hundreds of people. Jennifer wandered over to the edge of the stage, peeking out. She was shocked to see even more people than she imagined. Even from her restricted view, she could make out fans dressed in hideous Christmas sweaters, leather jackets, Hawaiian shirts, Mardi Gras beads, sideways red snapbacks, '80s shell suits, Plucky masks from Douglas's movies, and, of course, bushy mullets. Her heart hammered in her chest. Nausea rolled in.

A hand touched her shoulder. She turned to see Luna, who was smiling at her, her green eyes glistening.

"Breathe," Luna said softly. "It's going to be okay."

"I don't know if I can do this. They didn't care about me a year ago, and I don't think they really care about us now."

Luna wrapped her arms around Jennifer. "Look, even if they are here just to see the freaks from the fucking Tinseltown Massacre, think about who we're doing this for, okay?"

Jennifer rested her head against Luna's. A gentle warmth spread across her face and her heart gradually slowed. She kissed Luna.

"I think you're making *me* nervous," Luna said.

"Nah, we've got this."

The women took a deep breath and walked out together.

They squeezed each other's palms as the crowd erupted into applause. Jennifer winked at Luna before letting go to wave at the sea of faces. As the applause gradually subsided, a young woman approached them carrying microphones.

"Thanks, Sarah," Jennifer said.

The woman's eyes widened. "You remember me?"

"Of course I do." Jennifer touched Sarah's elbow. "It's great to see you again." She leaned closer and whispered, "I want to apologize for being a total bitch to you a year ago."

Sarah smiled and gestured for Luna and Jennifer to take their seats.

As they sat, the crowd erupted into applause again as Thomas stepped onto the stage. He looked great. Wearing a tailored cream blazer, dark chinos, and a silk patterned neck scarf paired with a matching pocket square, he waved to the audience before spotting a few guys dressed as his character. Striding to the front of the stage, he pointed at them and made a playful gesture for them to leave. The crowd laughed, and Thomas accepted a microphone from Sarah and settled beside Luna and Jennifer.

Jennifer leaned over to Thomas. "Thanks for coming."

"Of course, I wouldn't miss this." Thomas squeezed her hand.

"Ladies and gentlemen," Sarah began. "I'd like to welcome Thomas Barnett, Luna Watson, and Jennifer Hawkins to the stage."

The crowd responded with an even louder applause.

"We really appreciate you all for coming. Honestly, I am such a big fan. Much like everyone else here."

The crowd cheered again in agreement. The trio smiled.

"First off, congratulations on such a fantastic tour, we've seen everything you're doing on social media and you're smashing it–you must be so proud."

"Thankfully, Luna's granddaughter is a pro with all that, so we've had some help," Jennifer smiled, waving over to Luna's family in the crowd.

Jennifer caught the subtle shift in Sarah's seat, knowing that she was about to politely move on from the small talk. Meeting her gaze, Jennifer offered a reassuring nod and a gentle smile. Sarah returned it, a flicker of ease softening her expression.

"Now, I want to address that we all know how difficult it must be for you to be here. For you specifically, Jennifer, this must bring back a lot of memories. You used to be a regular on the convention circuit and, understandably, you stopped after the incident. Can you explain why you've decided to return and talk today?"

"I'm going to be honest," Jennifer said, bringing the microphone to her mouth. "I didn't want to do this. Coming back here is quite jarring. Not because of you guys, but because of how I saw myself at that time, before the incident. As well as, of course, knowing that I'd never see Doug..." She paused to compose herself and Luna gently rubbed Jennifer's back. "See

Dougie again. Celebrating film, stories, art, and escapism is a joyous thing, and it's something he always appreciated and wanted to contribute to, especially for his fans. So, that's why I'm here, to do that for him...and I guess for myself, too."

She took a breath before continuing. "I'm here for the people who can't be, and they would want their stories to be told. They're not just characters in a movie. They're real people with families and lives. So, we wanted to create a fundraiser in honor of the friends we lost. Every single cent earned here today will go directly to the families of Dan, Johnny, Christy, and Doug..." Jennifer's voice caught again. She sipped a glass of water waiting for her on a small table. "Douglas King loved his fans. He would have done anything for them. And I know he's looking down at us with that cheeky, sometimes-menacing grin of his."

"I'm sure their families will be very thankful," Sarah said. "From ticket sales alone, we've raised $90,000."

The crowd erupted in applause.

Sarah paused before continuing. Turning to Luna and Thomas, she took a deep breath and then read her cue card. "Now, it has been a year since the Tinseltown Massacre claimed four innocent lives. I won't ask you to relive that painful experience again, but could you tell us what happened after?"

Luna spoke first. "When I finally came to, I found Jennifer on the ground with the bodies of Vincent and George Lutz next to her–"

A few boos rippled through the crowd.

"Thankfully, she was somehow still alive," Luna continued, her eyes glazing over with tears as she recounted the memory.

"We were both in bad shape, barely able to walk. We went back to get Thomas. He was barely conscious. Still, we managed to wheel him back through the park using an old prop mail cart. We found the keys to the bus where we'd been sleeping in Vincent's pockets. We got it started up, crashed right through the gates of Tinseltown, and got ourselves the hell out of there."

Thomas lifted his mic and continued the story. "It would have felt like a euphoric moment if we all hadn't had fucked-up arms and legs. But we somehow drove the bus an hour to the nearest hospital, where we received medical treatment. I had a dislocated arm, and the doctor said if that bastard had cut a few centimeters deeper into the back of my knee, then I wouldn't be here today. We gave our statements to the police at the hospital."

Sarah shook her head. "I'm so sorry you all went through that. But what you are doing now–telling your stories–is so important. Thank you." The crowd cheered.

"On a brighter note, can you tell us what you've been up to since then? What does life look like now?"

"Going through what we went through, it made me appreciate the important things in life," Luna began. "So I've been spending time with my daughter and grandkids. But I've also been giving myself time and purpose again. I've allowed myself to be happy, and introducing Jennifer into my life has greatly helped with that."

"Although you both now live in Texas part-time, you haven't given up acting completely, have you, Jennifer? Rumor has it you've got offers lining the street," Sarah said.

"Well, they've been calling, but I haven't really confirmed any *just* yet," Jennifer teased, smiling to the audience.

In a twisted way, the Tinseltown Massacre and the release of the snuff film had put Jennifer back in the spotlight. Even her sleazy agent, Andrew, resurfaced, eager to cash in on her newfound attention. However, Jennifer canceled her contract with him, choosing instead to work with Carole J. Evans, a Hollywood agent known for securing career-defining roles–ones that could revive her career in a way that reflected who she was now, not who she was as a twenty-year-old scream queen.

"Are you able to give us a little clue as to what may be coming up for you?" Sarah asked.

Jennifer wanted to phrase this right. She took another sip of water. "Well, even though Rebecca Sommers is undoubtedly the highlight of my career, I think I've proved to myself that I can be a strong 'final girl' even when the cameras aren't rolling–wrinkles and weak wrists and all." She laughed to herself as she rotated her wrist. "So I'm very excited to find roles that reflect my life now."

Jennifer's gaze hovered over a large poster that covered the entirety of the back wall: herself, as Rebecca, frozen in time and unable to age.

"...I want to represent those who the movie industry overlooks. I want us to be seen."

A smatter of applause erupted into cheers, encouraging Jennifer to look up at the crowd. It was only now that she could take in the diversity of faces and ages all brought together by their love of a project she had always felt embarrassed by.

A pang of guilt hit her for all those years she'd resented the franchise and its fanbase.

As Sarah moved to questioning Luna and Thomas, Jennifer let herself soak in the moment, looking on at the fans that Douglas always appreciated. Her eyes darted from one person to the next.

But just as she was about to pull away to engage with her peers, one figure dressed as Plucky stood motionless amongst the jovial crowd.

Unlike the other Pluckys in the crowd, this fan wore a sagging, torn, and dirty white mask, with stitching to revive a once cheerful grin. The same mask that had haunted her nightmares for the past year. Her breath caught. Her heart pounded. She looked over to Luna, who was fully engrossed in Sarah's next question. Jennifer turned back to Plucky, and as quickly as she had spotted him, he was gone–replaced by yet another fan in a regular *Evil Elf* Plucky mask. She let out a deep breath.

Get your shit together.

She squeezed Luna's hand.

"How about you, Thomas?" Sarah's voice went from muffled to clear in Jennifer's mind. "I know photos of the actors in their hair and makeup were also leaked and you got a pretty exciting call."

"Yes, despite the horrific circumstances, it seems people couldn't help but love my work. And since then, I've been the chief makeup artist for three major movies. A lot of eighties and nineties looks, but I'm working on my first sci-fi next month. But then, I've heard that working in space is bad luck..." Thomas played to the crowd and Luna pretended to smack him.

"Only in horror, Thomas, only in horror," Jennifer chimed in.

Sarah shook her head before turning to the audience. "Right, guys, Jennifer, Luna, and Thomas will be signing autographs right after this. Once again, all the proceeds will go to the victims' families–an important cause that I'm sure we all want to support."

After the talk concluded, the three of them made their way over to their booths. Over Jennifer's table hung a big, bright, shiny poster. She was happy to see it was a headshot from the present day. She turned around to address her visitors. An impossibly long line stretched before her, and she couldn't help but think how much Dougie would have loved this. She took a deep breath, and with a bittersweet smile, Jennifer uncapped her gold pen and gestured for the first person to step forward. When they extended their palm for a handshake, she made her way around the table that separated them and clasped the fan's hand with both of hers.

Her gaze swept the sea of excited faces–until it froze. At the very back, the mangled mask had reappeared. Jennifer forced herself to look away, to breathe, to remind herself it was only the echo of her nightmares. But when she looked again, it was still there. Watching.

And then she heard it–the whir. Slow. Mechanical. She tilted her head skyward. A drone hovered above her, poised for the shot. Its single red light forever lit.

ACKNOWLEDGMENTS

Thank you to Mango Publishing for helping us achieve our dream of publishing our novel, and to Chief Content Officer Hugo Villabona, who believed in us from the start. Also to our copyeditor, Robin Miller, who gave us incredibly helpful notes and feedback.

We'd also like to thank the amazing people who took the time to beta read our book: Ben Poulteney, Charlotte Tar, Kiz Moncrieff, D.R. Forge, and Nicole Kirsch. Your feedback was invaluable in shaping this book.

To everyone who regularly watches our YouTube channels, *The Simpsons Theory* and *Lydia Loves Timelines*, your continued support means the world to us. We appreciate each and every one of you.

Finally, thank you to our wonderful family: Helen, Tracy, Phil, David, Darren, Charlotte, Alex, Ben, Erin, Max, Jade, George, Asmara, Drew, Chel, Kresh, Keona, Xavier, and Logan.

This book is dedicated to our beautiful daughter, Freya. We love you so much.

ABOUT THE AUTHORS

James and Lydia are a husband-and-wife duo, each holding a Bachelor of Arts in Film and Television. Together, they run the popular YouTube channels *The Simpsons Theory* and *Lydia Loves Timelines*. They are also the authors of two nonfiction books: *The Simpsons Secret* and *Collecting the Simpsons*.

In their free time, they enjoy traveling, watching movies, attending film conventions, and spending time with their little bundle of joy, Freya.

Follow them on Instagram @jamesandlydiahicks.

Mango Publishing, established in 2014, publishes an eclectic list of books by diverse authors–both new and established voices–on topics ranging from business, personal growth, women's empowerment, LGBTQ studies, health, and spirituality to history, popular culture, time management, decluttering, lifestyle, mental wellness, aging, and sustainable living. We were named 2019 *and* 2020's #1 fastest growing independent publisher by *Publishers Weekly*. Our success is driven by our main goal, which is to publish high-quality books that will entertain readers as well as make a positive difference in their lives.

Our readers are our most important resource; we value your input, suggestions, and ideas. We'd love to hear from you–after all, we are publishing books for you!

Please stay in touch with us and follow us at:
Facebook: Mango Publishing
Twitter: @MangoPublishing
Instagram: @MangoPublishing
LinkedIn: Mango Publishing
Pinterest: Mango Publishing
Newsletter: mangopublishinggroup.com/newsletter

Join us on Mango's journey to reinvent publishing, one book at a time.

www.ingramcontent.com/pod-product-compliance
Lightning Source LLC
Jackson TN
JSHW030547251025
92378JS00001B/1
9781684818969